Web of Death

by

Samantha Quinn

Lightcastle Cove, Book 2

Web of Death

Cover Art by *Rae Monet, Inc.*

The Wild Rose Press, Inc.
PO Box 708
Adams Basin, NY 14410-0708
Visit us at www.thewildrosepress.com

Publishing History
First Edition, 2023
Trade Paperback ISBN 978-1-5092-4948-0
Digital ISBN 978-1-5092-4949-7

Lightcastle Cove, Book 2
Published in the United States of America

She swiped at a wayward curl that had escaped and was hanging down her forehead. He wondered why she didn't just let it be free. He imagined it framing her face in soft ringlets.

"Come on inside," she called over her shoulder but when she reached for her door, Todd stopped her.

"Wait," he corrected at her questioning expression, "Aren't you forgetting something?"

"What? Oh, sorry. I guess I did for a minute. How do you want to do this?"

"I'll go in first. You wait here."

"Nuh-uh. No way." She shook her head. "I know how these things work. It's the one who is left behind-- the one who is told to 'wait here' who ends up getting her throat slashed. Where you go, I go."

Todd stared into twinkling blue eyes and realized she was making a joke. His countenance was meant to tell her he didn't think it was funny, although it was hard to hide his own smile.

He heard her sigh but she complied, leaning against her car as he opened the door to her home.

With a glance over his shoulder, and a twinkle in his own eye, he whispered, "If you're worried, maybe you should get in the car and lock the doors… Just in case." And then he was gone.

Other Wild Rose Press Titles By Samantha Quinn:

Never Say Die

Dedication

This book is dedicated to my family both by birth and by choice.

To my sisters Nan and Cate. We have always been able to count on each other, whether we needed a sounding board, a talk off the ledge of panic or just a rational voice to help see things clearly.

To Karen, my sister of the heart. I know you would have loved this one. I miss you like crazy but until we are together again, I will meet you on memory lane.

To my parents, who have always encouraged me to follow my dreams. I don't know where I would be without you.

To Guapo, thank you for fielding dinner or errands while I wrote… and wrote… and wrote some more.

And last but not least, as always, to the two amazing humans I call my children. Bud and Doodle, you make me proud every day and I love you to the moon and back.

Chapter One

"Fire!" The call rang out, just as the shrill of the fire alarm jolted Cara Kane from deep concentration. "Oh Jiminy Cricket." She jumped, placing her hand over her heart. "God I hate that noise."

Paige Simpson, her personal assistant moaned. "Not freakin' again. That's the third time in two weeks."

"I don't have time for another false alarm," Cara said as she grabbed her purse and her keys, locking the door on her way out. "Let's go, people," Cara continued as she walked, herding those who were doing more chatting than exiting, in the hallway. "Paige, can you please check with property management to discuss this? I swear I'm going to start charging them for my downtime." She shoved open the fire door at the end of the hall and stomped through, passing the elevators and continuing down the stairs and through the foyer, toward the front door.

"Top of the 'to do' list as soon as we get back inside. In fact I will call them while we wait."

On their way out, they ran into someone from maintenance wearing a hard hat and coveralls. "Hey, is this a false—"

The worker was through the door before Cara could get her question out, running at break-neck speed. "Maybe it's real this time. They sure seem to be in an all-fired hurry."

Brightwell Manor, one of Lightcastle's oldest mansions, was converted to exclusive business offices ten years ago. That's when Cara decided to move *Perfect Life Design by Cara Kane* downtown instead of working out of her home. It was a decision she'd never regretted. It provided legitimacy to her business and at the same time, provided a visibility to the clientele who could afford her. She'd had five-star ratings ever since, with very happy customers. Her business had taken off and now she could coast a little if she wanted. She didn't want that, but she could. It was nice to not have to worry about getting her bills paid anymore. Instead of coasting, she chose to do some philanthropic work, like mentoring young women in business who were just getting started and helping them see their own potential. She'd seen too many women with the dream beaten out of them--both physically and emotionally and it struck a nerve in her. Her sense of justice and fair play screamed each and every time. So she helped where she could. Women needed to uplift each other.

The midday sun warmed her skin as soon as she exited the building, a stark contrast to the air conditioning inside. It wouldn't be long before the humidity would arrive and it wouldn't be nearly as comfortable for most people, though Cara, having been raised in the South, loved the weather here in Lightcastle, South Carolina. But seriously…the hair…that was a challenge. She could already feel it trying to escape and curl.

Paige headed over to talk to the occupants of some of the other offices. She was a bright and friendly young woman, just starting out in the interior design field. She was taller than Cara's five foot six inches at close to six feet and wore flats because she was self-conscious of her height. She was athletic and strong with a pixie cut that made her look like a faerie. She reminded Cara of Tinker Bell but Cara would never tell her that. Paige wouldn't believe her anyway. Hiring Paige as her assistant was the best thing she'd done, next to leaving law school. Mentoring young women brought her real joy in life, and in this case, it also made her life easier.

Down the street she could see the ocean and yearned to take some time off to spend there. When was the last time she'd been to the beach? At first it had been the challenge of starting up her new business. Everything other than work had taken a back seat in the beginning. What was her excuse now? Paige did a great deal of the running around she used to have to do so she should be able to make time. People prioritized what was important. It was time to review her own list of priorities, just as she instructed her mentees.

With a deep breath, inhaling the glorious sunshine filled air, she looked around at the other occupants of the building. Their reactions to the interruption seemed to vary from excitement to annoyance to out-and-out hostility. With a shrug of her shoulders, she walked over to the park, across the street. There was an old sycamore tree with a welcoming bench beneath it. *Perfect. Just enough sunlight shining through to get some vitamin D.*

Sitting, leaning back, she raised her face toward the sun and closed her eyes, reveling in the moment of sunlight and nature. It would actually be peaceful if it weren't for the screaming alarm. It shut off at that moment, thank God.

"What's up over there?"

The question came from a tall man standing behind

her. She tried to shade her eyes from the sun by holding up her hand to allow her to see the stranger. He had short, dark blond hair, streaked by the sun. With the sun's rays directly on him, he appeared to have a halo. His face was cast in shadow. St Michael meets Ryan Reynolds, eat your heart out.

"Fire alarm. Third time in two weeks," Cara answered, shrugging her shoulders, working to let the stress release from her neck.

He gave the impression he was trying to delve into her innermost secrets. Maybe it was because she couldn't fully see his face or maybe it was just the mood he was giving off, but his vibe remained intense, and she touched her face as she felt the tell-tale warmth of a blush creep up her neck.

She looked closer at the stranger in his nicely tailored suit--one he wore with ease. Coming from a family of lawyers, and feeling like she had somehow let her family down after leaving law school, she was determined to support herself and pay her own way. She'd worked in retail to afford her degree in interior design. She recognized quality. And as a designer, she knew fabrics better than her own skin. That suit cost some serious cash.

She was about to speak again, when he excused himself and crossed the street, eyes apparently glued to something--or more like someone. The building's receptionist, Ivy Romano was beautiful. She'd give her that. No matter where she was, men flocked to her like moths to a flame. Some people just had that "it" factor. Ivy had it in spades.

"And another win for Ivy. You go girl."

With a heavy sigh, she watched as Ivy noticed St.

Michael's twin approach and broke away from her adoring fan club to greet him. That girl could spot money a state away.

Well, they would make a cute couple, and dear God, gorgeous babies.

As Cara watched, 'Mr. tall, blond and incredibly attractive' sailed right past Ivy. Her eyebrows raised. *Well, that's new.* Wait a minute. She'd seen him before. If she wasn't mistaken, he was the best man at her client, and friend Miranda's wedding. It was Todd Mitchell, and he was here to see her. She giggled.

He spoke with one of the firefighters, then made his way back across the street. Ivy placed her hand on his arm to detain him but he waived her off and pointed directly at Cara.

"Well, that's weird," Cara muttered.

The fire chief turned, yelled, "wrap it up," and everyone started returning to the building. Cara threw her purse over her shoulder and headed back across the street. It took a few minutes for everyone to filter through the doors and make their way up the stairs or to the elevator and Cara eventually made it to her office at the end of the hall.

She touched her key to the lock and the door nudged open.

Startled, she pulled her hand away from the door and took a step backward. "I wonder how that happened."

"How what happened?" came a very deep response at the same time hands grabbed her arms.

Cara whirled around, bumping Todd again with her elbow. "Oh my word."

"Whoa, you okay?"

She placed her hand over her heart, stepping back.

5

"Sorry, you just startled me."

"I guess you could say we're even then." His lips widened in a devilish grin.

"Even? For what?"

"You left me with the clinging-vine downstairs, not even trying to rescue me," he said, laughing when she smiled. "You knew what I was in for and didn't even try to save me."

"Most men don't want to be saved from Ivy," she replied still surprised and fighting the blush that was doing its best to crawl up her neck.

"Well, I'm not most men."

"You can say that again," she whispered as she turned to walk into her office. When their eyes met again, she had the feeling that he'd heard her last comment. *I think I'm losing my mind.*

Straightening her shoulders, she met his gaze dead on. She would not be embarrassed. "Come on in, Todd, and have a seat. I will be right with you."

His eyebrows raised, and a grin lit his face, showing dimples that made Cara's insides go to mush.

"I'm sorry. Have we met before? You are Cara Kane, aren't you? I didn't recognize the name but you do look a little familiar. Anyway, I'm sorry I was supposed to be here sooner but I got held up. Todd Mitchell. FBI and current attaché to the Lightcastle Police Department."

"Sorry, yes. I'm Cara Kane." She held her hand out in greeting. He had a firm handshake and maintained eye contact. That said a lot about a man. "And no worries. Miranda and your cousin, Hunter said you would likely be a little late. Have a seat and we can discuss where things are with their house build and what you need from me while Miranda and Hunter are honeymooning in Italy. I don't want to step on anyone's toes while they're gone but I do want to keep an eye on things to make sure everything flows smoothly. Design choices for the space have been made and it's important that we follow the plans. I want to make sure their home is exactly what they want.

I can provide you with the design as soon as I have final approval from Miranda. That should be tomorrow if that works for you. I can email you everything if you'd like and save you driving over again. Come on into my design room and have a seat. I can pull up a few items I wanted to go over now before things get too far ahead in the build."

Cara walked to the other side of the ten-foot solid wood, live edge, oak table she used to display swatches, tiles and samples to clients to get a feel for what they liked, and how things would look together. She pulled a chair out for herself while grabbing her laptop to drag it closer. She was about to sit when she stopped mid squat.

Cara gasped and then the air whooshed out of her. She stared at the chair, trying to process what she was seeing.

"What?"

It was as though time sucked her into a tunnel. She was present and aware of her surroundings but it was like she was watching it all happening to someone else…as though it were happening in a movie. Her vision blurred for a moment and tears pricked her eyes. She was aware of Todd coming around the table. Felt his strong arms as he took hold of her shoulders and moved her aside, but everything remained in slow motion. It was Cassidy, her grandmother's doll.

"You…broke your…doll?" he asked, apprehension evident in his stilted tone as he took a step back. "Do you always keep dolls at work? Is it a design thing?"

"No. It was at home in a cabinet," she added, taking a deep breath. "It's not overly expensive. It was, however, very special to me. It was a gift from my Grandma Josephine."

She knelt down beside the broken doll and reached to pick it up but a strong grip on her arm stopped her from touching it.

"Don't touch anything, Cara. I'll put the call in."

"A call to whom?" Still staring at the once treasured doll that now lay with its head severed from its body she added, "I can probably fix it." Tears rolled down her cheeks. She wiped at them and tried not to let the stranger see. She needed to be professional, but the distress was overwhelming. Who would do this? Why? What did Cassidy ever do to anyone?

"To the police. Your office was just broken into and a doll you left at home turned up here. That means that someone was there, too. You need the cops, Cara. You should never touch a crime scene until the professionals have reviewed everything."

"Crime scene?" She snapped up, her back ramrod straight. "My office can't be a crime scene." She moved toward him, her pointer finger in the air, to emphasize her point. "No, no, no, my office can't be a crime scene. I don't have time for that. I have deadlines and clients. Well-connected clients who have very high expectations. No. I don't have time for this at all. It's just a doll." Her head was shaking back and forth to emphasize her words, as though that would make any difference. "And I'm sure I can fix it."

8

Todd's face softened and she saw pity in his eyes. She remembered watching her parents interviewing crime victims to prepare them for court and viewing pity in their eyes. She didn't want to be one of them. It gave her anxiety and brought back memories of her own experiences of prepping for court. She stood a little taller, her chin raised a little higher.

"Don't give me that 'I feel sorry for you' expression. I don't need anyone's pity. I'm a strong, capable, professional woman. There is no dead body. There is no blood anywhere. This isn't a real crime scene. No. The police have more important things to deal with than chase a doll killer."

"Let me help you with this." His hands splayed outward, palms up in supplication.

"And what can the police do anyway?" she continued as though Todd hadn't said anything at all. "The doll is already broken. There's no doll doctor on call for the police force. No. The damage is done. I can fix it myself. I won't waste tax dollars on a doll. Don't be ridiculous."

"Cara, I'm FBI and this falls outside my jurisdiction, because you know…as you said…dolls…" He paused and smiled. "Too soon?" he added with a grin.

If he hadn't smiled she might have been able to hold it together but his kindness was her undoing. Her eyes blurred and her attempt at a smile wobbled, but she didn't let the tears fall. With a deep inhalation, she filled her lungs and worked on releasing the tension in her shoulders. It was easy in yoga class but much harder than anticipated in a real life stressful situation. She knew she wasn't thinking clearly. She knew Todd was right and she should call the police but she couldn't seem to make her mind go there. She couldn't believe she was one of those people who needed the police. Again. No. Just no.

"The police can check out your home and office and see if there are any fingerprints that don't belong. Then they can ask around to see if anybody spotted anyone who shouldn't have been here. There's a process that needs to be followed to preserve the crime scene."

She snorted. Not the most lady-like of actions and her mother would be horrified. "The reality is, I have a ton of clients and since the cleaning staff doesn't do nearly as good a job as they should, there will more than likely be fingerprints from every one of them. And as for strange people in the building, we just had a fire alarm. Third time in two weeks, I might add. Who would be paying attention to who was supposed to be here and who wasn't? Besides, they won't do anything. I already called once when I had the feeling I was being followed. I kept seeing the same black sedan driving slowly down my street. Then it would speed up once it passed my house. They said they would increase the patrol in my neighborhood, although I haven't seen any evidence to support it." She took another deep breath. "Sorry. Did I just roll my eyes out loud?"

"Who did you talk to at the department? I can't believe a detective wouldn't at least come by your house to investigate." He turned to the door running his hand along the edge and bending to get a closer inspection. "There's no damage to the lock or the door jam. Are you positive you locked it when you left? I'm sure you were eager to get out of the building with the fire alarm going off and all."

"Someone named… I can't remember. It was Irish though." She started pacing back and forth. "And yes I know I locked it. I always lock it. I have confidential files and expensive samples in here so I never leave it unlocked when I leave. It's a habit."

"Good."

"You believe me? Just like that?"

"Sure. Was it Reilly?"

"Yes, that's him." She snapped her fingers and pointed. "He said there wasn't much anyone could do at this point. And he's right. There's isn't any real evidence that suggests I'm in any kind of danger."

Although she said the words, she wasn't sure she really believed them because sometimes at night, when she was alone in her house, she sensed she was being watched. Telling herself that it was because she was so isolated, was one thing, and believing it, another, but if she didn't let the fear in, she could overcome it. She was strong. Capable. She would not be crippled by the actions of someone else. Standing up to evil was always the right thing to do. Always.

Her stomach rolled and a lump formed in her throat. Deep breathing usually helped calm the nausea but as her vision waved in and out she grabbed her purse and turned to Todd. "I think I'll go home." She knew her voice sounded weak but she couldn't do anything about it. "I need to make sure no one broke into my house and stole anything of value."

"I can follow you if you'd like."

"That's not necessary. I'll be fine... Really."

He reached for her arm to guide her out. "Good, then you won't mind if I follow you just to be sure." Determination was clear in his voice.

She tensed and stepped away from him. "And your reason for following me would be...? I can assure you I am perfectly capable of taking care of myself." She knew she was probably pale but she would not allow him to see her fear. She must never show her fear. After all she didn't really know this man other than he was a relative of a friend.

She heard him swear under his breath as he held his hands up, palms out. "Call the Lightcastle Police Department and ask for Special Agent Mitchell. They'll tell you he's out of the office and when they ask if someone else can help you, tell them you want to leave a message. When they patch you through, you'll hear my voice."

She hesitated.

"Just do it so you can put your mind at ease."

"Fine."

She did as instructed and when she heard the voice of the man standing beside her, she knew it was him. She could see the surprise on his face as she left a message. "Special Agent Mitchell, I just wanted to apologize for my momentary lack of trust, but a girl can never be too careful." She smiled at him as she continued. "If the offer is still valid, I'd love to have you follow me to verify no one has broken into my home."

She hung up the phone, embracing the humor in the situation if only briefly. "That was just silly. You know it would have been easier to just give me a business card."

"Anyone can have a business card printed."

She stopped in her tracks, and stared at him.

"True enough. Well… Let me just send a message to my assistant and then we can go."

"Before we leave, do you have a paper bag? I want to see if we can get anything off this doll." He was snapping pictures of the doll with his phone.

"What are you doing? I'll fix it tomorrow. Just put it on the table."

"Come on. Let me do this my way, just this once?" He winked.

"Fine. But are you sure you want to use your 'one time' this early? I mean…"

Smiling, she handed him a bag from Neiman Marcus, removing the shoebox that was inside. He raised his eyebrows at her and she shrugged and watched him carefully use his pen to maneuver the broken doll into the bag. Then, doll in hand, he escorted her out of her office, waiting while she locked the door.

Todd held her elbow as if to guide her. She might have shaken it off under different circumstances but she was exhausted from the ordeal of the afternoon, and yet another fire alarm. She just didn't have the energy. She was worried about what she might find at home and recognized the tension flooding back in, her shoulders tightening, and rising higher around her ears. They walked past the front desk in reception and Ivy called out asking if everything was okay. Cara did her best to smile at her and gave a weak wave.

"Taking the rest of the day off. We can chat tomorrow. Remember we have our meeting first thing in the morning."

She fought tears again and turned her head away from the rest of the people in the lobby so no one would see her. As it happened, that meant turning toward Todd. The warmth of his body and the strength of his hand at her elbow comforted her somehow. Something solid to stand by her. And that irritated her.

Chapter Two

It wasn't far to Cara's home. She was true to her word when she said she lived in the same historic district her office was in when she had provided directions just in case he lost her. Like that would ever happen. The streets were lined with ancient trees that stood watch over those passing by. They provided shade that cooled the air several degrees and Todd opened his window to get some fresh air.

He hadn't been sure Cara was going to let him check out her house, but when she'd agreed, he'd made sure they left immediately before she could change her mind. He'd followed in his own car, going over in his mind, the things he'd seen today and conversations he'd had, starting with the stunning woman sitting on the park bench.

He'd known who she was before he approached her. Miranda, his cousin's new wife, had described her perfectly. Pretending he wasn't sure, gave him an advantage to see how people introduced themselves. It had been easy enough to pick her out of the crowd, but Miranda had said she was a little skittish where new men were concerned. Why, was anyone's guess. She'd been sitting on the bench, her face to the sun and she just appeared so at peace. So natural. He hadn't been able to see her face until she'd tilted back her head to face the sun. She was dressed professionally but he'd sensed a different side of her. When she turned toward the sun there was something sensual and earthy…something real about her that had truly caught his attention. This was a woman who enjoyed feeling her way through life, not just sitting on the edge. She was open. He liked that.

When she'd turned and stared at him, he'd been stunned for a moment by her bright, blue eyes. They were clear, crystalline –sky blue- with a deep blue ring around the outside. Dark lashes framed them, and above, perfectly sculpted eyebrows. He'd thought she was pretty, until she smiled, and then he'd been momentarily dumbstruck. She was beautiful. Her entire face lit up and she radiated an unearthly beauty. Keeping it all real, and making her appear more approachable, were adorable dimples.

He knew she'd been in shock when she'd found the doll in her office. What kind of a sick bastard would do such a thing? Severing a head from a doll, though juvenile on the surface, was a clear threat directed at Cara. She didn't seem to see that, though he knew she'd get there once the shock wore off. He wondered if she had an ex-boyfriend who was seeking revenge or maybe a new boyfriend with a jealous ex. He hoped there was no new boyfriend, though he had no right to hope. He would be leaving town, once he finished up some loose ends here and then would have a new assignment. The FBI could send him anywhere, though it was likely he would go back to DC where he was hoping to get that promotion his superiors kept dangling in front of him. He wanted his own team and he would get it. He'd worked his ass off for it.

Todd followed Cara into her driveway. Her house was Georgian style and while newer than the century old homes that lined the street, the builder had clearly taken care when building, to ensure it fit in with the neighborhood.

He stepped out of his car and ducked under the garage door as it began to close.

"Sorry about that. It's a habit to hit the button before I get out of my car."

Todd watched her pull her briefcase and purse from the back seat. She appeared to be struggling with the briefcase so he reached for it. "I can take that."

"I don't know why it's so heavy. I didn't even bring any work home. I'll just leave it in the car." She tossed it back and closed the door. "It's been sitting in there since last night anyway. No point in dragging it into the house only to drag it back out again in the morning."

She swiped at a wayward curl that had escaped and was hanging down her forehead. He wondered why she didn't just let it be free. He imagined it framing her face in soft ringlets.

"Come on inside," she called over her shoulder but when she reached for her door, Todd stopped her.

"Wait," he corrected at her questioning expression, "Aren't you forgetting something?"

"What? Oh, sorry. I guess I did for a minute. How do you want to do this?"

"I'll go in first. You wait here."

"Nuh-uh. No way." She shook her head. "I know how these things work. It's the one who is left behind - the one who is told to 'wait here' who ends up getting her throat slashed. Where you go, I go."

Todd stared into twinkling blue eyes and realized she was making a joke. His countenance was meant to tell her he didn't think it was funny, although it was hard to hide his own smile.

He heard her sigh but she complied, leaning against her car as he opened the door to her home.

With a glance over his shoulder, and a twinkle in his own eye, he whispered, "If you're worried, maybe you should get in the car and lock the doors… Just in case." And then he was gone.

Todd explored the house that Cara called home. The kitchen was modern and spacious. Nothing seemed out of place. There were a pair of shoes in front of the sink and a coffee cup on the counter, a dishtowel beside it. He imagined she'd left that there this morning before leaving for work. A round wrought iron table and four chairs with iron grillwork on the backs and leather seats sat in the breakfast nook. The island in the kitchen held a butcher's block of knives. All appeared to be there. A good sign.

The family room was adjoined to the kitchen. A white throw lay over the back of the mint green L-shaped leather sofa, and two sleek white wingback chairs sat as sentinels across the room. The focal point was a marble fireplace that appeared old yet still fit in with the updated décor.

He continued through the house. Checking out Cara's bedroom seemed like snooping however, nothing appeared unusual. There were a few clothes on the floor of her room and everywhere he went he saw shoes, discarded wherever she seemed to have taken them off. He smiled at the personal insight he was getting into Ms. Cara Kane.

The office wasn't quite as neat, with files stacked on the desk as well as samples on the floor. There were bills lying on the desk, probably awaiting payment. A banker's lamp had been turned on. Was it on a timer? It was this room that housed Cara's collectibles. Was that a Fabergé egg? Todd stopped and stared. "What the hell?"

****

It seemed like forever before he finally returned. Cara had opened the car door and was sitting on the front seat with her legs hanging out. When Todd opened the door again, she jumped, hitting the horn on her steering wheel, causing her to jump again.

"Jiminy." She placed her hand over her heart. "I think I just scared ten years off my life."

"Come on in. I want you to see something."

Cara searched his face for a smirk, anything to say he had something very funny to show her. She tried to remember if she'd picked up her underwear last night before bed. She really hoped she had but never in a million years would she have imagined she'd have St. Michael searching her personal space.

There was no smirk and she was suddenly very nervous about entering her own home.

"What?" she asked. "Did he wreck anything?"

"Just come on."

She knew she was moving slowly.

"Nothing's, been damaged. In fact everything seems to be as it should be. Only you can know that for sure, of course, but I want you to take a look at something."

Hurrying her step, she followed Todd through the laundry room and down the hall to the kitchen. With every step, she searched for something out of place. All seemed to be in order.

When he led her to the cabinet in her office, she stopped. There in plain view, was the doll her

Grandmother had given her. Not a head out of place.

"Oh my God. It's not broken. But how is that possible?" She placed her fingers over her lips.

"How many people know about that doll? It's my guess it's someone who knows you well enough to know it's of value for sentimental reasons and although they didn't want to damage the doll, they did want to scare you -or perhaps get back at you for some reason. Is there anyone who's jealous of your relationship with your grandmother?"

"No. Who would be?"

"That's what I'm asking you," he replied. "A cousin? Aunt? Anyone?"

"No. My family is very close. We all have a great relationship with Grandmother. She's the matriarch of our family. Everyone adores her and she them. Well my cousin Barkley's wife doesn't like me much, but it's not a break into my house kind of dislike. Just a contradicting thing like she knows everything about well…everything kind of annoyance."

"Do you have an ex-boyfriend who's mad you dumped him?"

Cara thought of her last date. It had been a while.

"No, my last date was John Russell and that was…" she placed her finger on her lip "about six months ago… no… it's… wow… it's been a year already… And he dumped *me* because I worked too much. Not that I would have wanted to continue dating him. But the nerve of that guy. He actually said he wanted a wife who would have time to take care of him and his home. I told him I was *so* not the girl for him and suggested he hire a maid." Oh she was so over John Russell. Who wouldn't be though? Yes, he was wealthy but he was an arrogant ass. Her sisters had hated him on site, but then again, they didn't like anyone she brought home.

"What about a new boyfriend? Are you seeing anyone now? Someone with a jealous ex-girlfriend?"

Red crept up her neck and she felt warm under Todd's gaze. For a split second she thought he was asking for personal reasons. Good thing she realized her mistake before she opened her mouth. She prayed her thoughts weren't written across her face. "No... I'm not seeing anyone right now, so no jealous ex-girlfriend hiding in the shadows with an axe."

"Who knows about the doll?"

"Anyone who's known me for any length of time and had a tour of the house would have seen it. And that includes clients and friends. Anyone I went to college with. Anyone who knows my parents, my grandmother... a better question would be 'who doesn't know?'."

"But what about this doll in particular?" he continued. "Who would know it's more special over say the Fabergé egg?"

She stared at him as though he were obtuse. "Everything in that cabinet is special. Each item has come from a family member or special friend. This one isn't really any more special than any other. I have several pieces that were given to me by my grandmother."

"Was anyone particularly fixated with this doll more than the egg?"

"You mean besides you?" she responded, sarcasm slipping through. She knew she was being ridiculous and potentially rude, but she was so relieved to discover no one had been in her house.

Todd wasn't amused and she realized that he was just trying to help. "Look, I think it's just like officer 'O'Read'im-his-rights' said when I called about the sedan. It's probably just some kids goofing around. Nothing to worry about."

Todd laughed. It was quick and deep, and stirred feelings in Cara's middle that she didn't think should be stirred.

"'O'read'im-his-rights'?' Where did you get that?"

"Well I couldn't remember his name and I had to call him something."

"Well it suits." He continued to chuckle.

"So now at least we know that he wasn't in my house. That's good. Want some coffee? A Soda?"

"Are you kidding me? You can't just wash your hands of this as though it's all done and over with."

"Why not? No one was here."

"What about the fact that the dolls matched perfectly? Just because it wasn't your doll doesn't mean they weren't in your home."

"It's probably just a coincidence. Come on and set a spell. What can I get y'all to drink? You're wound up tighter than an eight day clock."

She felt his sigh more than heard it.

"A soda will be fine, thanks," he said as they reached the kitchen. "Nice place you've got here."

"Thanks. I bought it a few years ago but I swear, I'm hardly ever here. The pool sure is nice though. It's only ten minutes to the beach… in bad traffic, yet I never make it. Here, I can at least use the pool to cool off at the end of a long hot day. I have my privacy and can swim whenever I want."

"That would be nice."

With drinks in hand, they moved out to the terrace by the pool.

"Earlier, you said that you thought you were losing your mind. What did you mean by that?"

"Oh. That was my outside voice?"

"Musta been, unless I've developed ESP." She stared at him and he continued. "It's my job to listen carefully."

"Well, yes I suppose it is. There have just been weird things goin' on lately. Things moved from the place I was sure I had left them…" she paused for a moment then snapped her fingers and pointed at Todd. "The air-conditioning being turned down to a temperature that was far too cool. The door to my office being open when I was sure I had locked it. Stuff like that."

"Is that all?"

"Well it may not seem like much to you but there are times I've thought I was going crazy."

"That's not what I meant. Is that all that's happened?"

****

The phone rang. Cara went into the house to answer it while Todd continued to look around. He rose from his seat and walked over to the pool bending to feel the temperature.

The yard was vast and even though there was a fence, it wouldn't be difficult to get in. There didn't seem to be a security system. No dog. Nothing that would hinder someone from gaining access if they wanted it enough.

Cara returned and Todd stood, shaking the water from his fingers. "Nothing important. My assistant was

22

just checking on me to see if everything was okay." She smiled "I'm not in the habit of leaving work early."

"Me either."

"Oh. I'm so sorry. Here I am monopolizing your time and you should be getting back to work."

"Nothing to be sorry about. I had no intention of going back to work," he lied. It was a small lie and one he didn't feel guilty about in the least.

He watched her, taking in her curly hair that was barely controlled by a butterfly barrette. He wondered again what it would be like down, flowing around her face and shoulders.

"What?" Cara asked, her head tilted slightly.

Todd choked. "Nothing, I was just thinking that I should get going so you can enjoy your afternoon off."

He didn't like where his thoughts had gone. He wasn't a player and getting involved with anyone wouldn't be smart when he knew he wouldn't be around much longer.

"Would you like to have dinner?"

No one was more surprised than he, when the words came out of his mouth, but he meant them. That too surprised him.

"I'd like that."

"I'll pick you up at seven then?"

"Perfect."

The phone rang again so Todd waved good-bye. He let himself out the front door and backed out of the driveway. As he drove down the street, he once again took in the large majestic homes with mature trees. It really was a great place to live.

With a refocus on the situation, Todd headed straight for the Police department. No sooner was he through the doors, than he saw Reilly and let him have it.

"What the hell kind of cop are you anyway? A woman calls and tells you she thinks she's being followed and you don't even go out to check out the story? How lazy can you be?" He wasn't shouting but he was enunciating every word as he stood over Reilly, knowing his 6' 4" stature, not to mention his posture, was intimidating.

"What the hell are you talking about? Never mind, don't bug me, Mitchell. You think you're such a hot shot, whoever it is, you deal with it. We've got enough real police work here to keep us busy, we don't need to follow any ghost runs."

Todd was disgusted with the man he'd had to work with briefly while undercover and searching for leaks in the Police Department. Reilly had certainly been fit to kill when he'd found out that not only was Todd, Hunter's cousin, a man he despised, but he was also an FBI agent sent to 'spy', as Reilly put it, on good cops. There had been antagonism between them before; now it was palpable.

"Well at least you don't deny your stupidity," Todd mumbled. "Your ghost, as you put it, left a calling card in Ms. Kane's office today and although it wasn't deadly, it wasn't friendly either."

"Ah… Ms. Kane… What sort of calling card? And why did she call you? Is she one of your tarts, Mitchell?"

"Ms. Kane is no tart. Where the hell is your respect for women?" he asked through gritted teeth, hands on his hips in a clear 'don't push me' posture.

"Oh, so that's the way it is. I see. You're doin' her and now you think she should get special treatment. Well it doesn't work that way. No matter who she's sleepin' with."

Todd grabbed Reilly by the shirtfront and pulled him to his feet. "I wouldn't push it, Reilly or you're liable to end up flat on your ass… again."

Both men remembered the time Todd's cousin had sent Reilly on his butt because of a comment made about Hunter's wife, Miranda. Todd smiled an evil grin which just made Reilly angrier.

"You threatenin' me, Mitchell? I got witnesses this time," he added as he looked around the room.

Todd too glanced around the room and saw a number of people put their heads down or turn in the opposite direction. Reilly wasn't a man who was well liked by his fellow officers and Todd was being given a break. However, he also knew that if push came to shove, and it was that blue line against the FBI, there was enough of a rivalry between them that he wouldn't want to test that loyalty too often. Still, he took a chance.

"Doesn't appear as though there are too many witnesses ready to jump to your defense, Reilly. I wouldn't test me again."

"You and Sloan think you're so much better than everyone else."

Todd let go and Reilly plopped back down onto his chair. The animosity had increased between the two men when Todd, along with his cousin Hunter, had made a huge drug bust several months ago. Reilly had been sitting on his ass and didn't pay attention to any intel that showed his partner was dirty and missed the bust completely. He could have worked with Todd and Hunter and been included in the bust, but had chosen not to. He'd been reprimanded by the police chief and blamed the cousins for the embarrassment he felt at being duped by his partner. Reilly had been very vocal about this but Todd didn't give a shit.

Reilly brushed the wrinkles from his shirtfront and mumbled under his breath. "God damn pussy whipped agents… always doin' somethin' for some skirt."

Todd heard what Reilly said but chose to ignore it as he headed for his temporary office to make some phone calls. He closed his door for privacy.

"Rae," he spoke into the phone. "I need a huge favor. I need you to run some tests."

"What kind of tests are we talkin' about, sugar? I certainly hope it's none that involve a rabbit dying." Rae laughed.

"Ah, honey, you seem to have that on your mind a great deal lately. You worried yourself? Who is he? I'll take care of him for you."

"Fat chance. I'm much smarter than that. Nobody's trapping me. Not this girl."

It was the same thing whenever Todd called Rae. They had worked together a few years back and had become friends. Neither one of them had ever entertained the idea of more than that. They were both concentrating too hard on their respective careers. Now she worked for Lightcastle Police Department and they had reconnected.

"Well congratulations on the good news then." He paused. "Seriously, Rae, I'm sending a package over to you. I need to know what, if anything, you can get off it."

"What kind of package?" she asked again.

"You'll see. There's no investigation yet but I've got this weird feeling that it's more than it appears to be. Call it a hunch."

"You and your *hunches*. I swear you and Hunter are so much alike it scares me."

"I always knew you were a chicken at heart."

"At least I've got a heart."

She was quick on the responses. He had to give her that. "When can you get to it?" he asked turning serious once again.

"As soon as it arrives, I'm on it."

"Thanks, Rae."

"Yeah, you owe me."

****

Cara was disappointed to be called to the phone as Todd was leaving. Removing her earring she waved goodbye, and spoke into the receiver.

"Hello?"

There was silence.

"Hello?"

She hung up, remembering the other thing that had been bothering her. It was all the phone calls, and then silence when she said hello.

"Not serious," she told herself as she sat down at her desk in her home office to do some work.

She sat daydreaming for quite some time before she turned on her computer and pulled up her email. So much spam. God save her from unauthorized mailing lists. She deleted them without even looking.

Chapter Three

Cara struggled with what to wear. She should have asked where they were going so she would know if she was to dress casually or with more sophistication. "Get over it Cara. He's beautiful, yes, but you are a successful woman. You don't need to impress anyone."

She was still rooting through her closet for the perfect outfit when the phone rang.

Leaning her head through the door of her walk-in closet, she listened to be sure she had indeed heard the phone. When she heard the ringing again, she walked to the bedside table to answer the call.

"Hello?"

There was silence once again on the other end and she was about to hang up when a voice spoke.

"What took you so long?"

"I'm sorry you must have the wrong number," she said as she hung up the phone and turned back to her closet. One outfit was discarded after another. What was she doing? It was just dinner.

A black sleeveless dress was pulled from the rack. With a slightly tailored body and hem that went to her ankles it would be perfect for either occasion. All she had to do was pick the shoes to dress it up or make it casual. She would just wait until Todd arrived and choose then.

"You're brilliant," she told herself. *You're an idiot* her mind responded and she laughed at herself.

Fifteen minutes later, she was waiting in her home office. Todd wouldn't be there for at least another half hour so she decided to see if she could get some work done. There was a never-ending supply of email. She answered a few letters and requests, until she found one that disturbed her. It was an apparent love letter and she felt awful for having read it. Some poor soul had evidently poured his heart out to his love and then made a slip-up when typing in the email address. She thought about replying to the sender to let him know that he had made an error, but decided against it and instead, deleted it. There was no point in embarrassing him. He would probably just assume it had gone missing in cyberspace and send another one, hopefully getting the address correct next time. In any case there was no harm done.

She heard the car just as she saw the lights shine through the crack in the curtains of her office. Turning out the light, she peeked out the window to see what Todd was wearing. If there was a need for a last minute change, she would need every second she could get. With a sigh, she allowed the curtain to close and began to make her way down the hall toward the front door.

She tried to tell herself the sigh was for her choice in attire-she would wear the gold strappy sandals to dress up the outfit. But her logical mind wouldn't let the excuse take hold without acknowledging the real reason. It was for those broad shoulders. Broad shoulders in a tailored navy suit. She sighed again.

The doorbell rang and she hurried her steps to get to it, slipping on her sandals as she opened the door.

****

Todd ran his eyes up and down the beautiful woman standing in front of him. The dress clung just enough to give a hint of the shape beneath it.

He whistled, a slow sound coming from his lips and Cara blushed. "I didn't mean to embarrass you," he said when he noticed the pink tinge to her cheeks, "but you're a knockout."

"Pfft. Hardly. But thanks."

Todd chose not to comment further as he was already affected enough by this woman. He watched as she pushed a stray strand of hair away from her face. He put his hands in his pockets to keep from reaching for the strand himself. The intense need to touch her was something he wasn't accustomed to dealing with. He had always prided himself on his self-control, yet here he was fighting a need so strong he had his hands, still in his pockets, fisted tight with restraint.

What, exactly, was he doing here? He had gone back to the office to take care of a few things that couldn't wait, or rather things he didn't want to wait, and used as an excuse to take his mind off the woman who seemed to have entered his awareness, against his better judgment. He reminded himself, again, that he would be leaving soon. Things were just about wrapped up here, and he would be moving on to another case, in another town. He didn't have time to get involved, even if he wanted to. Okay so he wanted to, more than he wanted to admit to himself, but it wasn't smart.

"Did you want to come in for a drink before we go?" she asked. "Or do we need to get going right away?"

"A drink would be good," he said, even as he told himself it would be smarter to leave right away; smarter to get to the restaurant where they would be in plain view of other people and he wouldn't be as tempted to take her in his arms and kiss those full lips.

"Todd?"

"I'm sorry, what did you say?" he asked, realizing that he had been staring.

"I asked what you would like."

"Anything's fine. Whatever you're having."

Cara poured another white wine and then turned to hand one to Todd. He had stepped closer, taking in her scent and because of that, he nearly wore the contents of the glass.

"Sorry," she said as he took the delicate crystal from her fingers. For the briefest of seconds, their fingers touched and heat shot through him.

"My fault," Todd apologized. "I have a habit of startling you."

"You are a very quiet man. I don't seem to hear you move at all."

His ability to move quietly had saved his life on several occasions but he wouldn't mention that to her. Most women didn't want details of the danger he faced on a regular basis. Well some, he supposed got off on that, but he didn't think Cara was one of them and honestly, those that did, didn't interest him.

"Where are we going tonight?" she asked filling the silence.

"I thought we would head up to Barefoot Landing in Myrtle Beach. It's a nice night and I figured we could walk around after dinner."

"Gosh I haven't been there in so long. It's such a quaint place. I love it there."

Todd had asked around for a good place to go to dinner and Barefoot Landing had been mentioned a few times for a casual night that didn't carry a lot of commitment. It was a bit of a drive, but he was assured it was worth it.

"We should probably get going then. Let me grab a wrap -just in case it cools off."

They were about to leave when the phone rang. Todd stopped, assuming that she would want to answer it.

"No. It's probably just another hang-up. And if not, it will be a family member and then it will be hours before I can get off the phone. If it's important, they'll leave a message."

"You've been getting a lot of hang-ups?"

"Some. It happens." She raised her shoulders in a shrug then waved her hand as though to brush it aside.

"If you say so." Todd held the door open for her.

"Nice car. How did you find one in such great shape?"

Todd viewed his car with pride. The sun was glinting off the chrome and the paint was bright and shiny –not a spot of dirt, let alone rust, in sight.

"Actually it took hours upon hours of manual labor. I still have calluses to prove it."

"You mean you did the restore yourself?"

****

He seemed so at ease in his expensive suit, she was surprised by the new image; that of a man in jeans and a greasy tee shirt lying beneath a car. She had to admit she liked both images.

"Don't sound so surprised. Should I be insulted?"

"Oh Lord. That's not what I meant. I just didn't picture you in tight jeans and… well… I mean you look so good in your suit… and… Oh my word. I'm completely embarrassed."

"Nothing to be embarrassed about. You see

someone in a certain style and you assume that's the only mold they fit into. It's human nature. Why should you assume they have a different style, or a different life, if you've never seen it?"

"Yeah, that's exactly what I was trying to say," she lied, sarcastic tone slipping through.

"But seriously, my grandfather used to have one of these," she continued trying to smooth over her blunder. "I used to love to sit behind the steering wheel pretending I was driving to some dance. Of course I was only eight so it was a complete stretch."

She stroked the dash of the 57 Chevy Corvette remembering her granddaddy and the fun they'd had pretending she was a racecar driver, or his chauffer.

"He even let me drive it once when Mom and Grandmother weren't around."

"At eight?" Todd asked amazed. "Was he nuts?"

"Grandmother thought so when she found out about it. She was madder than a wet hen. I thought she would string Granddaddy up by his toes." She smiled wistfully.

"And I take it she didn't... string him up that is."

"No, she eventually forgave him because she loved him but she warned him that she had better not hear about another driving lesson until I was old enough to do it legally."

"You kept the other times secret then, did you?" Todd chuckled.

"You got it. No way I was getting Granddaddy into trouble and losing a chance to drive such a sweet car. I'm no fool."

There was a moment of silence before she asked, "How did you guess?"

"I don't know, I guess it just made sense. And don't

forget, I'm trained to hear what people aren't saying."

"So how long have you been a special agent?" Cara asked. "Or is that classified?" She smiled.

"Well you've heard the saying, 'I could tell you but then I'd have to shoot you', right?" At her laugh, he continued. "Fifteen years… any private roads nearby?"

Cara snorted. "None at all. They're all very well populated."

"So how did you get into Interior Design?"

"Well I was enrolled in law school –because both my parents and my sisters are lawyers- but I hated it. I helped to redesign our sorority den and I loved every minute of it. So I switched up classes and didn't tell my parents for months. I didn't want to disappoint them. Not that they would ever be anything other than supportive. Now my sisters –well that was another story. They didn't feel I gave it enough of a chance but it was plenty as far as I was concerned. Certainly enough to know it didn't float my boat. I am happier with the artsy side of life. It's far more fulfilling for me. Décor isn't just something frivolous or superficial. It defines how our home feels and it should be a reflection of who we are. It should offer comfort at the end of a long day."

Once they arrived, Todd found parking and they walked to the entrance of the restaurant, hands touching every now and again as their arms swung. They were ushered to their table immediately and conversation was easy and enjoyable. They talked about their childhood, college, and family. Todd shared stories of antics with his cousin Hunter that made Cara laugh so hard, her ribs ached.

"And dessert for you both?" the waiter asked with what Todd said he was sure was a fake French accent.

"Oh goodness. Not for me," Cara gasped, placing her hand on her stomach. "If I eat another bite, I'll have to waddle home."

"None for me either," Todd replied

"I'll get your bill then."

As he walked away, Cara laughed. "Could he look down his nose any further?"

"He is a bit... what's the word I'm searching for?" he asked as he searched his memory.

"Arrogant? Pompous? Ostentatious? Take your pick."

"Sure any of those will work nicely."

They laughed, trying without success to smother their chuckles when the waiter returned with their check.

"Thank you for dining with us."

"You're welcome," Cara answered and then started laughing all over again when the waiter's face registered his annoyance.

"Why the heck would he work here if he doesn't enjoy it?" she asked. "Life's too short to do something you find distasteful."

"Who knows why people do the things they do. There's always some reason somewhere that they feel justifies their choices."

"Yes but... Oh never mind. Like you said, who knows?"

"Why don't we walk around a little bit? It's a nice night."

"I'd like that."

They pretended they were tourists and fed the huge carp in the pond. Cara asked Todd in a rather loud voice if they were sharks and then listened to the squeals of laughter of the children beside her.

"Well, darlin', I'm not sure, but I think they might be. Sure looks like it to me," Todd answered enjoying the game.

They were about to enter the candy store when Cara's cell phone rang. "Oh nuts," she exclaimed. "That's my phone. Just hold on a second while I see if it's family. My sister is expecting."

With her arm in her very large handbag, she searched for her phone. "Here it is," she said pulling it out and swiping to answer.

"Hello?"

"What took you so long?"

"What?"

"What took you so long to answer the phone?"

The words came back to her. They were the same words she had heard earlier in the evening when she had assumed it was a wrong number. Only it obviously hadn't been.

"How did you get this number?"

"Are you having a nice night out?"

"Who are you?"

"You don't remember me? I'm hurt."

Cara didn't wait for another word, she just hung up. Feeling disoriented and a little lightheaded, she reached for Todd's arm only to find that it wasn't there. With dismay, she felt as though she were floating.

Todd swept her up into his arms, carrying her to a rocking-chair outside one of the small stores.

"Cara," he called her name tapping her face lightly to get her attention. "What is it?" he asked almost shouting in her face.

"It was him again."

"Who again? Cara, it was who again?" he repeated

when she didn't answer.

"The man on the phone. He asked me what took me so long to answer the phone. He asked me that earlier -at home," she clarified, "And I thought it was a wrong number. How did he get my cell phone number? Only my family and my assistant have that number."

"Anyone can find a number if they work at it hard enough. It's not that difficult."

Cara stared. She said nothing at all. Her breathing shallowed. Her heart raced.

"He knows I'm out. Oh God."

"I think we should go home. We'll call the police from there."

"They can't do anything."

She was shaking. Todd pulled her close hugging her-holding her as though he wanted to protect her from the world.

The phone rang again and Cara jumped.

"Don't answer it," Todd snapped. "Sorry, I didn't mean to sound so surly but I'm worried about you."

"I have to. It won't be him again. He won't call twice in a row." She tried to sound confident but wasn't certain she had pulled it off. She hoped and prayed she was right.

"How often has he called?"

"Hello?" she answered quietly, ignoring Todd.

Chapter Four

"Hello?" she repeated a little louder and more shrill.

"Cara? Sorry. Timmy was talking to me and I didn't hear you answer. Is everything okay? You sound upset."

"No I'm fine," she lied. "What's wrong?"

"I just needed to confirm that you're going to be able to make it to Mom and Dad's anniversary party a week from Saturday. The date's been changed... again, and I wasn't sure if you remembered. I hope it's still going to be okay. You did remember didn't you?"

"Of course I remembered, Em. It's their fiftieth. I couldn't forget that."

"And you're taking care of the flowers right?"

"Oh nuts," she mumbled.

"What was that? You did remember you were taking care of the flowers right?"

"Don't worry about it. The flowers will be there."

Todd held his head close, listening.

"Listen, Em, I have to go. I'm in the middle of something here. I'll talk to you tomorrow."

When she hung up, her eyes were filled with worry and seemed more intense. They glistened, as though she were on the verge of tears and that made the blue, bluer somehow.

"It was just my sister, Emily. I forgot I have to get flowers for my parents' fiftieth wedding anniversary for next week. God I hope it's not too late. How could I have forgotten the flowers? Thank God Em called. I'll take care of it tomorrow."

Todd watched as she put her head in her hands. She shook like she might be sobbing and he felt useless. Rubbing his hand up and down her spine, he tried to comfort her. It was a useless effort, he knew, but he tried it anyway.

"Let's get you home," he said as he searched the area around him. There wasn't a great deal of chance that whoever had made the call was actually watching them as he instinctively checked to be sure he was never followed, but he still would prefer to get her in her own home where she wasn't so vulnerable. There was a crowd beginning to gather as well and he didn't really think Cara would appreciate being stared at.

Standing a little woodenly, Cara allowed herself to be guided back to Todd's car, but she straightened her posture as she did so. Once inside she fastened her seatbelt and waited for Todd to get in the other side.

"He asked how I was enjoying my night out and told me I should enjoy myself. It sounded threatening. You know…the way he said it."

"Any idea who it is? Did you recognize his voice?"

"No, at least I don't think so. It sounded like it was electronically enhanced or something; distorted maybe, but not in a huge way so it still sounded like a normal voice. Yet somehow, it all seems familiar."

"Have you gotten calls before?"

"No. My family says I can't remember anything but I would remember that. I know I would. I'm not ashamed to admit it. I'm scared."

"You should be," Todd told her. "If you're scared, you'll be more careful and that could save your life."

He heard the inhalation of her breath and chastised himself for his bluntness but he wouldn't take the words back. He couldn't. She needed to be on her toes.

"What part of it do you think sounds familiar? The voice? The words?"

"I think it's the voice. It was sinister sounding… in tone… if that makes any sense. It must be the voice. But if it were distorted, that's impossible."

"Did you notice anything in the background noise? Traffic? Music? Anything?"

Obviously, she was feeling a little better because she rolled her eyes at him. "I wasn't exactly listening for background noise, but if he calls back, I'll try to pay more attention."

"Just a shot," Todd said. He forgot sometimes that others weren't trained as he was. He spent so much time with his cousin, and now Hunter's former partner, Alex, that he was just used to people who thought like he did.

"I know you're just trying to help and I appreciate it. I'm sorry I was sarcastic."

Todd used his own cell phone to call the police. He wanted them there when they arrived, just in case there was a surprise waiting.

****

They pulled into Cara's driveway and Todd shut off the car.

"When we go inside, you stick to me like glue. Got it?"

"Yes sir." She sighed. "I'm sorry, it just seems silly to have the police coming because of a phone call. Ridiculous, really."

"Obviously you forget how frightened you were when you got that call. I certainly remember you going as white as a sheet. We wait for the police and then we go together."

"But…"

There was no time for another protest as the police arrived, lights flashing, but thank God, no sirens. The cars that would fit pulled into the driveway. One of them had to park on the street.

Todd snarled when he saw who was getting out of one of the cars. "God dammit. What the hell is Reilly doing here?"

"Hopefully his job," Cara answered. "Sorry I can become sarcastic when I'm under stress. It's not an attractive quality.

"Mitchell," Reilly acknowledged Todd. "Ma'am." He nodded in Cara's direction.

"My name's Officer Reilly. Would you like to tell me what this is all about and why we've been called in?" he asked, his chest puffed out with self-importance.

"I thought that was why *you* were here. To find out what was going on. If I knew, I could have done something about it, couldn't I?"

She knew she sounded petulant, even childish, but she didn't like this man. Partially because he had ignored her and treated her like a dim-witted female when she had called the first time, but now that she had met him, she realized that was only part of it. He was a short man by most standards, barrel-chested with thick beefy hands, but the reason she disliked him was because she had seen him in the supermarket the other day demeaning his wife. She had been completely embarrassed for her and had to stem the urge to walk right up to her and tell her to leave the turd.

She hadn't though, so the poor woman was probably

still putting up with the arrogant idiot. She could recommend a good lawyer for her. She had sisters, and several of her friends who had gone into family law and they were all very good at their jobs.

"Reilly, why don't you go inside and check the place out and then we can get Ms. Kane in and out of the night air."

"Why don't you mind your own God damned business and let me do my job, Mitchell? This is my case. Butt out."

Turning to Cara, he continued his questioning. "Are you involved in anything you shouldn't be? Unsavory boyfriend –other than present company I mean?"

"Mr. O'Leary," she said purposefully getting his name wrong, and ignoring the fact he was an officer. "I am a very successful interior designer. I have no need to be participating in or with anyone 'unsavory'. I am not a criminal and I will not be questioned as such. Are we clear? Or would you like me to call either one of my parents, both of whom are lawyers with the Department of Justice?"

"It's Officer Reilly," he corrected, anger rising and coloring his skin.

"Whatever. If you would be so kind as to make my home available to me, I know we could all be more comfortable throughout this process. Chief Aldrich certainly felt comfortable the last time he was here."

Todd choked as he watched Reilly's face turn a dangerous shade of purple. Cara seemed so easy going, laid back, so it was a surprise to see this side of her. He liked it. She wasn't a shrinking violet and could certainly hold her own when she needed to. He supposed though, growing up in a home filled with lawyers, she would have picked up a few things.

Turning on his heal, he marched over to the front door and entered. Todd just hoped he didn't compromise any evidence.

"You did a great job of putting him in his place. But what I don't understand is, if you know Chief Aldrich, why didn't you call him when you didn't get results earlier?"

"I've never met the Chief."

"You lied," Todd exclaimed, eyes wide and his hand over his heart? "I'm usually an excellent judge of character and I wouldn't have known."

"I most certainly did not." Cara sounded offended, as she picked at an invisible piece of lint on her dress.

"What… did you buy the place off him?"

"No. Actually his sister owned it."

She smiled then and Todd wanted to kiss her. It was like a craving. He didn't do it, but oh God, he wanted to.

Hours later, Cara's home was once again declared her own.

"You know that… Reilly," she said his name as though it were too distasteful to even speak, "is a butthead."

"You don't have to tell me that. It took me all of about fifteen seconds to figure that one out on my own."

"You're not real quick with first impressions then?" she asked innocently.

"I was trying to give him the benefit of the doubt at the time. I figured I had to be wrong about him because no one could be that bad."

"Well it's something you could work on. We all have our areas of challenge."

The phone rang startling them both. Todd checked

his watch and put his hand on Cara's wrist to stop her from answering it. "It's two o'clock in the morning. Your family wouldn't be calling now."

"Not unless my sister Lilly had her baby. I have to answer it."

"Don't you have voicemail?"

"Old school answering machine. It's in my office."

"Let it answer and then you'll know who it is."

They ran to Cara's home office and listened while the machine picked up. There was silence and then the voice began to recite Sir Walter Scott.

"Oh what a tangled web we weave…," then silence again.

Cara stared at Todd as he listened for something in the background. If there was anything that would help them, he was trying to hear it. At least he would be able to take the recording and see if he could get anything off it. Maybe with some of the equipment he had access to in the lab, he could get something…anything.

Cara pressed her hand to her lips as she waited in the silence.

"I can hear you breathing," the voice whispered.

Cara gasped. Todd held one finger to his lips telling her to be quiet.

With eyes wide, she waited. Her breathing was faster than it should be and she felt lightheaded again but still, she stayed, listening to what the voice had to say.

"Did you like my present?" It's just like the one you have. Just like you'll be."

There was an audible click and Cara's knees collapsed. "Oh my God. He could hear me breathing. Todd how could he hear me breathing? How could he do that?"

44

"Do you have an option on your answering machine that allows you to monitor your home?"

"I d-don't know. I don't think so."

"Then he couldn't hear you, Cara. He was just saying that to scare you."

"Well, it worked. I'm scared."

"Try not to let him get to you. That's exactly what he wants to do. He's trying to control you with fear."

"Like I said, he's good at it."

****

Todd distracted Cara by making small talk, trying to keep her mind off the caller until she calmed somewhat. It took some time, but she began to relax. He checked out the house again, just to be sure that all the doors and windows were secure.

"You really should get a security system. At the very least, a dog."

"I've never needed one."

"Well you should get one now. And call display too. Call your phone company tomorrow and get it. I thought everyone had it."

"I didn't need it either. No one except my family and my employees have my home number." She paused. "Well my close friends too."

Todd just stared at her.

"Okay so a lot of people have it, but it's not a listed number. I've never needed call display or security before." Sighing, she continued. "Fine, I'll call the phone company tomorrow."

Todd was giving instructions to Cara to lock the door behind him as he was leaving. They stood for a moment in the doorway staring into each other's eyes. Slowly, to give Cara time to change her mind if she chose, Todd leaned forward and gently pressed his lips to hers.

The electricity that shot through him was startling as was the desire that flared. He pulled back afraid that if he didn't do it now, he wouldn't be able to.

Cara placed her hands on Todd's shoulders as though to steady herself then gripped his shoulders as Todd's lips lowered to hers once more.

He would have said goodbye then, but when she reached for him, he was lost. He felt himself grab her to him, pressing her body against his own.

They were standing in the open doorway for all to see. Cara moaned, pressing herself harder against the firmness of Todd's chest. Her hands ran over his broad shoulders causing his muscles to flex beneath his jacket.

"Cara," Todd tried to speak through the kisses Cara was bestowing on him. "Cara, we need to stop or…"

Somehow the words made it through the sensual fog that clouded her thinking.

"I'm sorry."

Her eyes cast downward and a pink blush creeped up her neck and face. Todd tilted her chin up so he could gaze directly in her eyes. "I'm not. Not even close."

Cara smiled then, and Todd turned to leave.

"Don't forget to lock up."

Cara closed the door and was consumed by the silence. She was used to being on her own but tonight she wasn't sure she could handle it.

Every shadow was a potential danger, every creak an intruder. The wind outside was someone trying to break in.

She swung the door open just as the tail lights of Todd's car disappeared down the street. She was on the verge of panic but would pull herself out of it.

"Breathe," she told herself. "Just breathe. Count to ten and breathe."

Slowly she brought herself back to center and then proceeded to turn all the lights on in the house. Her electric bill would go through the roof but she didn't care and she could afford it anyway.

You're being ridiculous. What part of wasting electricity helps the planet? She rationalized it by reminding herself that doing deep breathing added carbon dioxide to the atmosphere and that wasn't good for the planet either.

As she paced back and forth across the kitchen floor, she continued her controlled breathing. She could get deeper breaths and that was a good thing. Her heart rate was slowly returning to normal. She would be fine. It had been a long time since panic attacks were a part of her life. She hadn't missed them, but the coping mechanisms still worked if she could get her mind to remember how to use them.

Something banged against the house in the back yard. Cara screamed, whirling around to face the French doors, placing her hands over her mouth.

A knock at the front door had her whirling back around the other way, panic taking over again.

"Cara?" came the muffled call from the other side of the door. "Are you still up?"

She couldn't seem to move at first but then she couldn't stop herself as she ran to the door, yanking it open.

****

Todd was just getting back into his car and was about to slam his door shut, thinking Cara had already gone to bed but as soon as she opened the door, he saw the panic in her body language. Immediately, without so much as a hesitation, he climbed out of his car and was back at her door.

"What's wrong? Did he call again?"

Feeling foolish now, she struggled for a reasonable explanation for her actions.

"I uh… um… no… I'm fine. I just panicked a little. I'm good now. Honest."

Todd saw her fear. She was obviously very successful in her chosen career but this was out of her wheelhouse. To be expected.

"I just freaked out a little when I heard something bang against the back of the house."

Without thought, Todd grabbed her hand and all but dragged her to the back door. "Wait here," he whispered as he quietly opened the door and headed into the dark.

Within minutes he was back, holding a piece of a broken planter in his hand. It was shades of blue and green and had contained some kind of palm.

"Was this broken before?

"Gawd," she sighed. "No. That too was my Grandmother's. How the blazes did that happen? Was there an animal?"

"Not unless it's of the two legged variety. There are size ten men's sneaker prints in the dirt. I'm guessing they were scared off when I arrived back here."

She was shaking again. He could see the signs of shock setting in so he grabbed the throw from the sofa in the family room and wrapped it around her, pulling her close and rubbing his hands up and down her arms.

"I will call this in again. I want forensics to get an imprint of that size ten. Come sit down. This will only take a minute."

The police arrived again, lights flashing. They bagged and tagged items from her garden and made a mold of the shoe print. After many more hours, they finally left.

"The neighbors are going to want me to move with all the commotion I'm causing."

"It's not your fault," he responded. "Hey… what's this?" he asked, tilting her head up and seeing tears.

"I'm fine," she said quietly-too quietly as far as Todd was concerned.

"Clearly you're more shaken than you realize. Would you like me to call someone? Your parents? A sister? Want me to sleep on your sofa?" he joked.

"Would it be too much to ask? I mean, I have a spare bedroom already made up and it's late anyway."

"Sure, I can spend the night if it would make you feel better."

"Seriously? Don't kid me now. My sisters would blow this all out of proportion and make things worse. And I wouldn't want to be responsible for you being in an accident on the way home." Smiling a tremulous smile, Cara thanked him. She knew he saw through her excuse. She knew he was staying with her because she was afraid to be alone in her own house.

"Thank you, but in all seriousness, I will be fine. I will check to ensure all the windows and doors are locked, and will keep my cell by my bed. I will be fine." The words were spoken quietly but they reached his heart.

"Anytime. I truly wouldn't mind. But call if you hear anything else. I mean it."

Chapter Five

Todd was surprised when Cara asked if he could stay the night and then was disappointed when she said she was joking. He would have stayed. He couldn't have turned her down if he'd had to. He would, of course, have preferred to be in the same room as her... in the same bed... but the timing wasn't right.

As it was, he was crazy enough to try to sleep in his car a block down the street to be close, just in case he was needed again. It was uncomfortable and while he was usually great at power naps, rest was not on the agenda. When things remained quiet, he drove home to try to catch a wink or two of sleep.

No sooner had he closed his eyes, than he opened them again; a bright light shining in his eyes. He dragged his exhausted body from his bed, stretching his back, one vertebrae at a time. He groaned, raising his arms above his head and strode toward the shower. Cold would wake him. It was painful, but he did it.

As he dried himself off, he wondered how Cara's night was. Why was he so concerned about her and why was she consuming his mind first thing in the morning? He had numerous other items on his to do list today, but still she filled his thoughts.

He inhaled his coffee and burned his lip because he wasn't paying attention. He would have taken it intravenously, if he could. With a glance at the clock, he grabbed his keys and headed out the door. He had time to stop at Cara's to see how she was doing, before he went to work.

****

The doorbell rang, causing Cara to jump. She sloshed her coffee, nearly hitting her top as she jumped back trying to get out of the way. It fell with a splat on the floor.

"Jiminy," she whispered as she threw a paper towel down over it and walked to the door, being sure to check through the window to see who it was before opening it. The stupid caller had her on edge.

"Oh, good morning, Todd. Come on in. Coffee is hot and strong. I feel like you could use it as much as me."

She bent over to finish wiping up the spilled coffee, speaking while her head was still down. "I'm just making some breakfast. Have you eaten? Would you like something to eat? A bagel? I have fruit too."

"A bagel and some of those strawberries would be great," he added pointing at them on the counter. "That would help my mood I'm sure, and a coffee would be a godsend. I can survive anything, as long as I have enough caffeine," he joked.

"Would you like anything else? Eggs? Toast? Cereal?"

"No this will be fine. I need to get into work soon anyway. And I want to pop out to the house to check on things there. You know—make sure I'm on the same page as Hunter with the build—but wanted to see how you were doing this morning and make sure all was quiet after I left last night."

"Ooh, I want to go out to the build too," she said right before tossing the last piece of a bagel into her mouth and walking toward the bathroom. "Just let me brush my teeth again. I have strawberry seeds stuck." She grimaced. "I hate that. And I didn't hear anything else," she called from down the hall.

When she returned, she had her hair pinned up and in place. Well, as much as she was able. It certainly had a mind of its own this morning –much like her brain. She had seen Todd at the door and for a moment, thought he was here to see her, but while she'd brushed her teeth – and flossed as that seed was not wanting to leave its secure space in her mouth -she realized he was just doing his job and was verifying there were no other issues through the night.

Todd was staring at her, and she glanced down, brushing her hands down the front of her top and skirt. Buttons were all closed and she didn't see any toothpaste on her shirt.

The tension in the room was thicker than a bramble bush. Maybe he felt she was overstepping.

"Are you okay if I come out with you? We can take two cars and I can then go to the office, but I want to make sure you and I are on the same page too." She paused feeling uncertain. "I mean, I don't want to insert myself where I'm not wanted or anything but I have a clear vision for the house and I pride myself on making sure my clients get what they want."

There was a buzzing sound and Todd reached into his jacket pocket, pulling out his phone. "Mitchell," he answered, holding up his finger as though to put her on hold, then walking toward the hall for some privacy. "Got it. On my way," she heard as he turned back, facing her again.

"Can we go after work today? They're pouring the

foundation this morning and I just got a call I have to deal with. I can meet you at your office, if that works and we can take one car. That work for you?"

"Sure. I can do that. I have clients until six though."

"Perfect. In the meantime, you've got my card." He pointed to the counter where he'd set his card. "If you hear anything at all, call that number."

When she picked the card up off the counter to show him that she did indeed have it, he took it from her writing another number underneath the one printed.

"This is my personal cell phone. Call me if you can't get me in my office. Do you want to give me your cell number so I can call you with the results of the tests? Or do you just want me to call your office?"

"What tests?"

She scrutinized this man and all thought seemed to flee her mind. She had trouble thinking. Heavens, she couldn't even sleep last night knowing someone was watching her and when she wasn't panicking, she was thinking of him and how she wished she would have accepted his offer of staying the night. She sighed. But she hadn't. Part of her knew she was being smart, but another part, a deeper part, was disappointed.

Now she was having trouble remembering what tests had been done. Try as she might, she couldn't recall what he was talking about. In her mind, she rewound the conversation but still came up empty.

"The forensic testing on the doll and the testing from last night. I'm not sure how long it will be, before they come back, but you never know. It could be today or tomorrow.

"Oh right." Was that her voice? Her words? You would never know she was a successful woman by the conversation she was having this morning. What was wrong with her?

Handing Todd a business card of her own, she added her home and cell numbers in ink.

"You can call me at any of the numbers. It doesn't matter which." As an afterthought, she added another number to the card. "This is my direct line to my office. It won't go by way of my assistant but ring directly to me. Give me a call when you're ready to go to the house. I really want to see the progress being made for myself." She paused and tucked a stray curl that had escaped behind her ear. "Or seriously, if it's a problem, I can go on my own later. No big deal."

Using the card to salute her, he turned to leave, then glanced back. "You'll be okay? Do you want me to follow you into work?"

"No thank you. I'll be fine. I'm leaving in a few minutes anyway. I just need to check my face and grab some samples from my office. Then I'm ready."

Todd strolled back and tilted her chin up to see directly into her eyes. "Your face is fine as far as I'm concerned." He kissed her. "Perfect, in fact."

Cara sighed as the door closed behind Todd. She needed to get a grip on her racing heart. What was it about this man? Well besides the incredibly wide expanse of shoulders, firm and thick with muscles that rippled down a flat stomach to very narrow hips… Sure he was attractive but she had seen attractive men before. Although he affected her in a very physical way, there was something else to it. She just couldn't put her finger on it.

When she arrived at the office, Ivy was already at her desk and flirting with a courier.

"Goodness that woman attracts an overabundance of testosterone. Ivy would say 'hashtag blessed'." Cara chuckled.

"Oh here she is now," Ivy said as Cara passed. "Ms. Kane, this handsome man was waiting for you to get here so he could deliver your package. Wasn't that dreamy of him?"

Dreams. That's why Todd seemed so familiar. Well she wouldn't ever tell anyone about that or they'd have her committed. She had been dreaming about him for years. It was silly, she knew, but it was him... At least it certainly looked like him. She began second-guessing herself.

"What?" she asked as Ivy called to her again.

"I said, wasn't that dreamy of him?"

"Absolutely dreamy," Cara mimicked the receptionist. "But you should probably let the poor man get his work done. You could have sent him up to my office. Paige is there and could have signed."

"Oh I'm sorry," Ivy said to the courier, batting her eyelashes. "I didn't even think of that. And here I've wasted all your time. Will you get in terrible trouble?"

Cara snorted, rolling her eyes, as she picked up the clipboard off the counter and found her own name. "I signed thanks, so I'll just take the package up myself."

No one was listening.

The elevator doors opened soon after she pushed the button and Cara relished the silent ride by herself. She was about to step inside when Ivy yelled over to her "Cara, can we meet at lunch instead today? Are you free? My treat. I swear I won't be late this time."

"Let me check with Paige but I think that will work."

Stepping inside the elevator she pushed the button

for her floor. Just as the door was about to close, the accountant from one floor above hers, grabbed the door and stepped inside. She sighed, saying good-bye to her few minutes of solitude.

"Good morning, Cara," he said barely above a whisper. He stood directly beside Cara causing her to move closer toward the wall. She could feel the heat from his body, smell his cologne and thought she would gag with its pungency.

"Good morning."

For the life of her she couldn't remember his name. She hoped she wouldn't have to use it.

"I was wondering..." he started in a voice that sounded far too whiny for a man of his age.

Cara waited for him to continue. When it appeared as though he weren't going to, Cara debated ignoring him. In the end she prompted him to continue.

"You were wondering?" she asked.

"Well... Oh never mind. Here's your floor. I'll maybe stop by and talk to you about it later... If that's okay," he added.

"I'm in the office all day but I have appointments spread out throughout most of it. Whatever works... Give my assistant a call."

She let the rest hang in the air, not making any commitment one way or the other. The elevator doors closed behind her and Mr. Smith disappeared.

"That's his name," she said snapping her fingers. "Bill or something. No James. James Smith." She'd known it was something common. No sooner had the thought registered, than she let it go again.

"Good morning, Paige."

Paige stood up from her filing as her boss walked

through the door.

"G'mornin', Sunshine. How are you feeling?"

Cara ignored the nickname Paige had given her the first week she had started working for Cara. No matter how hard she had tried, she couldn't get her to call her by something more dignified. Eventually she had given up.

"Fine, Paige. Do I have any messages before the Marshall's arrive?"

"Actually, the Marshall's called to postpone their appointment. Mrs. Marshall isn't feeling well today and she said she would rather not throw up…"

"Never mind Paige. I get the picture. Did she set up another appointment?"

"She'll call tomorrow and if you don't hear from her you're to call her because she's forgotten."

"Not to worry, Mr. Marshall won't forget. Mrs. Marshall has a lot on her mind right now with her pregnancy but Mr. Marshall is being extra attentive," Cara said dismissing the mental note she had made to call two of her best clients. "I'll be in my office, if you need me."

"You got it."

As Cara closed the door to her office she could hear Paige humming along to a tune that was obviously only playing in her own mind. Cara smiled. Paige was such a sweetheart, so full of a fun loving attitude that all who met her were completely captivated by her. Cara was glad she'd had the good sense to hire her.

There was a knock on the door and Cara looked up just as Paige entered the room. You left this on my desk. It's addressed to you 'Personal and Confidential', but would you like me to open it?"

"No thanks, Paige. Just leave it on the table over there and I'll get to it later."

Paige did as directed and walked to the door where she stopped and turned to her boss. "Uh, Ivy said that…"

Cara waited.

"Ivy said what? And before I forget, change her meeting time to lunch. I think that should be okay, right? You are the schedule wizard. If it won't work, call down to let her know. And if Todd Mitchell calls, put him right through."

"That's what I want to talk to you about," Paige told her.

"What?"

"Well Ivy said she saw you leave yesterday with a man and I just wanted to make sure you were okay." Pausing briefly, she waited for Cara to give some sort of explanation. When it wasn't forthcoming, she stammered forward. "It isn't any of my business, but it isn't like you to leave in the middle of the day, especially with a man. And a very attractive man at that, I hear." The last was added in an exaggerated whisper. "Ivy said you looked upset."

"Paige, there is nothing to worry about. I just had some things I needed to take care of outside the office. You remember what that was like when I was just starting out. It was nothing more."

"If you say so. But Ivy thought…"

"Don't pay any attention to what Ivy thought. Trust me, it's nothing to worry about." She smiled but didn't feel like the smile reached her eyes. She was edgy this morning and didn't know why. Maybe her lack of sleep, but she didn't want to take it out on anyone else. She added an apology for her grumpiness.

Paige went back to her desk, and Cara returned to her work. She had a great many things to take care of and although she was disappointed the Marshall's had canceled their appointment, she was somewhat relieved to be able to catch up on the work she hadn't completed when she'd left early.

The morning flew by and true to her word, Ivy was there with sandwiches and salad for lunch.

"I told you I wouldn't be late. And aren't these the best sandwiches? It's a new place across the park."

"So good Ivy, thank you. Now what have you accomplished on your 'to-do' list we made last session. Have you drawn up any designs? Struggling? Reviewed any schools and accreditations to finish your courses? If you want to be a designer, and own your own business, one of the most important things is setting your priorities to get things done."

"Well I did do up a drawing. I did one of your house. An outdoor kitchen," she clarified. "It was so pretty back there when our group met last week but I thought it would be great to have the additional space defined. Not that you have to do one but I wanted to practice on something that would be closer to home for you, so I could gage how I'm doing on getting what other people like, instead of what I like. Just like you told me to do. It isn't about my tastes, but about the clients, and Paige said you were wanting to make some changes..." Her voice trailed off.

Tentatively, she pulled a page from a folder and handed it across the table to Cara, her head down, not making eye contact.

Cara turned the page over and sucked in her breath, causing Ivy to glance up, eyes wide.

"It's terrible, isn't it? I knew it. I can't do this. I'm not talented like you."

"Ivy, it's beautiful. You've done a fabulous job of creating the new area but making it appear as though it was always there. That's a great feat, and so important, especially in an historic district. Well done, girl."

"Really? I mean…Thank you." Ivy blushed and lowered her head again.

"Girl, you need to start believing in yourself. Don't ever sell yourself short. You are so much more than your beauty. You're smart and have so many talents. And never let anyone tell you differently."

"Well that design is for you… if you want it, that is. I wanted to say thank you for all you've done to help me. I gave notice this week and will be gone by the end of the month. I'm moving back home. My family needs me, but I promise I will keep working at this and I will even register for school as soon as I'm home and settled in again."

"Oh wow. I had no idea you were considering leaving us. We will miss you. The office building won't be the same but you add so much to our meetings as well that I know others are going to miss you too."

"Thank you. I'm going to miss you and everyone else too."

Her head lowered and she fiddled with her fingers as though it were a sad memory so Cara didn't push it.

"And this has been brewing for a while now but it's time," she continued. "You've been so kind to me, taking me under your wing, and building my confidence in myself. I just want you to know how much all of that means to me. I wish I could stay, but I can't. Gawd, I'm so going to miss our meetings… and your friendship."

Tears swam in her eyes.

Cara stood and walked around the table to give her protégé and friend a hug. "If you ever need me, I'm here for you. Just please Ivy, don't sell yourself short. Ever. You have real potential." Tears gathered in her own eyes so she cleared her throat. "And I'm going to frame this drawing and hang it up in my office at home. It will go perfectly there. I am just so proud of you, Ivy."

Several hours later, Paige stuck her head in the office. "I'm leaving now, Sunshine. Do you need anything before I go?"

Eyeing the clock on her computer to see that it was indeed that time, Cara answered. "No thanks. I'll be leaving soon anyway."

It was funny how just a few short years ago, Cara had put her career first. Nothing was as important as getting herself established and her name out there. She supposed a great deal of that push had come from her leaving law. Some had said she was nuts to give up such a great career, including her sisters; both of whom had followed their parents' path, and were successful lawyers, and she'd always felt the need to prove herself.

Some of her 'friends' from law school had written her off when she left, so she'd been on a mission to prove she had made the right choice and had gotten caught up in the materialism of her career a little. She had purchased the grand house, the silver Mercedes. She had the pool and the 'right address'. Even though she had all the 'things' that proved her success, she felt more and more each day, that something was missing. That was when she had started mentoring young women to believe in themselves. There were several in her inner circle now but Ivy was special. She had shown such promise and it was evident she had talent. Somewhere along the line, someone had beaten down her self-esteem, but she'd come so far. Cara hoped she continued to grow and wished her all the best.

Mentoring filled a hole she was feeling but she still sometimes wondered if life had passed her by. Was it too late to catch up and fulfill the need for a family of her own? She was thirty-three years old, soon to be thirty-four. Could she find someone who wanted the same things she did? Someone who would take her, corkscrew hair and all?

Blowing one of the mentioned corkscrews out of her eyes, she heard shuffling in her outer office and froze. Oh God. Someone was out there.

There was nothing she could find in her office to use as a weapon except a crystal decanter she used to serve her clients water. She was loath to break it but break it she would if she needed to. It was very expensive but that was irrelevant when compared to the value she placed on her life.

Slowly, she rose from behind the desk and crept to the door. Sticking her head around the doorjamb, she came face to face with Bill... no John Smith. James, dangit.

"Jiminy cricket. Mr. Jones, you frightened me half to death. What are you doing here?" She didn't realize she had called him by the wrong name until he corrected her.

"Smith. It's James Smith and I... Well..." he stammered." I was uh wondering if you would like to go out for dinner with me."

Cara couldn't have been more stupefied if he had asked her to get naked right then and there. She was speechless and therefore didn't get a chance to answer as he moved closer to her.

"I thought we could go to that new Greek place over on Main Street."

Cara stepped back, coming up against the wall. "Well thank you for asking, Mr. Smith. I'm sorry but I do have to decline. I have other plans." Her southern accent always got a little thicker when she was trying to let someone down easy.

Thinking he would now back up and give her some room, she began to relax. He didn't back up however, and she felt his breath, which smelled of peppermint, against her cheek.

"I'm sure we can work around your schedule. Can't we?" he asked, one arm leaning against the wall above her shoulder.

"Uh no. We cannot. Now please kindly take a step back before I have to call security."

Her back was pressed so tightly against the wall, she was sure the wall would have indentations of her butt. Sweat was dripping down his face and off his chin. Cara thought she was going to gag from his cologne.

"We don't have to get security involved. I know what you really want to say is yes. You're just shy, like me."

Wait, what? Where had he ever gotten such a ridiculous idea?

"But I've been taking assertiveness training classes and I know what to do to make you feel better."

Cara inhaled, ready to give him a blast of her mind. "Let's be clear. No never means yes. Ever. She raised her hands and pushed him back."

"She'll feel better when you take your slimy hands

off her," said a deep voice.

Cara exhaled, admitting to herself she was relieved but she was still spitting mad. She could see over Mr. Smith's shoulder that Todd had arrived and was exuding intimidation. Way back in high school, she remembered taking some self-defense classes but in all honesty, she hadn't paid much attention. She knew there was one spot she could do a lot of damage to a man, but she hadn't wanted to use that method unless it was absolutely necessary.

Mr. Smith whipped around, startled and embarrassed. It was obvious he had waited until there was no one left in the building, or at least within earshot, so he wouldn't have a witness see him practice his new techniques.

"It's against the law to harass someone. No means no. No doesn't mean try again. Cara I'll need to get a statement from you."

"A statement?" Mr. Smith squeaked.

"You do know that no means no, don't you?" Todd continued grilling the sweating man. "By the way, where were you last night at about ten o'clock?"

"I was at home. Why?"

"What were you doing?"

"Watching TV. What's this all about?"

"Who were you with? Can anyone corroborate that?"

Cara placed a hand on Todd's arm and felt heat shoot through her fingers. As if shocked, she removed them again. "Todd, I think we can let Mr. Jones go. He sees the error of his ways, don't you? And I trust you will listen next time a woman says no?" One eyebrow raised to clarify she actually required a response.

Mr. Smith was so nervous; he neglected to correct Cara's use of the wrong name.

He nodded and Cara turned back to Todd who in turn, squinted his eyes as though trying to see if the little weasel was telling the truth.

After an awkward pause, he relented and let the man in front of him go.

"Fine, but don't leave town," he added as the little man actually squeaked and all but ran from the office.

Chapter Six

Todd regarded Cara, taking in every detail of her face and eyes. He was searching for signs of stress and although he found them hidden in her features, he didn't think it was out of proportion to what had just happened.

"Are you okay?" he asked just to be sure. "Any calls today?"

"None of the variety you're referring to," she answered. "Although I think I could have done without this little scenario." She waved her hands randomly through the air.

Todd stepped directly in front of her and rubbed his hands up and down her arms. "Do you know him well?"

"No. That's the really weird part. I can barely remember his name. More often than not, I get it wrong. I almost never talk to him and if I do it's just a 'good morning'. I can't figure out what could ever have given him the idea that I would like to go out with him, let alone why he would think I 'really meant yes' when I clearly meant no."

"So he hasn't ever bothered you before?"

"Never."

"But you've never had threatening phone calls before either. Nor have you had dolls left with their heads ripped off."

"Todd I know what you're thinking but I really think he's harmless, if a little misguided. I don't think he's the caller."

"Well, I'm going to keep an eye on him just the same. Maybe I'll even have one of the guys down at the station bring him in for questioning."

"Whatever you think, but I still say it's not him. He doesn't have the gumption."

"Why didn't you just lift your knee and nail him one?"

"I didn't want to hurt him. I didn't really feel that threatened, otherwise I would have. It's never the first choice of a woman to make a scene, but next time I promise you, I will."

"If it ever happens again, don't hesitate. Just nail him and run. It could save your life."

"I never thought I would ever hear a guy tell me to 'nail' another guy." She laughed, trying to lighten the mood.

"Any decent guy would advise you to do the same thing if you were in danger."

"Well, be that as it may, I would like to have this conversation done, and go. Would you care to join me for dinner? I can whip something up real quick. It won't be fancy, but it won't taste bad either. First, though, we need to get out to the job site before it gets dark. I want to see the progress that's being made."

"You look tired, why don't we put off going out to the build site and pick up some take out. There's a really good Chinese place down by the beach. They have the best Moo Goo Guy Pan. Do you like Chinese food?"

"I adore Chinese food." Her eyes got big and her stomach growled to prove how hungry she was. "So deal, but I still want to stop by the build first. I talked to Charlie Davenport this morning and she said things are going well. Did you go already? I thought we were going to go now."

"We can, but I was out there yesterday. She seems to know her way around a construction site. And her team listens to her and respects her. Gotta admit though I was expecting a guy with a name like Charlie."

Cara snorted. "I get it. I would have thought the same thing, had I not gone to school with her younger cousin. She took over Davenport Construction when her dad died years ago. She's certainly made a name for herself with quality work. She had another great loss when her husband passed away in an accident four years ago. He was such a good man, and they were devoted to each other. Her kids are amazeballs too, but they didn't seem to feel the need to build like she did. Anyway, she's done a remarkable job of keeping the business running up to, and beyond the standards set by her father."

She yawned and her stomach growled again.

"Seriously, I was just there. Let's just get some take out and get you home. You seem beat."

"I guess if you were just there, we can wait until tomorrow. I just really want to make sure the build goes well for Miranda and Hunter. This is important to me. It's not just another job."

She thought about her friend Miranda, a bestselling author and her new husband Hunter, who was also Todd's cousin. They had been through so much with someone trying to kill Miranda last fall. They truly deserved their happily ever after. She would do her part to make sure their new home was exactly what they wanted.

Touched by the consideration she saw in Todd's eyes, she accepted his hand, linking their fingers as they left her office. When had anyone been concerned about how tired she was? Other than family, she amended. Family was always concerned, sometimes too concerned, about her welfare.

****

"I'll just grab some dishes from the kitchen and we can sit in the family room. It's more comfortable in there," Cara said as they entered the front door of her home.

"Forget the dishes. We can eat out of the boxes. It's more fun that way and I swear it tastes better. Somehow it loses something when you put it on a plate."

"I'm game if you are. Just let me get changed."

When she returned, Todd had changed as well. He had removed his suit and was now wearing a pair of worn jeans and an old Michigan sweatshirt; his sleeves pushed up to just below his elbow, revealing strong forearms, covered with golden hair.

Cara sucked in her breath and Todd looked up, chopsticks paused in front of his mouth.

"You changed," she said lamely. "Now this is a man who knows how to restore a classic car." The heat of a blush crept up her face. Dang her filter for being broken. If it entered her mind, it exited her mouth.

Todd chuckled. "Yeah this is more comfortable. I always carry extra clothes in the trunk of my car. You never know when they might come in handy."

"Your 'go bag'? I suppose you need one, in your line of work."

"You better get something to eat before it's gone." He plopped himself down on the floor in front of the sofa, legs outstretched and crossed at the ankles.

"That hungry, are you?"

"You never can tell. I've worked up quite an appetite chasing bad guys all day."

"Sure you have." She smiled, tucking a stray curl behind her ear again. "Thanks for chasing away my bad guy today."

"By the way, the test results came back on the doll. There was nothing. It was wiped clean. Not so much as a fiber out of place. And no problem, but you should probably take some self-defense classes. All women should have a working knowledge of how to protect themselves."

"I'll check into it tomorrow."

The phone rang just as she was about to take her first bite of food.

"Oh Nuts. That'll be my sister and I forgot to order the flowers for the party." Without hesitating, she reached for the phone.

"Wait to see who it is," Todd told her, holding her arm back from the phone. "Where's your call display?"

"Oh Jiminy Cricket. I forgot to call the phone company. Just let the machine pick up if you want to, but I know it's my sister."

Todd was surprised she hadn't thought to get the service set up, but he laughed at her expression. "Jiminy Cricket?"

"Oh shut up." She swatted at him and reached for the phone. "I know it's my sister."

Todd made no further protests. He knew it had rung enough times to get a fix on the line with call return. However, there was no one on the line when Cara picked up the phone.

"Just another hang up," she said as she set the receiver back down in the cradle. "Pass me the rice, please."

Seconds later, it rang again, only this time, Cara tensed.

"Let the machine get it this time," she told Todd.

He wondered at her apprehension this time as opposed to last time, but made no comment, allowing her to make her own decisions. "I'll just go listen to see who it is." He left the room.

Seconds later, he returned with the answering machine in his hand. "I hope you don't mind, but I brought out your machine, so we wouldn't have to get up and run to your office every time your phone rang. I'll return it later."

"No, that's fine. Who was it?" she asked tentatively.

"It was another hang up. No one was there. No noise in the background. Nothing. I hit call return but it was a blocked number."

"Maybe I should answer it next time."

"No. That's not a good idea. Better to let him think you aren't at home."

The two of them polished off the food, and Cara made coffee. It was an hour before the phone rang again. He felt Cara tense as she waited for a voice to speak.

"Cara? Why aren't you home yet?"

Cara lunged for the phone, answering and stopping the machine at the same time. "Em? Sorry, I didn't make it in time to answer. What's up?"

"Lilly had her baby. It's a girl."

"Is she all right?" Cara asked, concern in her voice.

Todd heard her anxiety and tensed, ready for action. What action, he wasn't sure, but he was ready.

"When?" Cara asked.

"Just about an hour ago. She said she tried to call

you to let you know she was in labor but got your answering machine. She's okay though, as is the baby."

"Have they chosen a name yet?"

"Not yet. Lilly is so excited she will still be able to make the party… You did remember the flowers right?"

"I said the flowers will be there and they will. You insult me."

Todd had relaxed when he realized no one had been hurt. He noticed now that Cara was twirling a strand of hair that had come loose from its bindings. He also noticed that although she said she was offended, she showed no signs of it. He relaxed completely.

"Tell her I will be over to see her tomorrow and that I love her."

"She's staying in hospital for a day or two. The baby is a little jaundice so wait until she gets home."

"What? That doesn't sound good."

"It's nothing to worry about. They will just have the baby under the lights for a few days. No need to worry, I swear. She's great. Lil said so herself. So wait until she gets home. Morgan's request on that one. She should be home Friday. Gotta run for now though. Don't forget the flowers."

Todd could hear her sister's laughter as the line disconnected.

"My sister had a baby girl." She beamed at Todd. "I'm so excited for her because she's been trying for so long to get pregnant."

"Hey there's something to be said for practice."

Cara laughed as the phone rang again. "That'll be my parents," she explained, "calling to tell me about the baby."

"Hello Cara. Did you have a nice dinner?"

Todd watched as Cara's face drained of all color. She slammed the phone down, missing the cradle, even as she began to shake. He reached for her, replacing the phone on its hook.

"That was him?"

She did nothing more than nod. Wrapping her arms around herself, she sat on the floor, right there beside the phone.

"Cara, what did he say?"

Eventually, her breathing slowed and she was able to answer.

"He…he j-just asked if…If I had a n-nice dinner? He's w-watching me, isn't he?"

Todd wanted nothing more than to wrap her in his arms and sooth away all the fear. He knew though, from experience, that he needed to make eye contact with her; knew he had to make sure she could hear what he was saying and see the words being formed on his lips.

"Not necessarily," he answered. "He could just be assuming that you had dinner. It's a logical conclusion, given the time of day."

This seemed to make her feel a little better. "Do you really think so?"

"It makes sense. Think about it."

The ringing started again and once again, the machine picked up.

"You shouldn't have hung up on me. That only makes me angry. You'll have to pay for that too. You haven't found the gift yet. I'll know when you find it. You'll know when you find it, too. You'll have to let me know what you think… although I will be able to tell from your reaction. I'll always know. Enjoy yourself, your time is running out."

The call ended and Cara sagged against the sofa, wringing her hands in her lap. Todd reached out to hold them still.

"I told you he was watching me. He says he can tell by my reaction. He has to be watching to know what my reaction is. I want to move. I want to sell this place, pack up my things and move. Tomorrow, first thing," she continued, "I'm calling the real estate agent and listing. Then I'm calling the phone-company and getting a new line… and call display. I have to get call display… Why don't I already have it? Everyone has it. And what else did you say? Oh yes, a dog. I need to get a dog."

She had barely come up for air and Todd pulled her close to ease her rambling. It seemed to have little affect for she still continued to talk. At the same time she shook as though a cold had set deep into her bones. He rubbed her arms, kissing the top of her head as he did so.

"Cara, don't get carried away. You're doing exactly what he wants you to do. You're panicking. Don't give him the satisfaction of knowing he's terrorized you. You can't give in to the fear. I won't let anything happen to you."

"You won't?" She glanced up at him with tear filled eyes and his heart seemed to melt and freeze at the same time; melt at the trust he saw and freeze at what? What was it about her expression that frightened him? It didn't make any sense he knew, but nothing made any sense where Cara was concerned. Only the fact that she was in his arms-and although the circumstances were wrong, holding her felt very, very right.

"No I won't let anything happen to you."

"I'm going to hold you to that." She sniffed. "I've got a really big party to go to next weekend and my parents won't be pleased if I'm dead or something."

The chuckle that rumbled through Todd's chest went through Cara's as well, the vibrations causing butterflies. Instead, she held on to the strong, warm chest that was offering comfort.

"We need to call this in, Cara."

"Why? The police can't do anything anyway."

"We can order a tap on your phone line. I should have done it already, but your life has definitely been threatened now and a phone tap is a sure way to find out who's been doing it; is still doing it. But first I want to try the call return again."

The phone rang but even before there was an answer, Todd knew it was a long distance number. He could tell from the number of beeps as it dialed. He admitted he was surprised when the answering voice was in French. The person they were dealing with was obviously very experienced in the art of bouncing calls. He really doubted their caller was in France... Or even far enough away to be long distance.

"Would you like me to sleep on your sofa?"

Cara felt the kiss on the top of her head and shivered. "You wouldn't mind? I have a spare bedroom that would be more comfortable but I'm a little freaked out about the thought of being watched. I know you said they aren't but I feel like I am."

She turned her head upward causing her lips to meet his, when the trilling of the phone was heard again. He felt her tension immediately. No one moved as they waited for a voice to begin speaking.

When Cara's own message was finished, there was silence except for the breathing which could be heard from the caller.

"I'm so sick of this," she shouted as she picked up the phone asking, "Who is this?"

"Cara?" Came the quiet voice. "Is that you?"

"Who is this?" she repeated.

"Why it's James. James Smith. I thought I'd give you another chance to get together and discuss our relationship. Maybe tomorrow at lunch. Less pressure for you, maybe."

Sputtering was the only way Todd could describe the noise Cara made, but then she found her voice. "Mr. Smith, we have no relationship to discuss. I will not have lunch with you, I already have plans, as is the case with dinner and lunch and all of my meals for the near future. I. Am. Not. Interested. Do not call me again."

"Perhaps after work then, before you go home, we could get a coffee or something."

Todd had his head close enough to hear the conversation but moved a little closer so his mouth was directly beside Cara's; their lips almost touching. The guy just didn't have a clue, but he knew what would work.

"Are you coming to bed, darlin'? I'm waiting."

The question seemed so intimate and even though he intended it for Mr. Smith, he struggled to think with his lips so close to hers. If he turned his head a little more to the right, they would connect and share a kiss like the one last evening. But again, his timing was off. He wouldn't take advantage of her vulnerability.

"I'm sorry, you have company. I'll call you back another time."

"That won't be necessary. Please don't," she replied and hung up the phone.

Todd moved away with the disconnection of the

call, but stared into her very clear blue eyes. He saw the heat there. He knew that she had been as affected as he had been.

"We should get some sleep. You're exhausted." His voice sounded loud to his own ears; breaking the spell they both seemed to be under.

Todd walked her to her room, gently kissing her cheek as he closed her door. Once the barrier was between them, he had hoped he would be able to think again. It hadn't worked out quite as he had planned because all he could think about was opening the door again and stripping away all pretenses along with their clothes.

He moved through the house checking all the doors and windows. He had completed this earlier but he did it again; more because he needed to get away from Cara for a few minutes and regain his sense of control, than for any other reason. He knew the house was as secure as it would be tonight.

Heat flashed through him once again as he walked by the sofa. He had placed his mouth by the phone only as a means to an end. A way of getting Cara off the phone and letting Mr. Smith know she wasn't interested at the same time. It wasn't so he could stake his claim, but that's how it felt once he was done. He shouldn't have had to do what he did to ward off any interest from any man, let alone one who had already been told she wasn't interested. Men needed to listen when a woman said 'no'. But he had done it…and when their lips had touched ever so briefly, he had been struck with such desire-a want so deep, that it almost left him debilitated with need.

He knew that if he approached Cara she would be

willing but again, he reminded himself that he would be leaving soon, and that wouldn't be fair to either of them. Long distance affairs were more trouble than they were worth, and he was hoping for a transfer to DC.

As he walked back to the room where he would spend the night, he stopped outside Cara's door. With his hands in fists, and a muted curse, he reached for the handle. It was cool to the touch. He knew it would provide relief to them both. He pulled back and moved on to the guest room.

He lay in his bed, as comfortable as he could possibly be considering the state of his arousal and wondered what Cara's response would have been had he opened the door. It hadn't been easy to pull his hand away. It had been damn hard, but there were too many things against a relationship for him; the largest being his imminent reassignment.

When he had signed up with the bureau, he had known that a normal lifestyle would be a challenge but as time went on, and he moved from one assignment to another, he began to realize for the first time, how slim the chance really was. Too many agent friends had tried to make a go of it and he'd seen the majority of them fail. It didn't seem to matter if the agent was male or female. Either way, relationships were doomed. He didn't want to be another statistic.

That was why, up until recently, he had kept his relationships light and without commitment. The women who entered his life, knew up front what could be expected of him. It was much simpler that way.

Out of nowhere, he heard his maternal grandmother's words. *Nothing worth having is going to come easy.*

"You would have liked Cara, Grandma Hailey," he whispered in the night.

Then what's keeping you from her, Baby Boy?

The endearment from his days as a child, startled Todd, and he sat up. He must have fallen asleep and been dreaming. Wiping the sweat from his brow, he examined the room trying to get his bearings. He was in Cara's house, he knew, and she was next door.

And if he was one of those people who believed in such things, he had just had a visit from his grandmother, who had been dead for years.

Good thing you don't believe in that sort of thing.

Chapter Seven

Cara lay in bed, listening to Todd as he made his way through the house. She didn't have any worries with him there. Somehow, she knew he would keep his word and protect her. Why it was so important to her, a woman of independence, she couldn't say, but it was. She supposed it was because she knew she wasn't alone in this. It was different for a man than for a woman. Years of walking to her car with keys between her fingers as a weapon, just in case something happened. Always being aware of her surroundings. She had learned that lesson years ago and had nearly paid dearly for a moment of carelessness.

Her family should probably be told what was going on, but they would insist on her moving in with one of them and she didn't want to have to do that. Alternately they would suggest that one of them, perhaps her one and only brother, Sterling, move in with her. She didn't want that either. She was used to living on her own and wanted to keep it that way.

Why then did it make her feel better to have Todd there when one of her own family members would have caused her discomfort, at the very least, and annoyance at most? Maybe because they would baby her. She didn't know and didn't really want to investigate it further for fear of what she might discover about herself and her feelings toward Todd.

Todd was walking down the hall. She could hear his every step. As he passed by her bedroom door, he paused and Cara imagined him reaching for the handle, but then his steps continued. He was probably only listening to be sure she was okay.

With a heavy sigh, Cara rolled over and closed her eyes. Sleep would be a long time coming but she had to try. She had a client coming in tomorrow morning and she needed to be both alert as well as coherent. If they were going to go to the build before that, it would be an early start.

Punching her pillow, she rolled over again, getting tangled in the covers and having to get up to straighten them. She watched the door, wondering what Todd would do if she went to his room. Wondering if he would take her hand and pull her toward the bed, or turn her away.

Climbing back into bed, she sighed, placing her hands beneath her cheek as she curled on her side.

The words of her caller came back to her. *Oh what a tangled web we weave, when first we practice to deceive.* What did it mean? She knew it was Sir Walter Scott but what was the significance to her? Why had he chosen those words?

The questions continued to go unanswered in her mind. It seemed that every question she thought of, only led to another question, none of which had answers.

****

Morning eventually arrived, after very little sleep. When Cara arrived in her kitchen, Todd was sitting at her table cradling a mug of coffee in both hands. He knew he looked bad. He was a little annoyed that she appeared wonderful.

"Good morning."

The words were spoken softly as though she were unsure of her welcome. Hell, it was her kitchen, what did she have to be hesitant about?

He knew his surliness was showing but there wasn't a whole hell of a lot he could do about it at the moment. The coffee would help some, once it had absorbed into his system, but that hadn't happened so far.

"Are you okay?"

"I just didn't get much sleep last night. I get grumpy when I'm tired. My cousin, Hunter, would say something worse but we won't go there."

"I'm sorry Todd, that you're not feeling well. Or that you're tired," she corrected when his look intensified.

"It's not your fault. It's my own. I have no one to blame but myself. And this coffee. I can't figure out why it hasn't jump started me yet."

"Which coffee did you use?"

"How the… I don't know. I found it in a container in your fridge. There was no label."

"Was it the one with the green or blue lid?"

"Green."

Cara smiled. "I'll get you some *real* coffee. That's decaf."

"Well shit."

****

Cara and Todd had delayed visiting the job site again, given neither of them had much sleep and she was running late. The office was already busy by the time Cara arrived. Ivy was surrounded by three men as she passed. Cara just smiled and shook her head. The men in the building were sure going to miss her. Probably as much as Cara would. Okay, maybe they would miss her more, and for very different reasons.

Her clients had arrived early and were waiting with her assistant. She told them she would only be a minute and unlocked her office.

Sitting on her table was the package she had received the day before, and she made a mental note to check it and see what it was. She didn't remember ordering anything so she was mildly curious.

"Later, Cara. You've got clients waiting."

As she stood behind her desk, she had a strange feeling she was being watched again. It was silly she knew as there was no one in her office, nor was there any chance of being observed. She brushed it off as leftover jitters and walked into the waiting area to bring in the Darby's.

They discussed business and walked through the markup of the design Cara had worked on. There were a few changes requested and she made them right away then confirmed they were okay to move ahead. The changes were super simple and didn't affect the overall look and feel of the final product so Cara was pleased with herself.

"Paige, can you prepare the contract for the Darby's and then add them to the job calendar for next month. Plan on six weeks for the renovation, but confirm with Davenport Construction to be sure of the timeline. Pretty sure Charlie said they were good with taking it on, but just make sure." She turned to the Darby's, holding out her hand. "Thanks for coming in. I am very excited about this design for you. If you have any questions between now and the start date, please don't hesitate to let me know. This is your design and we want you to be completely happy with it."

There were several other clients throughout the day. She ignored her phone, allowing her voicemail to take the messages. There was just too much to do.

Having thrown herself into her work, she was surprised to hear Paige stick her head in the door asking, once again if there was anything else Cara needed before she left. She always lost all track of time when she was being creative.

"Well holy smokes, Paige, where did the day go?"

"Time flies when you're having fun I guess."

"Sure that's it. Any messages that need to be taken care of today?" she asked her assistant.

"Nothing that can't wait until tomorrow. Except that one guy who called like twenty times today. I kept putting him through to your voice mail. Have you picked those messages up yet?"

Cara stopped with her pen in midair. She had been about to sign some forms but the pen didn't make it as far as the paper.

"Who was it? Did he leave a name?"

"No, just said you would be expecting his call and would know what it was about."

Again the feeling of being watched was strong, Cara had to resist the urge to glance over her shoulder. There was just a window behind her and the blinds were pulled to keep the sun off the antique desk. There was no way, someone could see through. She was just being paranoid. Todd had told her not to panic because that was exactly what the caller wanted her to do. She would not panic. She refused. If she reminded herself often enough, maybe she would believe it.

"Cara, are you okay? You're lookin' a little peaked all of a sudden."

"No, I mean yes." Cara took a deep breath. "I'm fine. Really," she added for reassurance. "I'll check the messages before I leave. You go ahead. It's already past quitting time. Have a good night and I'll see you in the morning."

"If you say so, Sunshine. Have a good night."

Once the office was empty, Cara felt a sudden chill. "You're just being silly. Grow up."

Picking up the phone as though she were afraid it might bite her, she held the receiver to her ear and pressed the numbers that would bring forth her messages. There were twelve of them. *Good Lord.*

"Cara, it's me. James Smith. Give me a call when you have a minute."

"One down and eleven more to go," she said aloud as she hit the button to delete the unwanted message.

"Cara? It's James again. Call me when you have a minute."

"Cara. It's James. I'll call you later."

"Cara, are you even in the office today, because I haven't seen you at all and although your secretary says you are there you don't seem to be returning my calls."

The next few messages were just mumbled curses where Cara could hear the phone being banged against something as it was being hung up.

"Cara, it's James Smith. Your secretary is incompetent. I'll stop by the office before I leave. I'm working late, so feel free to drop by if you want."

Cara shivered and checked her watch. Would she have time to get out to her car before Mr. Smith came searching for her? Or was she already too late.

His assertiveness training classes had done wonders for his persistence, although she didn't think this was

85

what the trainer had in mind when he was instructing the class.

Perhaps she should find out who was teaching the class and give him or her a call. They should be aware of the havoc they were causing in other people's lives.

Without waiting further, she rose and walked to the door. Footsteps sounded in the hall and she froze for a moment. When her wits returned, she reached for the lock and slowly, very quietly, turned it so no one could get in.

Once she was securely locked in, she inhaled a deep breath and brushed her hands together. "Well that should keep him out."

As she stood at her door, she watched as her doorknob, turned, slowly. Once again she held her breath, waiting to be sure she had indeed locked the door and not unlocked it. There was a slight rattling of the door as the person on the other side tried to open it, but it was secure.

Thank you, God.

Her hands clasped together, in front of her chest, she returned to her office to listen to the last of her messages. The next three were James again, but he'd hung up before leaving a message.

Then there was the last one.

"Having a good day? Make every minute last. You don't have much time before you must pay. We all must pay for our deceptions. You especially."

Then there was a brief pause in the message before Scott was recited once again.

Cara deleted the message, cursing her stupidity as soon as it was done. Todd would probably want the police to hear the message, or he would want to listen for… Son of a biscuit box, she forgot to listen for noises in the background.

Feeling the lightheadedness that had been far too much a part of her life lately, she put her head between her knees. The black waves soon subsided and she began to feel a little more stable.

A knock on the door sounded just as she was about to sit up, causing her to jump and smack her head on her desk.

"Jiminy, that hurt."

"Cara? Are you in there? Are you okay?"

The door was being rattled. "Cara. Let me in."

Chapter Eight

"Just a minute, Todd," Cara called from beneath her desk, still rubbing her head.

"What was that sound I heard? Are you hurt?" he asked through the door.

While continuing to rub the bruised and ballooning area--she was certain she had a goose egg the size of Atlanta- she walked to the door.

"I'm fine," she answered as she opened the door. "I just bumped my head on my desk."

"How the hell did you do that?"

She thought about telling him of her visitor but was ashamed of her skittishness. She was used to being much more self-sufficient, and she didn't want to rely too heavily on Todd. Special agents came and went. He had already told her he would be moving on soon, and when Todd left, she still needed to be able to take care of herself. Besides, if she wasn't careful, he would take her heart, or at the very least, a piece of it, with him. She needed to keep that in mind.

"I dropped my pencil." Sure, she lied, but at least she didn't appear as though she were a simpering idiot.

Todd chuckled. "You need to be more careful. Heaven forbid you should hurt that beautiful head."

Cara froze, then realized Todd was only being sweet. She should know better. She'd lived in the South her entire life. That was just how things were done down here. Men were very good at sweet-talking.

"Well, it's a little late for the warning, but thanks just the same. I'll keep it in mind next time I crawl under my desk."

Todd laughed again.

"I'm glad you find it so amusing." Cara couldn't keep from smiling.

"So here's my thought... First, are you hungry? Because I thought, if you wanted, maybe we could run out to the build and then have dinner at the Beach Barbeque. It sure smelled good the last time I drove by. And I think the waves are calling,"

"That sounds wonderful, but I'll have to go home and change first. Do you have beach attire in your trunk as well or do you need to go change too?"

"Always. It's on the list of recommended agent attire when living in a coastal city."

"Sure it is. Should I meet you there?"

She held her breath, thinking about entering her house alone.

Shake it off Cara. You can handle anything you set your mind to. Your daddy always says so.

It was as though Todd could see her fear and jumped to her rescue... again. "Why don't I follow you home and then we'll take one car. Besides, parking at the beach can be a pain."

"You're sure you don't mind?"

"No problem at all. Besides," he added, "If you liked my '57 Corvette, you're gonna love my '63 Mustang."

"Can't wait to see it. Just let me get my things and lock up."

The package which had arrived the previous day, still sat on the table where she'd left it. With a heavy sigh, she decided to wait until morning. If it was work she'd only end up doing it at home and she much preferred to enjoy the evening.

With one last glance over her shoulder, she closed and locked her inner office, then closed and locked her outer office.

Shuffling came from the end of the hall, but Cara gave it no more than a cursory glance. A bit of brown was seen as someone exited the hallway, into the stairwell.

"I guess someone else is working late, too," Todd said, watching the hall as they walked.

"It happens a lot in the building."

****

Cara rolled down the window of the Mustang and let the breeze blow her hair. It would be an unruly mess when she was done, but just this once, it was worth the freedom.

She had made the quickest change in history, except maybe when Grandad had offered to take her to the fair when she was eight. Her mom and dad had told her she couldn't go because she'd pushed Suzie Knott in a mud-puddle. It hadn't mattered that 'Suzie Snot' had shoved Lilly down causing her to scrape her knees. She should have known better than to behave that way. She could still hear her parents giving her a lecture that had seemed to go on for hours. Most of the words had been tuned out, at least until she heard the words that had broken her eight year old heart. 'And there will be no fair this year either, missy'.

It had seemed so unfair, but then Grandad had snuck her out and taken her to the fair anyway. Years later she realized that her parents had known about the escape and defiance of their rules. They had in fact probably suggested Grandad take her. She had been punished because she had done something wrong, but her parents were equally proud of her for standing up for her sister.

But right now, she was riding in a classic car with a very handsome man. A drop-dead gorgeous man. The same man who had spent last night sleeping in her guest room, while she spent the night in her own lonely bed, not doing much sleeping at all.

"So how long are you going to be in town? And where is home anyway?" If she were honest with herself, she was hoping he would be stationed in Lightcastle permanently.

"Who knows? I'm almost finished everything here, so I imagine it won't be long before I get my new assignment. I will be here until Miranda and Hunter return from their honeymoon at least but after that, it's anyone's guess. Home is here for now and has been for the last year while I worked a case. Hunter and I grew up not far from here in Wilmington."

"Where are you hoping to be transferred? What would be your Shangri-La?"

"That's a very good question. I would like my own team and am up for a promotion in DC, but I really don't know where I will get sent yet."

"Oh." If she was disappointed, it was her own fault for getting her hopes up. She wouldn't let it show though no matter how much she wished it were otherwise.

"Do you mind if I turn on your radio?"

At his nod, she turned it on, searching for a station that offered an upbeat sound. She wasn't paying attention to what was being played on the radio until Todd's hand grabbed hers, turning the dial back to a station she had by-passed.

"I like this song. Do you mind? It's called 'Broken Halos.' "

"It's lovely. I love Chris Stapleton." Cara relaxed in her seat, slipping her sandals off.

The smell of salt in the air was one that Cara had loved from an early age. She was happiest when she was by the water. It had been a dream to live right on the beach. To be able to walk out her back door and take a stroll on the sand with the water lapping at her toes. She'd gotten sidetracked by trappings of her career though and just now realized she had given up on that dream.

"What are you thinking about?" Todd interrupted her musings.

"I was just remembering how I used to always want to live right on the beach."

"Why don't you then?"

"Oh, I don't know. Life… that thing that happens while you're making other plans." She sighed. "I found a great deal on my house and I couldn't turn it down. It was practically a steal, for the price of other houses in the neighborhood, so I grabbed it while I could."

"It really is a great house."

They pulled up to the house being built for Todd's cousin and his wife. Acting on his cousin's behalf, Todd had already been out to see the progress but Cara hadn't seen it yet.

"My house is nice but this… this is extraordinary." If she sounded wistful, she didn't care. "The view is to die for and the house is going to be so amazingly gorgeous and elegant and… well perfect. I can see it in my mind's eye and once it's done, it will be exactly what they wanted."

"I'm sure it will be beautiful. You do great work. I saw the write up in Architecture Digest about you. Saw what you did to those homes they showed. They were stunning when they were done. Quite the transformation. And from the plans I've seen and the designs you've drawn up, this is going to be magnificent as well." He paused, pointing to the foundation that had been poured three days ago. "Another couple of days and they will begin framing. The primary suite will be back there, facing the ocean and will have fabulous sunrises. Then roofing will go up. After that, I was hoping you could come out and check out the electrical and plumbing to make sure we get everything in the right spaces per your design. I want to make sure it's right and better to get everything in the correct spot the first time rather than have to rip something out to move it."

He turned back to Cara. "Happy with the progress so far? It's a little delayed but permits were a pain in the ass to get."

She smiled, envisioning the final spaces. "It's going to be amazing. Hunter and Miranda are lucky to have you here looking out for them. And I'm so happy we could get Davenport Construction to do the build. They are the best in the area."

They walked back to the car and drove five minutes to the public beach and the barbeque joint.

"So, do you want to eat first, or walk?"

"Oh, eat, please. I'm starved."

"I like that about you Cara. You're not afraid to eat. So many women either don't eat, or don't eat when they're out on a date. I mean seriously. Food is such an enjoyment."

She was surprised into laughing. A real belly laugh. It was just so unexpected. God it felt good to be so at ease with someone.

"I could pick at my food and be all dainty and stuff like so many of my friends, but seriously, I love food way too much." She laughed again. "Besides, it's not pretty when I'm hangry."

A small lineup waited for food, but they were served with little wait. Taking their food in hand, they walked down the beach a bit and sat in the sand to eat. A breeze came off the water, cooling the air to make it not only comfortable, but soothing. It wasn't blowing enough to make them feel like they were being sand blasted, but enough that the waves were big, knocking swimmers over if they weren't paying attention.

"I wish I'd thought to bring a blanket," Cara said, setting her plate carefully on the sand as she sat, then picking it up again and placing it in her lap.

"We can always eat at one of the tables, if you'd prefer."

"No. I'd prefer to sit here, if you're good with that. If not, we can get a table. Either way I can have my toes in the sand."

"Not—"

"Oh my God. That woman's drowning," she yelled as she jumped up grabbing her food before it dumped on the sand. Todd's words were cut off by Cara's scream.

She needn't have spoken further, as Todd was already in the water and swimming toward the floundering woman. A group of people had gathered on the shoreline with Cara right in the center of them. She was shoved aside as someone bumped into her.

She smelled someone's cologne and felt sick to her

stomach. It was Mr. Smith.

With a look over her shoulder, she realized it wasn't Mr. Smith at all, but instead, someone who had the same poor choice in cologne. She expelled a heavy sigh.

Todd carried the woman into shore, setting her on the beach. Everyone made room for them, one man offering his coat to wrap around her.

Cara noticed the woman's arms were still wrapped around Todd's neck and she wanted to pry them off him. The jealousy surging through her was surprising. It was not something she had ever felt before, and she had no right to feel that way. Still, she was relieved when Todd removed the woman's arms himself. The relief was just as disturbing as the possessiveness. She had no right to feel any of it where Todd was concerned. He was just a nice man who was protecting her from a psycho. That was all. There were no other feelings entering into the equation. *Yeah right.*

The crowd clapped and the woman thanked Todd, asking if he needed to do mouth to mouth.

He declined gently, turning toward Cara. "You ready to finish eating?"

"But you're soaked. You'll catch a cold."

"I have my sweatshirt in the car if I get cold but it's a warm enough evening. I'll be fine. Besides, you promised me a walk on the beach and a walk is what I intend to have."

"You're sure?" At his nod, she agreed. "Okay, but don't say I didn't warn you."

When they had finished eating, they did take that walk, strolling down the beach. They had removed their shoes and walked barefoot, sandals swinging from their fingers. The sand was still warm on their feet, and every now and again, a wave would come further onto the shore, getting their feet wet. Todd didn't take long to dry out at all, given the warm breeze. It was a perfect evening and the sun was just starting to set when they reached the old lighthouse. It was no longer in use as a newer one had been built years ago, and was run by computer but it stood as a sentinel; a beacon even still. The salt water had ravaged it and it was due for upgrades again, but it still stood tall and straight, reminding those who passed on by of a time when things were simpler.

"Isn't it beautiful? This is where the name Lightcastle came from. It used to be called Lightcastle Cove because of this little cove where it sits. It kind of looks like a castle, don't you think?" Cara asked, staring off into the night.

"Gorgeous, Todd answered, not taking in the lighthouse at all.

"I'd forgotten how beautiful it was. So many memories here."

"I could never forget," Todd said, stopping his walking and taking Cara into his arms. "Never."

Cara sucked in a breath seconds before Todd's lips touched hers. She was swept away -torn from her surroundings by a maelstrom of emotions. Her knees were weak, her heart racing, and her breathing rapid and shallow. And she clung to Todd, terrified he would stop.

****

When their lips parted, Todd was breathing heavily. He needed to get some self-control and he needed it now. What was it about this woman that had him acting like a high school kid out on his first date? Cara scared him. Frightened him because of what she represented. A stable life with no career in the FBI. That was what terrified him most of all. In order to have a life with Cara he would have to give up his life as an agent.

He couldn't do it.

"Maybe I should take you home now."

"Uh, okay," Cara replied, trying, but not succeeding, to hide her disappointment.

Todd had to give her an A for effort, but he knew she had been as affected as he had, and was having a hard time getting her emotions under control. Maybe it would be a good idea for him to keep his distance for a while. Maybe it would be a good idea keeping his distance from her for good.

And maybe it would be a good idea if he didn't lean forward again, touching his lips to hers once more. Definitely a good idea if he didn't do that, but even as the thoughts ran through his head, he bent forward, taking her firmly in his arms and deepening the kiss.

Warning bells sounded in his head, but he ignored them, reveling in the sensations this woman stirred in him. Sensations he hadn't felt in a very long time -if ever.

The waves splashed on the rocks they were standing on, spraying them with a mist of ocean water, bringing them both out of their trance.

"I'd better get you home."

"Of course," Cara acquiesced.

The drive home was silent, while Todd tried to figure out what his next step would be -a step forward or a step back. He imagined Cara was trying to figure out the same thing. Damn. He needed to keep a clear head, and that meant no more kissing her. When she kissed him, nothing was clear at all.

"I'll walk you to your door."

Disappointment was evident on Cara's face, but he

was sure she would die before she would admit it.

"That's not necessary, Todd," she told him, using her 'former lawyer voice'...the voice that spoke with authority. "Thank you for a wonderful evening."

"I said I'll walk you to your door. In fact I'll just make sure you're all tucked in safe before I go home."

"Nothing has been unlocked since the last time you checked. I only used the front door, and it was locked before we left for the beach."

"Just the same, I'll sleep better knowing you're safe."

"Well, at least one of us will be sleeping," Cara mumbled.

Todd hid the smile that tugged at his lips. He'd heard what she said and knew without a doubt that she was as affected by the kiss as he'd been. It lightened his heart somehow to know this.

"Let me have your key."

"Nuh uh. I go with you," she said. "I refuse to be intimidated any longer by this goon. It's time I took charge of my emotions and my life."

He wondered if she meant more than the emotion of fear. He liked that she lost a little control like he did.

"Fine by me, but stay with me."

"Where am I going to go?"

"Just do as I ask, please."

The house was dark, every light turned off.

"You should leave a light on when you go out," Todd told Cara.

She gulped, grabbing hold of Todd's arm.

"I did."

Chapter Nine

Todd stopped dead in his tracks. "What?"

"I said I did leave a light on."

"Which one," he whispered.

"The one in the laundry room. That's where I enter the house from the garage."

The house was pitch black. No glimmer of light from any source. Clouds had moved in, covering what little moon there was, and because Cara's closest neighbors were quite far away, there was no light from those sources either.

"I'd tell you to stay here, but I know you won't. Keep behind me, and if I tell you to do something, you do it. Clear?"

"Crystal," she responded, grabbing hold of Todd's shirt with a death grip.

Quietly, Todd unlocked the front door. With a turn of the handle, he gave a slight push, sending the door inward with a slight squeak.

Cara gripped tighter to the man who stood between her and whomever had been in her home. "Maybe we should call the professionals," she whispered.

"I am the professionals," he answered, insulted.

"No need to get your shirt in a knot, I know you're FBI, but maybe some of your friends would like to join us. We wouldn't want them to miss out on all the fun."

"And if it's a blown lightbulb, what then?"

Cara bumped into Todd's back, when he stopped to stare at her over his shoulder.

"Then I suppose we appear quite silly, but we'll have spread some joy to your fellow agents. It'd be a shame to laugh all by ourselves. Where's your sense of sharing?"

There was a moment when Todd just stared at Cara. It was as though he were considering her idea. Or maybe she had offended his pride to such a degree, he decided not to go in at all, and would in fact leave her to her own defenses.

"I'm sorry if I dented your ego," she added.

"No, I'm just wondering if you're right. Maybe I should go back to get my cell phone. It's in the car. Uh, you wait here," he said, turning to leave.

Cara tried everything to keep from squealing, but it still squeaked through, though muffled by Todd's sweatshirt which she had in a death grip.

"No. 'You'll do fine alone', or 'we both go back to the car'… or 'Whatever you think is best,'" he added.

She could feel the rumbling of Todd's silent laughter, and realized he'd been teasing.

"Creep," she said, but without rancor.

They were in the front hall, and Cara asked Todd if she should turn on a light.

"Give me a minute," he whispered back. "I want to check something out first."

Turning around, and grabbing Cara's arms he pinned her to the wall. She was so startled, she opened her mouth to utter a 'Jiminy cricket', but Todd's lips were on hers before a sound could escape.

Cara felt the kiss course through her, her knees weakening and her hands gripping firm broad shoulders.

The passion in that kiss was like no other -like nothing she had ever experienced, nor could she imagine anyone else experiencing. It was deep. It was breathtaking. It was arousal at its fullest.

It was love. *No. The hell it wasn't.*

She stiffened and Todd followed, doing the same in reaction.

"If you're worried about an intruder, the power's off in your whole neighborhood. Didn't you notice?" he asked. "Oh jeez, you didn't see the lights out, as we passed your neighbor's houses, did you?" he continued.

"I did, I was just embarrassed for you, because I didn't think you really noticed."

"Good. You want to get some candles, or do you want to go back a few minutes in time and pick up where we left off?"

He released a heavy sigh as she stood there, her indecision evident. "So much for my ego. Let's get some candles lit."

"They're in the kitchen. I'll get them."

She was gone, disappearing in the blackness, certain of her step.

Once she reached the kitchen, she sucked oxygen into her lungs. Oh, God. She was in terrible trouble. She had stood there in the hall, listening to what Todd had to say, but when he had mentioned the kiss, she'd forgotten how to think. She had felt his passion, all over again, and all thought had abandoned her. If he hadn't taken control of the situation and propelled her out of her stupor, she'd still be standing there, staring at his shadowed face, her mouth open in a stupefied fashion. She envisioned a fish, mouth opening and closing. Not an attractive thought whatsoever. *What an idiot, Cara. You know better than*

101

to give a man your heart so quickly. Especially a man who's only in town for a short period of time. Didn't she tell her mentees all the time that they should never give their control to a man?

"You find any?" Todd called from the hall.

"Hold your horses," she called back, chastising herself once again for getting lost in her emotions.

****

When she returned to the hall, candles and matches in tow, she held one out to Todd. "Hold this while I light it, will you?"

He took the candle from her shaking hands then wrapped his hands around hers to calm them.

"Hey, you're shaking. It's going to be okay. I swear to you."

This woman had an effect on him. He had no control. He didn't much like that, although he certainly enjoyed the kiss. He knew they would be good together. Knew they would be incredible together, was more like it. Time for something to keep his mind off her body and on something else. Exercise. That was what he needed.

"What time is it?" he asked, following her around the room, setting up candles.

"Nine-thirty, why?"

"I was just thinking I needed some exercise. You up for it? Or do you want to call it a night?"

He'd had every intention of dropping her off and leaving for the night, but now he couldn't seem to make himself go.

"What kind of exercise?" she asked, "I mean, I'm not really in the mood for Yoga, but I guess I could give it a whirl if that's what you want to do."

"Well, I was thinking we could start on your first

lesson in self-defense. You game?"

It wasn't on his list of things he most wanted to be doing, but she agreed, knowing it needed to be done. He preferred she learn from him than from a stranger.

"I'm up for it, I guess. What do I need to do?"

They moved out to her back terrace and Todd proceeded to show her the very basics of self-defense-how to break out of a hold, using her body weight and her assailant's weaknesses. She did very well, once she got the hang of it, and was soon enjoying herself.

"What's next?" she asked, ready to begin the next steps. She was bouncing back and forth from one foot to another, her hands palm up and fingers motioning in a beckoning fashion. She was eager to learn more. "Bring it on."

"I think that's probably enough for tonight. The most important thing you can learn, is to be alert to your surroundings. Constantly. Keep your eyes and ears open, always pay attention to what's going on behind and around you as well as in front of you."

"You mean like the fact that you keep coming closer, with every shift of your feet?" she asked, proud of herself for noticing his change in positioning.

"Very good, but you need to be able to be prepared for anything. Once you notice your stalker, you need to be prepared for his next move."

A scream, mixed with giggles, erupted as Todd lunged for Cara, taking her to the ground. He rolled beneath her so he wouldn't crush her when they landed, but he himself, for all his lecturing about being prepared, wasn't ready for the feel of her on top of him.

She stared down at him, her smile disappearing, her eyes going hot. Her hair hung loose around them both, a mass of curls shielding them from the rest of the world.

Todd was ready to give in. Ready to give up.

The phone rang, breaking the spell.

Cara tensed.

Todd cursed.

"I'll get it," Cara said, raising herself from Todd's chest.

"Let the machine get it," he said, grabbing her hand.

The shrill ring of the phone continued until they both remembered the power was out.

"Duh. I better grab it."

Todd held onto her hand, staying her one more time. Is there an extension I can listen on?

"In my office. It's line two."

"Okay wait and give me time to get to the other phone." He picked up the receiver.

"Hello?"

There was silence.

"Hello?" she repeated.

Silence.

"It's okay, Todd. I guess whoever it was, hung up."

Cara almost dropped the phone when a voice, distorted as usual, sounded through the earpiece.

"I wondered if the goon would be listening."

Todd heard Cara gasp and imagined her slapping her hand over the phone. Her stalker knew Todd was there, or he was taking a shot in the dark.

He watched the hall toward the family room, hoping Cara wasn't panicking. He couldn't see her because she'd moved slightly which placed her outside of his vision. The phone wouldn't reach far enough, and he wanted to listen to the call to see if he could hear anything that might give them an idea of who it was.

"He can listen if he likes. It won't do either of you any good, though it aggravates me. You don't want to aggravate me any more than you already have, Cara, dear."

The tone, though twisted, didn't sound angry at all.

"Who are you?" Cara asked panic obvious in her voice.

"Haven't you figured that out yet? I'm hurt. I was a big part of your life at one time. How could you have forgotten?"

"You're an old boyfriend?" she asked, stunned.

"Hardly."

Was that honest irritation? Was it someone from her past? A guy she had turned down? Todd made notes on a paper he found on Cara's desk, scribbling quickly.

"You didn't find my gift yet, did you?" I know you've received it. I'll know too when you've opened it. I know all, Cara. Remember that."

"Hang up, Cara." Todd spoke through the phone, in order to let her stalker know it was Todd and not Cara who'd made the decision.

"Did you like my little black out? Of course you did. You were surprised to find your lack of power weren't you? Well, you need to get used to it. When I'm ready I will have all the power, and you'll have none. And where you're going, it's going to be very, very dark."

When Todd returned to the family room, Cara stood staring at the phone.

"He hung up," she whispered.

Todd supposed the caller had done it so Cara couldn't hang up on him. It was a power play. Sometimes, when a killer was feeling out of control, it was the little displays of dominance that gave the illusion of self-mastery, and that meant her caller had a very loose grip on his emotions. He felt he was losing control of himself and his surroundings. It wouldn't be long before he made his move, and Todd would be there when he did. *Bring it, buddy.*

He took the phone from her grasp, lying it back on the cradle.

"It's okay, Cara."

"I don't know who it was. I really don't. He thinks I should know who he is. I've had lots of dates but very few that turned into serious relationships. My career has always been forefront in my life. Creating a successful business always the priority as I was discovering who I was and what I could become. I had little or no time for serious dating. Did I offend someone? Not pay enough attention?"

"Maybe a coworker? Someone who you passed during your career?" Todd added.

He was rubbing her arms because she seemed cold. Shock. He recognized the signs.

"He knew what I was doing. He's probably watching right now." She searched around her like there would be proof she was right. "He probably knows when I get up in the morning. And when I go to work. My life has become so predictable lately; it would be easy for him to figure out my routine."

"Cara are you all right?" Todd asked, shaking her gently.

"I'm, I, I'm okay. Tr-truly, I'm, f-fine."

"Sure you are, sweetheart. You're fine."

He pulled her into his arms and rubbed his hands up and down her back. She could feel the terror ease back into the recesses of her mind. She couldn't deal with this.

She was way out of her league. What would she do? What could she do? She had no clue who her caller was. None. He would figure it out for her, but he couldn't do it without her knowledge.

"Come and sit here beside me while I find out where your caller was calling from."

"Don't call him that. Please," she added. "He's not *my* caller. I don't even know him."

"Well let's find out how he knows you."

She watched him, never taking her eyes off him as he dialed his phone and spoke to someone.

"Who's Ray?" she asked.

"Thanks, Rae, you're a doll. I owe you."

Cara sat up straight.

"Yes, and let me know if you find anything else out, will ya? Why is it you haven't been snapped up yet?" Todd spoke into the phone.

"Sure you haven't met the right man yet, I know, I know. All the good ones are taken." He laughed and Cara felt her heart break.

"Who's Ray?" she asked again when Todd was finally finished with his call.

"She's a girl from the office. She's doing me a couple of favors."

"I see."

"I doubt that, judging from the expression on your face. Not to mention your body language says jealous woman." He tucked a curl behind her ear. "She's just a coworker."

"It's no business of mine anyway."

"Well, that's true, but she is doing us both a favor. She's put a tap on your phone- at my request," he added when she appeared as though she would object. "She

107

says the call came from South Africa. We both know that's not the case. That call was too clear to have come from anywhere overseas. It's my guess it originated right here in Lightcastle."

"Close enough to see what I'm doing," Cara said, beginning to shake again.

"Not necessarily. He could have seen you with me earlier and assumed I had come home with you. Or wondered if I was here because I asked if you were coming to bed the other night. It doesn't mean he's watching from across the street or from the tree in your backyard.

She sucked in her breath.

"Shit. I didn't mean to put ideas in your head. I just mean that he can't see through curtains, so he can't know exactly what you're doing. He's guessing."

Yeah, well, he's a pretty good guesser wouldn't you say?"

"He's probably been watching your routine for a while. You said yourself that your routine has become predictable. It's not hard to guess if you're not at home for dinner, you've gone out. Think about it."

She was thinking about it. She was wondering how Todd knew what she had been thinking. At least she thought those ideas had been only in her head.

If she had spoken those thoughts aloud, what other intimate ideas had spilled?

Chapter Ten

He'd had every intention of going home for the night, but Cara had been so shaky he'd offered to stay again. What it meant was another sleepless night, but what was one more? He took the phone off the hook before he went to bed. He didn't need anything upsetting Cara further. Not that he thought her caller would try again. He didn't think so anyway.

Still, knowing she was in her bed tossing and turning, gave him some satisfaction. If he was going to be uncomfortable, he was happy he wasn't the only one. She had no idea what she did to him. Of that he was certain.

He heard her get up from her bed, heard the floor creaking as she walked to her door. He should get up and see if she was okay. If she went down the hall, he would go with her, to make sure nothing happened.

He was laying on his back with his arms folded behind his head, when she entered his room.

"Can you sleep?" she whispered, in case he was sleeping.

"No. You?"

"Nuh, uh. Do you want anything?" she asked, "Water? Warm milk?"

His feet hit the floor and he had her in his arms before she could gasp. "Just you," he replied, giving in to temptation. "I want you so bad. I can't stand it anymore."

Cara returned his kiss, with all the pent-up frustration she felt. She matched his ardor, heartbeat for heartbeat, praying he wouldn't stop, afraid he would.

With a sweeping motion he had her in his arms and carried her to his bed. "I swore I wouldn't do this, but I can't help myself." He nuzzled her neck.

Shivers ran down her body, her reaction to his words almost as strong as her reaction to what he was doing to her.

"I want to make love to you." He stroked her breasts with his calloused hands. "Please don't tell me to stop."

"Please don't stop," she gasped. "I think I'll die if you do."

The fire inflamed them both as he reached between their bodies to find she was ready for him.

When Todd entered her, he thought he'd found his one true place on earth. He was home, where he was always meant to be.

The urgency with which Cara moved, told him she was as frantic to reach fulfillment as he was so he shifted his body causing a friction so intense she cried out with the sweet agony.

He continued the rhythm, increasing it until they both climaxed, then lay satiated in each other's arms.

Oh God. What had he done? For the first time in his entire life, he'd had unprotected sex. Not a bright thing to do. He hoped she was smart enough to have protected herself. And what kind of asshole did that make him that this had been his first thought? That *she* was smart enough. God knew he should be smart enough.

****

"Are you okay?" he asked, brushing one of her

glorious curls from her face.

"Just a minute." She sighed. "I think I'm dead."

"I didn't use anything, Cara. I meant are you okay with that?"

"Oh." Her heart fell. What had she expected? That the world had rocked for him too? "I'm fine," she said, trying to hold the tears at bay.

He had been on top of her and had settled between her legs…and when he had entered her, she wanted it with all her heart. *Oh God, not her heart.* She'd opened herself to him on a physical level not realizing her heart went with the package. She tried to shut that part of her off, but was unable to do it. She hadn't thought of anything more.

Todd pulled her into his arms, laying her head on his chest. "You're more than fine, sweetheart."

She heard the endearment, but knew it for what it was. A figure of speech.

"You're not too bad yourself," she joked. *Just the best damn thing that's ever happened to me.*

"What's this? Tears?" He raised her face to gaze into her eyes. "Cara? What's wrong?"

"Nothing." She wiped at her face.

"It's obvious it's not nothing. Did I hurt you? I know we took things a little fast, but I'll be better next time, I promise. Tell me I didn't hurt you."

"You didn't hurt me." Next time? He wanted to make love again? Of course he did. Guys always wanted to have sex. *It's just sex Cara.*

"You swear? I couldn't bear it if I thought I'd hurt you."

"I swear." *You've done nothing but steal my heart.*

"Nope something's up. I can tell. Are you really

worried about our lack of protection? I swear, Cara, that's the first time in my life I've gotten so swept away, I didn't even think to use protection until it was already a done deal."

"You were swept away?"

"Hell, yes," he all but shouted. "And don't look so smug, I wasn't swept away by myself, you seemed pretty intense yourself."

She carried him away. It was concern she heard in his voice, not regret. "Yeah, I'm perfect." She couldn't stop smiling.

"You're perfect all right." He grabbed her then, rolling her on top of him.

They made love again and again, until both were exhausted, but Todd grabbed a condom out of his bag so they were protected going forward. Dawn was beginning to lighten the sky when they finally went to sleep.

****

Todd sat at the kitchen table thinking about last night. He was too damn close and although he didn't regret his actions, he didn't think it was wise to repeat them. He saw his career disappearing on the horizon and it panicked him.

He needed to head up the coast to check on the contractors again today. The septic tank was going in and the gas line was being brought in as well. Maybe if he could get home early, he could run Cara through some more self-defense training. That thought appealed to him far too much.

"Hey, Cara, I think it would be a good idea for me to give you some more self-defense lessons tonight. What time are you going to be done tonight?"

"I have a late appointment, but I should be finished

by seven thirty."

"Perfect. I'll meet you at your office. I don't want you leaving by yourself."

"He wouldn't be stupid enough to do anything in the open," Cara protested.

"Think about it. How open is your parking lot. Sure it's not underground or anything, but it's at the back of your building, trees all around it—no other businesses that draw crowds at that time of day. The only people there would be leaving your building and it's usually cleared out by then. As far as businesses go, your building is rather quiet. Why wouldn't he do something?"

"I suppose, but—"

"No buts. Wait for me to follow you home. I think he's starting to lose control and that means he could make a move soon," he ordered. "I'll be there before you're finished with your clients."

With that said, he pulled her into his arms, gave her a quick kiss, and was gone.

****

A mixture of emotions stirred in Cara. She was torn between resentment at being ordered around like a child, and excitement at having Todd kiss her goodbye in the morning. She wouldn't think about the excitement though. It frightened her.

He was a kind man, but she knew he could be formidable too. There wasn't anything he had done yet that gave her evidence to prove this, it was just an instinctual thing.

She prepared for her day, dressing with care, as always. She tried to get her hair to behave, but was disappointed once again when it wouldn't do what she wanted. Maybe she should get it all cut off. She threw the brush down on the counter as the big clip she used to secure the mass of curls, slipped sideways, giving her a rather lopsided appearance.

"Blast it all," she complained as she stood in front of the mirror. "I give up. It'll have to do. I'm going to be late."

She was on the way out the door when the phone rang.

"Have plans for tonight, do you?" the voice asked. Cara hung up, shaking but sick and tired of feeling afraid. Was her house bugged?

She glanced around the house, to see if she could see anyone watching. She knew there was no one there, but she searched, nonetheless.

Just get in your car and go to work, she told herself. *There's no one lurking in the closets, he's just guessing again.*

She drove to work checking her rearview mirror, every few seconds. Was that blue car following?

Seconds later, she checked her mirror again, the blue car was gone.

By the time she arrived at work, her neck muscles were tense. It reminded her of when she was back in the district Attorney's office again, getting prepped for court when she was a witness in the murder of Tommy Gordon.

Her hands gripped the steering wheel and she felt lightheaded again. Was this something to do with that trial? She was only sixteen when her neighbor and friend Tommy had been murdered. *Was that what he'd meant when he said he was a big part of my life?*

Her cell phone rang, and she swerved, cursing the

creation of mobile phones.

"Cara, it's Em. What color of flowers have you ordered?"

"Why?" she asked her sister.

"Because the caterer said he would prefer doing everything in burgundy tones. Mom loves the idea, but I was afraid they might not look right with the flowers. You did order the flowers didn't you?"

"Of course I ordered the flowers, and they're white and burgundy, so it'll be fabulous," she lied. She hoped to high heaven, those colors were available this time of year.

Picturing what was in her neglected garden, she figured she was safe. They may not get roses, but there would be something available.

Flipping open her cell phone, she called her private line at work, leaving a message on her voice mail to call the florist. Hopefully, with a week's notice, there wouldn't be a problem.

That done, she relaxed until she took the final turn into her parking spot at the office. It really was a great spot, shaded beneath the trees as it was. It saved her leather seats from the scorching sun.

Her arms were full with samples and the smaller of her two briefcases, so there was no way she could carry the one she'd thrown in the back seat of her car the other day. It would have to wait again.

"Can I help you with anything, Cara?"

It was Mr. Smith/Jones. Cara groaned.

"No thanks. I'm fine."

"You left something in your back seat," he commented.

"I want it left there, thank you. Now if you don't

mind, I'm running late."

With that she sped up her walk to a point where she felt she was running. With her arms full the way they were, she had a hard time keeping the pace up.

Mr. Smith/Jones didn't seem to have a problem though, curse his hide.

Once she was finally in her office she checked her messages, thankful she had reminded herself about the flowers. She just had too many things on her mind. That was all it was.

It took a great deal of finagling to get the florist to agree to Cara's needs and her date. It also was costing her a great deal of extra money. Orchids and roses would be the main flowers, with some other, more common flowers, spread throughout the displays. It would be stunning, and more importantly, it would be delivered on time.

It was a quiet day, with few interruptions. Paige had taken any messages from Mr. Smith/Jones and fielded them for Cara. She hated to use her assistant to run interference for her and felt like a coward because she did, but was relieved not to have to deal with his persistence.

Todd called late in the afternoon, to say he would be a little delayed getting back.

"Wait for me at your office. Please," he added when his order was met with silence.

Cara sighed. "I suppose I have work I can do, but I really think it's ridiculous. I'm a grown woman, for crying out loud."

"Humor me," was his reply just before he said good-bye.

Now it was getting late and Cara was tired. She

wanted to go home but knew Todd wouldn't be back for at least another hour.

Her last clients of the day had cancelled, rescheduling for Monday, and she wanted nothing more than to go home and soak in the tub.

"This is stupid. I'm out of here."

She shut down her computer and locked her filing cabinets, then her office door.

She had the sensation of being watched, but that was ridiculous. She was just being paranoid because of Todd's lessons in self-defense last night.

She would pay attention to her surroundings, and get herself all worked up over every little noise.

Was that someone in the stairwell? She pushed the button to the elevator, praying it would hurry.

Someone was on the stairs. She was sure of it now.

The door down the hall opened, and Cara felt her breathing suspend. Then air couldn't be pulled in fast enough to feed her lungs. *You're going to hyperventilate if you don't get a grip.*

Finally, the elevator doors opened, and Cara jumped in, just as the cleaner entered the hall, her tote-box of cleaning supplies in her hand. Breathing a sigh of relief, Cara pushed the button to take her to the main level. What a twit she was. She would be fine. She *was* fine.

By the time she'd gotten to the main lobby, she had herself reasonably calm again. If it killed her, she would learn to conquer this fear, reducing her stalker's power and taking that power back for herself. It was all a matter of attitude.

The lobby was empty, the marble floors already shined spotless for the next day. The cleaners must have been early tonight. The clicking of her heels could be heard across the floor as she walked toward the entrance. She hadn't noticed before, how large the foyer felt. It was only because it was empty that it seemed so, she chided herself. The emergency lights were on, casting shadows in the corners, behind the massive pillars adorning the entranceway.

She stopped, thinking she had heard more footsteps, but she was only imagining it. There was nothing but silence.

With her key in her hand, she searched the property through the front door. She should have waited. It was getting dark outside, and although the parking lot wasn't far, it was dim and secluded.

Chastising herself for her foolishness, she unlocked the door, keying in the code for the alarm. Once outside, she turned and relocked the door behind her.

She moved her keys around in her hand so one key was sticking out, feeling empowered by the memory of her grandfather and his lessons on safety, in combination with Todd's training. She walked upright paying attention to her surroundings just as Todd had taught her.

Her thumb rested on the remote door opener for her key fob.

She was almost to her car door when she was grabbed from behind. They came out of nowhere, and she panicked, swinging her fist, keys aimed at her attackers face.

He wore a mask.

A roar of pain sounded, and she hit the remote to unlock her door. Another swing of her fist had the car locking again. Her head hit the car, and stars swam before her eyes, but she would not give up. Her legs kicked, but missed as her attacker dodged her foot.

With her shoulders pinned against the car, she raised her knee with all her strength, aiming for that one spot that would bring her assailant low and screaming for help. A grunt of pain, but still he held on.

Please God, don't let me die tonight. Thirty-three is too young to die.

Lights shone on the streets as Cara struggled for her life but no one came to help her. She tried to pull her arms out of their binding grip, just as she'd been instructed.

"You need to pull away, with a quick jerk. Pull toward the thumbs and you'll get free," he had instructed. *"That's right, just like that. Good for you."*

She heard the words again in her head. Tried again. *It's not working.*

One last try. Yes. Free.

With a shove at her attacker's chest, she angled herself toward her front door, pulling on the handle.

"Shit," she swore, completely unaware the word had slipped past her lips. "It's locked. No," she cried, pulling on the door with one hand and trying to push the button with the other. It didn't work.

Her head was smashed against the window, and that was going to be it. She was finished. Waves of black swam in and out before her eyes.

Chapter Eleven

A muffled curse sounded behind her and then she slumped to the ground.

From somewhere in the back of her mind she was aware of lights shining on her and the sound of screeching tires, but beyond that, she was cognizant of little. She guessed a blanket was placed over her, for she sensed warmth. Someone was calling to her. *No*, her mind shouted. *Don't make me wake up. It hurts too much.*

"Don't try to talk, sweetheart. Just lie still."

The words soothed her.

"I'm not going anywhere." She chuckled, then moaned as her ribs hurt. It was important to let them know she was okay.

"I'm calling the ambulance. The police are already on their way."

She tried to sit up. "I don't want an ambulance."

She knew he could hear the panic in her voice, and didn't care.

"Don't be ridiculous, you need to get to a hospital."

She was becoming more aware of her surroundings. It was Todd's coat that had been placed over her, and it was Todd's eyes she was staring into now. Eyes showing concern, and something else. What was that? His lips were moving and she was mesmerized by their fullness, the way they moved.

"What?" she asked, having been distracted.

"I said you need to be checked out by a doctor. You could have broken ribs, a concussion."

"I have neither. I'm just going to be a little bruised, that's all. Will you help me up? This pavement is awfully hard to lie on."

"I think it would be better if you stay where you are."

"There's no way I'm going to be laying on the ground when that fat Barney Fife shows up. I'll stand and face him."

****

Against his will, Todd helped Cara up. He thought he'd die when he saw her being attacked. He now knew how a heart could truly break. First it froze, then cracked and crumbled. His would have done just that, had Cara been killed. He would have wanted to die right along with her, and that terrified him. He'd faced criminals of all sorts, shapes, and sizes. Had come up against guns, large and small, and nothing terrified him as much as the possibility of losing the woman he loved. *Well shit.* He loved her. That was unplanned. He felt like his breath had been knocked out of him. How could he stop this? How could he take back his feelings? Damn it all to hell.

He ground his teeth, torn between giving her what she wanted, and what he thought was best for her. Staring into her eyes, he saw determination and inner strength.

Sirens in the distance had her pushing his hand away, and preparing to stand. She was going to do it anyway, so he might as well give her a hand up.

Gently, so as not to hurt her further, he helped her to her feet.

"Why don't you at least sit in your car?" he asked.

"Because then I have to look up at him. I refuse to do that."

He placed his arm around her as the police arrived. There were two cars, one carrying Reilly and the other a man Todd recognized but didn't know well.

"What seems to be the trouble here?" Reilly bellowed.

"Cara, Ms. Kane, was attacked. She could have been killed."

"Not man enough to save your dolls, huh?" Reilly mumbled.

She advanced on Reilly so quickly even Todd was caught off guard. Her finger was jabbing the air in front of her as she stepped forward.

"I'm no one's 'doll'. Nor do I appreciate you talking about me as if I weren't here. If you have something to say, you may address me, not your armpit, and stop mumbling under your breath."

"Ahem…" Reilly cleared his throat, his face turning red, "can you describe your attacker, ma'am?"

"He was about this tall." She held her hand up in the air at the approximate height of her attacker. "That would be, what, about five feet, ten or eleven inches maybe?"

"Any distinguishing marks?"

"He wore a mask. Black. The kind with holes for only the eyes. And before you ask, I didn't see the color of his eyes, it was dark, and the holes weren't that big. Besides I was busy trying not to die."

"What about anywhere else? Any marks?" Reilly asked.

"Not that I noticed. If I'm lucky, he'll have a scratch down his face from my keys. Maybe I was really lucky and poked his eye out."

Casually, so no one would notice, she leaned against the car. Todd tugged her closer to his side, searching her eyes to see if she was going to make it through this. She gave him a brief smile, to let him know she was fine.

"Where exactly did he attack you?"

"You're standing there. I was walking to my car, and had just made it when he jumped out from nowhere."

"Well you haven't given us much to go on. There's no video surveillance out here," he said, looking around, "so chances are we won't find this guy. You sure you didn't see anything?"

Sarcasm dripped from his voice. She could hear it, but calling him on it didn't seem worth the effort. She was tired, all of a sudden, and wanted nothing more than to lie down.

"Nothing, but then I was doing my best to keep from getting beat up, or worse and my mind wasn't exactly functioning at full capacity. Next time I'll try to get the details down, maybe get his name. Would that help?"

A cough sounded a great deal like a laugh, and Reilly glared at the other officer.

"If you think of anything else, call the station."

Todd watched as Reilly walked back to his car. His shift was probably up. What a useless bag of—"

"Can I see your keys, ma'am?" the other officer asked, once Reilly was back in his car.

Cara held out her hand with her keys in them. The officer placed them in a paper bag, and labeled it.

"Hey those are my keys," she protested.

Todd held her arm as she reached for the bag. "He needs them for evidence, sweetheart. There might be samples of skin embedded in them. You said you scratched your attacker."

"But how will I get home?" The shaking was starting, and she felt as though she were going to collapse.

"I need to get her home," Todd said, glaring at the officer as though he thought he might try to detain them longer.

"I'm Officer Beauregard Calloway, but call me Beau. Here's my card, in case you think of anything else. Don't hesitate to reach out. This number is my voice mail, so even if it's late, and you think of something, call and leave a message. That way you won't forget."

"Have you been talking to my family?" Cara grumbled.

"Excuse me?" the nice officer asked, uncertain if that statement was meant for him.

"Nothing. If I think of anything, I'll call."

"Agent Mitchell? You'll see Ms. Kane gets home? That's a question but also an offer, if you're not able."

"I'll see to it," Todd replied, standing a little taller.

Cara eased her way into the front seat of Todd's car. "This certainly isn't a muscle car." Cara snickered, then grabbed her side and moaned.

It was a brown sedan, older model, and rather beat up. Todd took no offense.

"This is the piece of crap car the bureau gave me for this case. It's souped-up under the hood, but looks like a pile of- well I agree it doesn't look great. Trust me though, this baby can run."

"Show me," Cara dared.

"You need to be checked out at a hospital, not flying all over the countryside." He saw her protests, and continued. "I know you don't want to go to the hospital, which is why I'm going to take you home."

"Chicken?" she challenged. "I double-dog-dare ya."

Todd smiled, and Cara's insides turned upside down.

"Now how can I resist a double-dog-dare?"

****

She couldn't explain the need she felt to fly down the road. Maybe it was having come so close to death, or maybe it was a need to run away, and escape reality, if only for a little while. She only knew she needed to get away from here and she didn't feel ready to go home just yet.

He was right. The car could move, and quickly. She rolled down her window, letting the air blow away all her troubles. Her hair was a tangled mess, but she didn't care. For once in her life, she didn't worry about her appearance. She relaxed and enjoyed the exhilaration of the drive.

"You hungry yet?" Todd asked, glancing over at the beautiful woman in the seat beside him.

"No, but you must be. There's a place just up the highway that serves good food. It looks a little rough, but it's not a bad place."

"Which one?" he asked watching for signs of it.

"It's on the right. Poncho and Lefty's."

He turned into the driveway, insisting that he would get take-out.

"Don't be silly. We can eat here," Cara insisted.

"No, we take it back to your place and you go to bed."

"Will you come with me?" Cara asked, unsure of her footing, yet not wanting it let the opportunity pass. If she was honest with herself, she also didn't want to be home alone. She was afraid of reliving her attack or worse, being attacked again.

"I think it might be a good idea if I sleep in the spare room tonight. You're going to be pretty sore come morning."

She was disappointed and knew it showed.

Todd reached over to brush his finger down her cheek, "You need rest."

She held his hand against her cheek, "I need you," she whispered against his palm.

Todd leaned over, kissing her gently, lips barely touching. It moved Cara, bringing the sting of tears to her eyes.

"Go get food, and while you're in there, I've decided I want one of their burgers. Go." she insisted when he hesitated.

"Lock the doors. I'll keep an eye on you through the window."

Todd was impatient in the restaurant, silently cursing the staff for moving too slow, even though his expectations were unrealistic. What the hell was wrong with him? He wasn't the impatient sort. That was his cousin, Hunter's job.

Damn he wished Hunter were here and not in Italy on his honeymoon. He'd thought about calling him after he'd seen Cara's attack, but he wouldn't do that to Miranda. He smiled thinking he didn't have a problem doing it to Hunter. But either way, there was nothing Hunter could do anyway.

What about Brad? Was he still in the area? He'd check it out as soon as he got back to Cara's. And Alex too.

When he returned to the car, food in hand, Cara was asleep. He'd known she was exhausted, or would be once her adrenalin level fell. It wasn't something 'normal' people were accustomed to dealing with, but it was a feeling which was no stranger to Todd. He hated it.

Cara stirred when he opened the car door. "Just keep your eyes closed. Your body needs rest," he told her.

"Food smells good," she mumbled, turning her head toward Todd.

"Don't worry, I'll save you some."

The ride home was at a much slower pace. Todd needed to think. How would he reach Brad? He'd try his hotel first, then through the Bureau given he too worked for the FBI, and as a last resort, he would call Miranda given Brad was her cousin. She would have an idea of how to get in touch with him.

When he finally pulled in the driveway, Cara was sound asleep. He shook her gently, trying to wake her just enough to give him her house key.

"It's on my key ring," she told him. "The police have it."

"Yeah, but where's your spare?"

"In the face stone that's sitting in the flower pot by the front door," she mumbled.

"What? Of all the—" he'd have to yell at her later. How could someone so smart do something so obviously irresponsible?"

Todd left the food in the car and carried her to her room, laying her gently on the bed. He pulled her shoes off, and the covers back, then placed her between the sheets. There was no way he was taking off her clothes. He couldn't handle it.

"Are you coming to bed too?" she asked, opening her eyes slightly.

"Later," was his non-committal reply.

In Cara's office, he ate his food, which was now cold. Accustomed to eating under such conditions, he didn't pay much attention to the temperature. It all tasted good to him.

Brad had checked out of his hotel. Damn. Well, he'd try him from the office tomorrow and see if he had returned to England, or was still on vacation. In the meantime, he would do a little investigating.

He stroked the keyboard of Cara's computer. She wouldn't mind, he was sure. He wouldn't open anything personal. He could if he wanted to, but it wouldn't be right. He wouldn't abuse his gift of, what was it Hunter had called it? Computer wizardry. There wasn't a computer Todd couldn't get into, given enough time.

Searching Cara's files was on the list for later. Now he would search James Smith. It would take some time. It was after all a common name, but there were ways of narrowing the search.

"Let's see Mr. Smith. What sort of information does the FBI have on you? How many of you will there be?"

The computer hummed and Todd waited while the information downloaded.

"Well shit."

"That many. James Smith is more popular than I imagined. Well, Mitchell, you'll just have to narrow it down some more."

Rolling up his sleeves, he felt the excitement surge through him. He was on the hunt. Give him a computer and a mission, and Todd was pumped. The ins and outs of computer searches thrilled him. Add to that a search for information, or a puzzle to solve and he was in heaven.

He thought about the woman sleeping upstairs. He

was crazy about her, goddammit. Yes, he wanted her, and he'd been stupid enough to allow himself to care deeply, but he couldn't give up his career. Couldn't leave behind the excitement of the chase, the progress in his career, the—

He just wouldn't think about it.

Chapter Twelve

"What are you doing?" Cara asked from the doorway, hours later.

Todd's collar was unbuttoned and his hair was messed. Cara could see where his fingers had run through it -in frustration, she imagined, and she'd never seen a sexier picture in her life.

She watched and as he observed her, his eyes lost that faraway look and focused solely on her. She melted inside.

"I thought you were asleep."

He pushed back from the desk and rubbed the back of his neck with his hands.

"I was, but I had a bad- I woke up."

"Bad dreams are to be expected, Cara. It'll take some time."

She sat in the chair that faced Todd across the desk. "But I always thought I could take care of myself -took pride in how I had always achieved things on my own- but when it really came down to it, I couldn't do anything. I was useless."

"You didn't have the control you're used to exerting, and that's hard to deal with. It would be for anyone."

"I tried the things you taught me. That's how I got away, even if it was for just a few seconds."

"Those few seconds saved your life, sweetheart.

Give yourself some credit." He added a smile.

"Will you show me more self-defense? I mean… something else that might cause some damage, rather than just getting away?" she asked.

"Did you kick him? Dead center like I told you?"

"I tried, but I missed and it didn't have the effect I was going for."

She tucked a stray curl behind her ear and Todd's gaze on her warmed. His eyes seemed to sizzle.

"I'll show you some more moves in a couple of days. When you're feeling better," he answered, trying to take his mind off her hair and get it on something more practical.

"I'd feel better now, if you could show me something. Anything."

"Why don't I get you something to eat? Do you want me to heat up your burger?"

She sighed, taking a deep cleansing breath, stopping short with a twinge in her ribs, then smiled. "Great food huh?"

"The best, but then it came with a great recommendation." He paused. "You up to eating?"

"Yeah, I guess I could eat something. It's weird but I'm starving."

"We have fabulous choices for you today, mademoiselle," Todd said with a thick French accent. "Might I be so bold as to suggest the beuf du jour?"

"Oh, it sounds wonderful. That'll be just what I'll have."

"Would you like a glass of Chablis, to go with that?"

"Perfect, garcon," she said pronouncing it 'purrfact garkonn' and an exaggerated Southern drawl.

Todd choked. "One moment, and I'll return with

your beverage, Mademoiselle."

Cara laughed, enjoying herself. She turned to her computer and opened her email program. The first message to download was another love letter from the poor soul who had made a typo on his girlfriend's email address.

Should she read it? Oh heck, why not? It was sent to her, even if it was a mistake.

She hadn't gotten two lines into the letter when she noticed how angry the author was. It was obvious he expected a reply and hadn't gotten one, and was now blaming his partner. "The turd. I hope she dumps you on your nasty butt."

"You hope who gets dumped?"

"This turd who sent this letter. I got a lovely letter from him before, if a little possessive, but he had the address wrong."

"You sure about that? Can I see?"

"Be my guest." She rolled her chair back so Todd could have a seat. "See? Right here," she pointed. "I don't know 'for_your_eyes_only'."

"That's just his email name."

"I understand that, but he only showed up a few days ago, and I have no clue as to who he is."

"Maybe it's your caller."

"That's stretching it a little don't you think? My caller wants me dead. This guy is sending love letters."

"There's a very fine line between that kind of love and hate or obsession."

He was serious. She could see it in his eyes.

A shiver traveled down her spine and she crossed her arms over her chest in an attempt to ward off a chill.

"But how could he have gotten my email address.

No one knows- Okay so we won't go there again. But it's not as if I advertise it. Only my business email is on my webpage.

"There are numerous ways to get your email address. The easiest way would be off an email that was forwarded to you and everyone else on their list."

"What?"

"You know, when they send one of those stupid jokes to you and everyone else, then that gets passed on to everyone they know and so on, until it happens to make it to that one psychotic who knows you from your past and has an axe to grind, or hackers post email addresses online on a regular basis. Companies pay money for that sort of thing."

"Well, put that way, I suppose it's easier than most people would think," she said, head tilted to one side in thought, lips pursed.

"What I don't understand, is why would he send a love letter then try to kill me? In fact, why would he want to kill me anyway? What did I ever do to him? Honest, I'm a very nice person."

"That's what we have to find out. Then we have your attacker. And it's obvious it doesn't have anything to do with being nice or not, when you're dealing with a psycho."

"Is that why you're investigating the slimy accountant from upstairs? You think he's a suspect?"

"There's something not right about him. I just can't put my finger on it, yet. Give me time, and I'll get it."

"I'm sure that's true. But I don't think it was him. I didn't smell his cologne and whoever attacked me was leaner and definitely taller."

"Leaner? You didn't tell Reilly they were lean?"

"I just remembered after my nightma –um… my dream."

"Did you remember anything else?"

"White hands. He was wearing gloves, but his sleeve raised and I saw his wrist. He was thin. That's all I can remember."

Cara finally picked up her burger and ate it, but it stuck in her throat.

"It's gotta be cold again. Want me to re-heat - again?"

"No thanks. I'm used to eating cold food. Though it does seem to taste different from this side of the desk, she teased."

****

Todd watched her sip her wine and eat her burger. She would have a lovely shiner by morning. That would be quite the talk for her office building. God he wished he'd been earlier. He put his hand on his gut, which was grinding. He needed antacids. He tried to hide the fear he still felt remembering the gut wrenching feeling of seeing her alone and being attacked.

Shit. If he hadn't been so late, she wouldn't have been in the parking lot alone. It was his fault, and he would carry the blame.

"What?" Cara asked. "You're staring at me."

"Nothing," he answered, not ready to admit to himself, let alone her that his heart ached every time he remembered seeing her lying in the parking lot.

"Tell me. You're staring at me like I'm some fragile doll, who will break if you move wrong."

"Actually I was just wondering what rumor would be going around your office building, when they see your shiner."

Cara sucked in her breath. "I have a shiner? Let me see."

She ran to the bathroom to see herself in her mirror. "Oh my Lawd. I do have a shiner starting. My mom and dad are going to be mad. We're supposed to have family pictures at the anniversary party."

She turned to Todd who had followed her into the tiny powder room that was just off her office. "How much makeup do you think I'll need to cover it up? My brother Sterling has already booked the photographer."

They walked back to the office, Cara gently poking at her eye and trying to determine how much it hurt –and by proxy, how much it was going to show.

"Makeup's out of my range of expertise. That's my cousin's specialty."

"Hunter?" Cara asked, stunned. "Hunter Sloan? That big bruiser of a man who scared me half to death the first time I met him, Hunter Sloan?"

Todd laughed, "That would be him. He's the best in his field at disguises. Of course I always tease him that the DEA's not nearly as good as the FBI. He of course, would tend to disagree and defends his agency."

"I don't think I'd want to be anywhere near either one of you when that happens. Give me plenty of warning if you're ever going to be so stupid, and I'll clear out of your way."

"You don't think I can take him?"

"I'm not sure either one of you can 'take', as you put it, the other. And I don't really think I would want to see it anyway."

"Your lack of faith in my manly abilities wounds me."

Cara choked on the sip of wine she'd been taking.

"Don't make me laugh. And don't fish for compliments either."

Todd was smiling at her. She appeared secure and relaxed.

"You should get some rest. You look tired."

He was rubbing his neck again. Cara got up and walked behind the desk to stand directly at his back. With strong, but gentle fingers, she began to rub the tired and aching muscles.

"You're very good at that," he said, tilting his head to one side. "God that feels good."

He reached up to hold her hand then led her around him. She sat sideways in his lap.

Cara's email beeped, letting her know she had a message.

"You want to check that?" he asked, nuzzling her ear.

"Check what?"

Todd chuckled, realizing she hadn't heard her computer. "Your message."

"It'll still be there later."

"You sure?" he asked again, nuzzling the other ear, then kissing his way along her jaw.

"Unless you think I should," she said, turning the tables on Todd.

"Should what?"

"Check the message. What if it's another love letter?" she asked, still in a dreamlike state, and not wanting to change that fact.

Todd stopped for a second, then said. "Let him get his own woman."

****

When Todd kissed her, she could think of little else.

There was nothing and no one in the world beyond this man sitting here in her office. The rest of the world disappeared, if only for a few moments, and she felt at peace.

Zero competition required. No need to prove her worth or her abilities because she was either a woman, or a Kane. Coming from a successful family had its drawbacks. She loved her family dearly, but they could be challenging and she always felt the need to succeed.

Todd's hand's moved up her thigh to her hip, then upward to her breast. Cara moaned, arcing into him, offering more.

"You're so beautiful," he said, adding pressure and hearing her responsive moan. His hand moved up to tangle in her hair.

Cara tried to move it out of his way by pulling it back over her shoulders.

"No don't," he whispered. "God, I love your hair. It's wild and free."

"And a curly mess."

Todd pulled back to see into her eyes. "Are you nuts?" he asked dumbfounded. "It's the most beautiful hair I've ever seen."

He leaned forward to nuzzle her neck again and stopped. "What the hell?"

Chapter Thirteen

Todd pulled back, drawing aside her shirt collar.

"What's wrong?" Cara asked trying to tug her collar closed again.

"Did that little shit do this to you?"

He cursed again as he inspected the raw scrapes on Cara's neck.

She hung her head as though in shame and Todd tilted her chin up to gaze directly in her eyes. "I'm sorry."

"What for? You didn't do it."

"Yeah, but if I'd been there sooner, it wouldn't have happened."

It was then he couldn't meet her eyes, and she used his own tactics on him. Turning his head slightly, so he had no choice but to look at her, she kissed him. "If you hadn't shown up when you did, I'd be dead. Please don't apologize, for saving my life."

"I swear to you, I'll hunt him down until the day I die."

The words were whispered, but no less deadly for their quiet. Cara shivered, seeing for the first time, a look of steel--of pure determination. She was glad she was not on the receiving end of Todd's anger. He was on her side, thank God.

Again she leaned forward to kiss him but before she could, he stood, picking her up as though she were as light as a feather. She wasn't. No one knew that better than she did, but for some reason, she almost believed it as he carried her to the chair and set her down. Then he was gone from the room. She heard muffled cursing in the bathroom and was confused.

Todd returned holding some salve. "This is all I could find. It will help it heal. That ass is going to be sorry he every laid a finger on you when I catch him. And then he'll be headed straight to prison." He reached for a glass of water that was sitting on the desk and passed it to her, along with a pill he'd also procured from her bathroom."

"I don't need that. I'm fine."

"Trust me, you're going to wish you'd taken it in a few more hours. It's just acetaminophen."

Todd seemed antsy. She hadn't yet seen him this way. It was as if he couldn't sit still, and he no longer seemed interested in making out. She guessed she was getting somewhat stiff so she took the painkiller and leaned back against the sofa.

As Todd walked behind her desk again, and sat in her chair, she sighed, giving up all hope of fooling around tonight. She didn't feel like making anything happen that wasn't going to happen naturally. She had enough on her plate with someone trying to kill her.

"Jiminy Cricket."

Todd looked up, eyes intense.

They stared and heat flared between them. The room went silent; the air seemed too still and Cara stood ready to throw her recent resolve out the window and walk toward her hunk of a hero but a loud bang followed by what sounded like broken glass, and then the sound of water in the backyard interrupted her.

Todd shoved her toward the desk then grabbed a

pistol from the back of his waistband. "Crawl under the desk, and don't come out until I say so."

How could she not have noticed he had a gun? She stood, frozen.

"Now, Cara," he yelled then ran from the room.

She moved then, pulling out the desk chair and crawling underneath, pressing her back against the wood; making herself as small as she could; breathing too fast, but as quietly as she could. Was that someone else breathing too? Was someone in the house?

Footsteps sounded in the hall and she held her breath. The floor creaked right outside the office and she slowly reached above the desk, searching for her letter opener. She wouldn't be caught off guard again.

Her fingers encircled the makeshift weapon and she brought it down into her lap. She wouldn't go down without a fight-that was for damn sure.

A crash sounded, followed by muffled cursing and scuffling, then Todd returned to her office, dragging a man she didn't know, but who seemed somewhat familiar.

"Alex, what the hell?"

"Sorry your message wasn't clear, dude. Don't get mad at me. I thought 'need your help –1247 Lundy Lane' meant you were in immediate danger so I came right over."

Todd turned to Cara who had crawled out from under the desk and introduced her to the stranger. "Cara, this is Alex. He's Hunter's old partner. I'm sure you met him at the wedding."

"Um…welcome?" She heard the hesitancy in her voice but was feeling disoriented. "You broke into my backyard?"

"No, ma'am. I came in through the front. I heard a crash out back but was already at the front door and it was open so I just let myself in."

"Wait, what? The front door was open?" Todd asked, hands on hips. "Is this like when you and Hunter said you 'found the door unlocked and let yourselves in'?"

"No, bro, this was legit open-like unlocked and open a few inches-open."

"Oh my God," Cara whispered. "Someone was in the house. Oh my God." She sat down heavily and Todd sat beside her, turning her head to face him.

"Look at me, Cara. We've got this. We will deal with it."

"Someone was in my house. I want to sell it. I have to sell it."

"Don't let them freak you out," Todd answered, maintaining eye contact. "Breathe, Cara. Just breathe. You're going to hyperventilate if you don't start taking deeper breaths."

"I'm fine. I'm fine. I'm fine," she repeated to herself. "I'm breathing. I'm fine."

Alex reached down to take the letter opener from her hand but she couldn't seem to let it go.

"What were you going to do with this?" he asked, slowly peeling away her fingers to release it.

"Use whatever you have as a weapon," she responded, finally starting to calm and staring up at Alex. "Todd taught me that."

"And what would you do with it," Todd asked gently as he rubbed his hands up and down her arms.

Cara noted the warmth that was returning to her arms. Todd's hands were warm. Hers were stiff and cold.

She could feel the difference and she began flexing her hands to get the circulation moving again. An imprint of the opener was in her fingers and palm. She rubbed, trying to make it go away, but it just made it sting more as the blood flowed back into her fingers.

She regarded Alex, who stood tall, above her. "Eyes, carotid in the neck, or groin. All will work. Use what you have." As she said the words, she started shaking again. "Oh my God I was ready to stab someone in the eye. This isn't who I am."

"Cara…" Todd was rubbing her arms again, massaging as he went. He paused as though waiting for some sort of acknowledgement from her. She wasn't sure what, so she watched him. He made her feel safe, whenever she looked into his eyes. After a moment, he continued.

"You do what you need to do to save your life. Do you hear me? You do whatever it is you need to do."

"Todd's right, Cara. You do whatever you have to do. It's on them if they break into your home."

"You broke into my home," she added starting to feel more like herself again.

"I told you the door was open," he insisted. "God. It's like no one listens to me anymore."

****

The color was returning to Cara's cheeks, so he asked her if she was okay and then called to Alex. "Come and take a look at this, now that you're here. I want to know what you think."

The men went out to the backyard and Cara followed behind.

A large wet patch beside the pool and then what appeared to be footsteps about three feet apart, as though someone were running. Todd bent down for a closer inspection.

"Appears as though someone hopped the fence to go for a swim," Alex stated.

Todd squinted at him as Cara asked "But why? Why would someone swim in my pool when all my neighbors have pools? They could swim in their own."

"A dare maybe?" Alex chimed in.

"I don't think so. See the splash mark and then that wet towel over by the fence." He turned to Cara. "Is that your towel?"

"It is. It was hanging over the back of the chair by the fire pit. It's been there for a few days now. Do you think whoever used it left DNA on it? Can we test that? Would DNA wash off them and remain in the foot prints?"

"This isn't a TV show. It doesn't work that way-unfortunately. But I think they used the towel to try to throw us off. I don't think anyone actually went into the pool. I think they wanted us to think it was just some kids fooling around. See the shape of the 'footprints' on the deck. They're too round and too big and uneven. I mean…it's possible, but I don't think so. Three feet between here and two there…more like four feet over there. It's like someone made them and wasn't taking care. And it's too much of a coincidence that kids would jump your fence on a dare while you have someone stalking you. I don't believe in that kind of luck."

"You're right, it doesn't make any sense anyway, when everyone has a pool," Cara added.

"I'll call it in." Alex sighed.

"My God, what are the neighbors going to think when the police show up again. Can you just call that guy we spoke to who listens? What was his name? Beau? He seems to know what he's doing and then we don't have to call everyone who will show up with lights flashing. And I really don't want that O'whatever his name is here again. I don't like him. And I don't trust him either."

When Beau showed up fifteen minutes later, Todd took him outside to show him where the water marks were and where the towel had been thrown.

"We also heard glass breaking but I couldn't find anything broken anywhere. Nothing inside, or out that's damaged and could have made that sound."

The three men investigated the backyard carefully, searching for anything that might be out of place. Todd kept an eye on Cara while she watched. She brought coffee as they were wrapping up. They had nothing new to show for their efforts.

"Whoever was here--and it's obvious someone was-- seems to have left no trace other than the wet towel and footprints. It is possible they made the footprints as they ran but given what you said about the gate it's unlikely someone actually fell in."

"If it's okay with you, ma'am, I'd like to skim your filters, just to be sure. Who knows… Maybe we will get lucky and some particles off their clothes will be trapped there." Beau added. I can have Rae put a rush on it."

"Rae? Rae Piccadilly? You know her too?" Todd jumped in.

"Yeah we went to school together. She just moved back, but she's the best at forensics. If there's something there, she will find it," Beau responded.

When Beau left, Alex and Todd talked in whispers in the office. Todd had tried to talk Cara into going to her room to get some sleep while he and Alex brainstormed.

She didn't, of course and his suggestion hadn't gone over very well.

"You don't get to tell me what to do. I have every right to be a part of these conversations as anyone else. Actually more so, given it's my life and I'm the one being targeted."

She had a point, and Todd knew it. He didn't want her upset though so he kept his voice down while she carried the coffee tray back into the kitchen.

"So what do we have?" Alex asked.

"Keep your voice down. I don't want to upset Cara any more than she already is. We have phone calls to her home and cell. I don't think she's received any at work but then again, I'm not sure. Her home number is unlisted so I'm thinking it's someone who knows her. Not that anyone can't find this stuff out on the internet if they know how to do a deep dive but that would take special skills. She's received a weird email too." He showed Alex a print out. "She thinks this was just a slip up and sent to her in error but it's too much of a fluke with all this other stuff going on. I just don't buy that."

"I would agree," Alex added. "Sonnets of love are pretty creepy when you think about it and this one is especially so."

Cara entered the room, drying her hands on a dishtowel. "Did you guys want anything? I think I'm exhausted and Lord knows you guys look dog-tired too so why don't we pick this up in the morning with fresh eyes. I feel like there's something I'm missing in all of this, but I can't seem to figure out what that is. Tomorrow will be better."

Alex left and Todd escorted Cara to her room.

"I'm going to do some quick searches on the

internet. I want to do a deep dive on you to see if anything pops up. Any skeletons you want to share before I do?" He was kidding, but Cara appeared uneasy so he added "What?" He asked as gently as he could.

"I remember what this reminds me of. When I was sixteen, I saw a murder. That's what has me so spooked. I was threatened then too. The murderer, a guy a couple of years ahead of me in school, killed a good friend of mine. I testified in court against him and he was sent to prison."

"Cara, what was his name? I need to check this out. Maybe this is who is threatening you."

"It can't be. He's still in jail as far as I know. They said they would let me know if he's ever released. He's got a minimum of ten years before possible parole with all the charges against him. It can't be him."

"Did he have any siblings? Friends who were loyal? Parents who were as messed up as he was?"

He had a younger brother, who was my age but he died in a car accident when he was eighteen. His parents are dead now I think. His mom was lovely by the way. His dad, not so much, but as I said, I think they're both gone now. I can't remember if he had anyone else. I don't think so though. There might have been a cousin who lived with them but I don't remember for sure. I have a trunk in the attic, though, with clippings from the murder and the trial. I can go get it out."

She was wringing her hands again, so Todd rubbed her arms and then pulled her in for a kiss on her cheek. "Try to get some sleep, Cara. We can inspect it all more thoroughly in the morning. It's not going anywhere and you need sleep."

She yawned, as though in agreement, then turned

and went into her bedroom.

Down in Cara's office, he did a search, reading everything he could on the trial. There had been a cousin but no information on what their name was, how old or what happened to them after the trial. He would search more, but for now, he needed sleep himself.

By the time he returned to Cara's bedroom, Cara was sound asleep so he went into the spare room for the night. He would have preferred to spend the night beside Cara, but he wanted her to get a good night sleep more, so he did the chivalrous thing and let her rest. He did leave the door open to his room though, so he could hear her if she needed him.

As he lay in bed, he wondered yet again, what he was doing. The last thing he wanted was to create a dependency. He reminded himself for the millionth time that he was soon moving on, but he wouldn't leave her to her own devices. His Grandma Hailey would be chuckling at him, knowing he wanted Cara to need him. He could leave at any time and know beyond the shadow of a doubt that Alex would be sure she was safe and that Officer Calloway would be more than eager to step up and watch out for her too, even if he was a little younger than she was. But he also told himself that no one else could take care of her the way he could. No one else was good enough to make sure she remained safe. That's what he told himself. He also knew he had fallen for her. This was not a good thing at all. He had plans and they didn't include Lightcastle, South Carolina. And sadly, that meant they couldn't include Cara Kane.

Chapter Fourteen

Cara awoke with a start. It was still dark, but the slightest pink was starting to shine as the sun started to rise. She had that feeling again that someone was watching her, but she could see no one in her room. She felt the bed beside her but it was empty and Todd hadn't been there at all through the night. Had Todd gone home? Maybe he was still up and in her office.

She shuffled out of her bedroom and into the hall, noting that the spare room had been slept in. She would start the coffee before getting dressed. Jiminy Cricket she needed coffee.

When she entered the kitchen, she had expected Todd to be there, but the kitchen was empty. After starting the coffee maker, she walked to her office. Also empty. The family room was the same but she found Todd outside, examining the bushes where the towel had been found the night before.

"I have…" Her voice was raspy from little use, so she cleared her throat and started again. "I have other towels, if you were wanting a swim." It was a joke that fell flat. Todd just stared at her until she realized she was still in her nightgown. It was just an oversized tee-shirt, but it was long. It didn't do much to support her breasts, so she crossed her arms, raising the hem a little.

"I just wanted to make sure we didn't miss anything last night, but a swim to start the day sounds amazing. I may take you up on that."

Cara stared, wondering if he would skinny-dip. That thought brought a smile to her lips.

"What's got you smiling, Cara? I hope I didn't wake you when I got up. I closed your door again, to keep it quiet."

Okay so they were back to being awkward in the morning and they hadn't done anything last night. She sighed. Maybe it was just her.

"I wanted to go over some stuff I found online last night.... You know... about the trial you mentioned."

"Sure. Just let me get dressed. We can talk over breakfast. Coffee is on, by the way."

"You are a goddess," he said as he left the bush and started examining the fence where it appeared the intruder had gone over the wall.

Cara showered and left her hair down to dry naturally. It wasn't because Todd said he loved her curls. It really wasn't. It was because it was already warm and humid and she didn't want to fight with it.

Makeup would have to be minimal today as well. She didn't have any client meetings given it was Saturday so it wouldn't really matter and goodness knew it would just melt off her face. She winced though as she added foundation, trying to cover her black eye. It wasn't as bad as she thought it was going to be, but it was tender to the touch. She prayed it wouldn't get any worse. Fingers crossed it would be gone before the party, or enough that she could easily cover it. She still had a week. Crisis averted. Well, one of them anyway.

Feeling more awake and more accomplished now that she was a little more put together, she padded off to the kitchen to get breakfast started.

"You okay with a breakfast wrap?" she called out the back door to Todd? "Bacon, egg, cheese, a little spinach, garlic and onion, rolled in a wrap and grilled?"

"You had me at bacon," he responded with a grin then turned back toward the fence, moving down closer to the other corner.

****

"Hey, how long has this fence been busted?" he asked walking into the house. "Man that smells good." He inhaled deeply enjoying the scent of breakfast cooking.

"The fence is busted?"

"Two of the wider boards are attached only at the top and will spread apart far enough to let someone through. Easier for someone smaller than me but still anyone could have gotten through without too much trouble. That would be how they got away so quickly last night. When the boards were put back in place, you couldn't tell unless you got up close and personal with it."

Cara stared.

"Sorry, didn't mean to start your day off crappy… How did you sleep?"

"I was tender whenever I rolled over and had a dream-which I can't remember by the way and that's annoying -but I managed to get back to sleep. How about you? How did you sleep? I hope you didn't stay up too late. You're going to burn yourself out if you don't get some sleep."

"I'm good. So would you mind if I dug around in your files in the attic after breakfast? You know, the ones you mentioned last night."

Cara peeked up from the stove. "No, by all means."

"I'm not cramping your style or anything today, am I? Did you have plans? I can take whatever I find home with me if you need me gone."

Cara's heart deflated a little. He didn't want to spend the day with her and she shouldn't have expected him to.

"Why would I need you gone?" she responded, her Southern upbringing creating a need to be polite, but she was also confused. "Do you have other plans? If so, that's totally okay. I don't want to monopolize your day."

"Never." He moved toward her then and kissed her neck being gentle so he didn't hurt the bruised area by her collarbone.

Cara tilted her head to the side, giving him better access but when she winced, he stopped.

"Still sore?"

"I guess I'm a little stiffer than I anticipated. Here, sit and eat," she said as she cut a wrap in two, stacking the cut ends over each other in a presentation much like a restaurant would do.

Once she was sitting as well, Todd started eating. "My God, this is good."

She smiled and it reached her eyes. She was doing okay.

"So this trial you testified in...the one where your friend was killed... What happened that you had to testify? There was a group of kids at the incident, but you were the only one who stepped up? Why was that?"

"Tommy Gordon was a couple years older than me but he was a good friend. He lived next door to me growing up and even though he went to a private school and I went to the public school-my parents wanted us to have a regular childhood-he managed to always be there whenever I got into trouble. Jeremy Flaxton was jealous of Tommy-who was great at everything by the way-and took every opportunity to antagonize him. One day I was walking home from school because my brother Sterling was supposed to pick me up but his car had broken down. Turns out it was sabotaged. Anyway, Jeremy was driving past me and stopped, offering me a ride. He and some of his friends were in the car and I didn't like any of them. They were too loud and obnoxious. I said 'no thanks' and he just got angry. He got angry a lot when he didn't get what he wanted so he got out of the car and tried to grab my arm while his friends all yelled something about showing me who was boss.

I tried to get my arm free, but couldn't so I just glared at him. That's when Tommy showed up. He told them if they didn't leave me be, he would call the cops and tell them about some stash they had out on Plantation Road. They left but Jeremy was pissed. Angrier than I had ever seen him, in fact."

She took a deep breath and held it for a minute. This was hard for her. The memories of that day –of all the days that followed- flowed through her. Her shoulders tightened and her jaw clenched, but she pushed through.

"That night, I went out onto the verandah while I waited for Sterling to come home from his date with Jenny-Lynn, his latest of many girlfriends. I wanted to know how it went because I didn't think they were a good match. Jenny-Lynn was all about appearances, cars, and money, so I didn't really like her for Sterling. Nosy little sister that I was, I waited up to see how it went. I saw Jeremy crawl under Tommy's car and yelled at him to get away. He told me to mind my own business when I said I was calling the police, but he just sneered and ran off."

"I told Tommy what I had seen, but he didn't think there was much Jeremy could have done. Turns out his brake line had been cut and he nearly got into an accident. Tommy was a great driver. The Police were called and Jeremy was arrested but was then let out on bail awaiting trial. There were rumors that Jeremy was mixed up in some gang or something out of Chicago. That seemed like way too far away to be real but he was nasty enough to have found the wrong type of people. Two days later, I heard a gunshot. I was back on the verandah waiting for Em to come outside. It was late. There were other kids walking by the street, but they were heading to Jeremy's place. Em and I were going to talk about the prom that was coming up and what we thought we would wear. A senior named Eduardo had asked me and I was so excited to be going. Just before Em came outside, I heard a gun go off next door. At first, I wasn't sure if it was a firecracker or a gun because I'd never heard a gunshot before, but then I saw Jeremy running away holding a gun in his hand and his shirt was covered in blood. He was running fast but he was running toward me until he saw me and then he made a beeline for the woods back behind Tommy's house. I screamed for Em to call 911 and ran to Tommy's to see if he was okay but he was already gone. I tried to stop the bleeding but I couldn't. I couldn't make it stop. Blood was everywhere. No matter how hard I tried I couldn't make it stop."

"It wasn't long after that, I started getting threatening calls, telling me I better be careful and I better mind my own business or it wouldn't go well for me. But I talked with my parents and we all eventually agreed that I would testify at the trial to say what I had seen. They were afraid for me, but they were with me the whole time –even when the DA prepped me for trial."

She was wringing her hands and Todd reached across the table to hold them still. She smiled a wobbly smile in response.

"He was tried as an adult because he was eighteen years old and convicted of first degree murder among other things. He's still in prison and will be for a long time yet."

Todd nodded. "I did confirm he is in prison and he's not up for parole. Even if he were, he's not had…um…exemplary behavior so he would be denied anyway. So it's probably not him. He can't make calls unless they're collect and his calls would be recorded anyway. He would know that."

Cara pulled her hands back and wrapped them around her mug of coffee. Todd took a sip of his, watching over the edge of his mug. He was watching her as though he thought she would break. She didn't then and she wouldn't now.

****

Cara had gone so white while she told her story. It must have been horrible for her. Losing a friend so young was bad enough, but to murder? No one that age should have to deal with that. No one any age should have to deal with that.

"Why don't we leave the treasure hunting in the attic until another time. I can see this has been rough on you; reliving it like this."

"No, it's fine. Maybe there's something up there that will help. Come on," she added as she placed her hands on the table, pushed upward, and stood. "The sooner I can put this latest upheaval behind me, the better."

"Okay, if you're up for it, I'm right behind you. We will do it together, Cara."

Tears welled in her eyes but she brushed them aside then waved at the dishes. "I'll clean this up when we are done. Let's go."

The attic wasn't what Todd had expected. It was cluttered for one thing, and everything was askew. The rest of the house was so tidy, but up here, things were tossed everywhere and piled high in places, falling over in others.

"Is this what it normally looks like?" he asked.

"Yes, why?"

"No reason."

"Oh because it's messy?" She grinned. "Yeah, this is the equivalent of my junk drawer. Everyone has one."

She moved some things around until she got to the old trunk that held her high school memories, and sadly, included the clippings from the trial. He could only imagine what it would be like to open up that trunk and face her past fully again. It wouldn't be easy. Her mood seemed more melancholy than stressed though. She continued to impress him.

He searched as well, moving things and stacking them in a more secure fashion. He was afraid they would tumble down on someone and trap them.

"Um, Cara," he called from behind some clothes hanging on a rack. "Can you come over here for a second please?"

Cara peeked over a pile of dusty albums. Those things would be worth some change if she ever decided to sell them. They should be kept somewhere safer, but he wasn't going to tell her what to do with them. Her house, her rules. But still, he just itched to get a look at them and see what she had.

She brushed her hands off and came around from behind the pile with a scrap book in her hands. "Found it."

She saw what Todd was seeing and stopped confusion clear in every line of her face.

"What's that?" she asked, eyes widened but showing no fear. That was a good sign.

"This isn't yours?" he questioned, waiting for her to recognize what she was looking at.

"No, and it wasn't here when I moved in. Is that a laptop? Why would there be a laptop up here? I don't understand. What are those wire thingies for?"

"Okay, Cara, I want you to remain calm and we are going to go back downstairs, and call the police. I want a forensic team up here ASAP."

"Has someone been—" She reached for the wire, but Todd grabbed her hand, turning her around and facing her back towards the exit.

"Let's just go downstairs. Don't touch anything else. Just go downstairs."

As he ushered Cara down the steps he was already on his phone calling Alex. When he got off the phone with him, he called Beau, telling him to bring a forensic team with him. Screw Reilly. He would just bungle everything anyway and probably wouldn't even show up for hours, given it was Saturday morning.

When he reached the kitchen Cara was staring at the ceiling, turning this way and that, as though trying to get her bearings. He already knew the hole in the floor of the attic was over her bedroom and the wires would have led to other areas of the house as well.

Chapter Fifteen

That rat-bastard had been in her house and she hadn't even known it. What the hell was going on? How could she not have known it? She had been right when she said she felt like she was being watched, but she had no clue they'd actually been inside her house. She was definitely moving. She was so livid, she was shaking. She needed to stop the shaking. Pacing and wringing her hands, she tried to breathe, but her breathing got more and more shallow, until she could barely pull in enough oxygen. The edges of her vision started to close in on her in waves of black. She put her head between her knees, and continued to breathe. She was fine. She was fine. She was fine. Okay she would be fine.

Todd bent down in front of her, pulling her head up to see her face and then pushing her head back down again when she was still white as a sheet. "Just breathe. I've got this. You're going to be fine."

Her head popped up. "You've got this? What exactly do you have because it appears as though someone has been spying on me. Yes," She continued when he looked like he would interrupt her. "That hole is directly above my bedroom. Someone was watching me sleep, at best and God knows what else they were watching me do. I can't even... I won't... I just can't... Just don't..." she enunciated when he reached for her.

Did they watch her and Todd? Did they get a kick out of that? She thought she would throw up.

She took a few breaths and stood, then paced back and forth again, her hands covering her stomach, trying to calm the churning. She wouldn't throw up. She wouldn't give anyone the satisfaction of throwing up.

"How did they get in my house without me knowing?" She turned grilling Todd. I told you they knew what we were doing but you said no. They were just guessing. Not guessing. Not even close."

"I'm going to do a sweep of your house to make sure there are no cameras or microphones. I should have done it sooner. I'm sorry Cara. I let you down."

She had started pacing again but turned back to him in surprise. "You didn't let me down. I wouldn't have even known that was up there, had you not asked questions and gone searching up there. I'm sorry. I don't know how to deal with this. I'm bungling it for sure, but let's make one thing very clear. You have not let me down. Not even close. So just stop beating yourself up. But sure…go ahead and check for cameras and bugs or whatever. I'm going to pack a bag and get a hotel room."

"Would it be better if you stayed with a family member?"

"I can't drag my family into this. They went through enough when I had to testify at Tommy's murder. That was hard on all of us, but I won't put them through this crap again. I can't take this to them and put them in danger too. I just can't. Oh my God I feel so violated."

The shaking began again, and she took a deep breath trying to regain her self-control.

"I know what you're probably thinking," she continued, holding up her hand when it appeared as though he was about to contradict her, "I would be safer there, but what about them? Right now this has nothing to do with them, so no way am I dragging them into it and putting them at risk. It's my parent's wedding anniversary for crying out loud. They should be enjoying this time, not worrying about whether some deranged psycho is going to burst into the house, guns a blazin' or sneak into their house and set up cameras. No. Just no."

"I was going to say it would be a good idea to move out of the house. I agree with you. But instead of going to a hotel, why don't you come and stay at my apartment. I can protect you better there, than anywhere. It's a controlled entrance, and on the third floor, making it more difficult to get to. I have a spare room you can use. You'll even have your own bathroom."

She hesitated, trying to process all that was going on. Making a decision this big needed planning; a pros and cons list. Pro, it would solve her issue of feeling isolated and ill equipped to protect herself. Con, she didn't want to inconvenience Todd, and sure as blazes, didn't want him to feel she was a wuss and couldn't take care of herself. *You really can't take care of yourself when it comes to this,* her mind responded. Pro, he could teach her more self-defense. Con, she didn't want him to think she was dependent on him, or expected this to be a permanent move.

"I know my place is clean of bugs and cameras. I know you are feeling violated right now and I'm sure you've got a pros and cons list going on in your head, trying to figure out what your best move is."

She glanced up sharply, scrutinizing Todd, to see if he could read minds.

"Don't look at me as though I'm a mind reader Cara,

I'm trained to know what people will do next. I've seen your notes in your office and know you make lists. It just makes sense you would make a pro and con list for this too."

She continued staring, not sure what to say. Her arms were tingling so she shook them and started pacing again.

"Look, you don't have to decide right now whether you'll stay at my place or not, but go pack some things. Pack enough things for a few days at least and whether you stay with me or we both go to a hotel—"

"I didn't say anything about you going with me. I would be safe there on my own. No one would know where I am. I don't want to inconvenience you."

"As I was saying –whether we both go to a hotel, because I'm not leaving you on your own, Cara. Forget about the fact I'm a federal agent, my Grandma Hailey would skin my hide if she were still around."

"Your who, would what now?"

She was feeling a little more like herself. She had control here. It may not feel like it and she was still feeling violated, but she had a plan. Well, she had two options for plans and that gave her back control.

"My Grandma Hailey," he continued. "She practically raised Hunter and me, and she would spit barbed wire if we ever didn't do right by a lady."

"Um… I don't even know what to say to that right now." She could feel the tears forming in her eyes but all she could do was blink to try to dispel them. If one slipped down her cheek, she tried to ignore it. "Allergies," she sniffed as she left the kitchen, walking to her bedroom.

She tried not to think about the hole in her ceiling.

She could see an air exchange vent in the wall close to the ceiling. That would probably be where it was because there wasn't so much as a mark visible from this side. She refused to search any more as she tromped into the spare room, returning seconds later dragging a large suitcase behind her. With her back to the vent, she threw the suitcase up and onto her bed, then began opening drawers and throwing things toward her bed, often missing the suitcase all together. The quicker she got this done, the quicker she could get her life back. She just wanted to feel normal again.

"I want my life back."

"You will get it back, Cara. I promise."

Cara whirled around, startled, bra and underwear clutched in her hands. "Jiminy Cricket, you scared me half to death."

"Sorry, just wanted to let you know Alex and Beau are here, along with some techies and I didn't want you to be surprised when you came back out. We are going to work upstairs in the attic for a bit and see if we can find anything to give us a clue as to who this is. The techies are going to see how the recordings or info is being transmitted to whoever is watching you."

She sucked in her breath. "God I just hate the thought of that. It sickens me."

"Sorry. Just keep packing and we'll be back down when we are done. It would be best if you wait downstairs so we don't further contaminate the crime scene."

"You mean so *I* don't further contaminate the crime scene," she responded automatically. "But don't worry. I'll pack and wait in my office until you're done."

Todd disappeared and Cara went back into the spare

room to get a bigger suitcase. She wasn't sure what she would need over the next few days so more would be better.

When she was done, she mixed up some lemonade and made some sweet tea in case anyone was thirsty. It was hot as blazes up in the attic. It wouldn't be fun searching and dusting for prints and whatever else they were doing. It made her feel a little vindicated knowing whoever had been up there…watching…would have been sweating like a stuck pig. Served them right. They deserved to roast in hades as far as she was concerned.

While she continued to wait, she checked her email. Nothing important except a picture of her beautiful baby niece.

Picking up the phone she called her sister. "Oh my lawd, she's such a peach. I just love her to bits already," she said as soon as the phone was answered. "How are you feeling? How was her night? Is she sleeping all the time? What's her name? I'm such a horrible Auntie not to have been out to see her already."

"We named her Josephine, after Nana, and chill. We just got home. Oh Cara, I just can't tell you how much I love her. I would give my life to protect her. This is like nothing I've ever experienced before. She's such an angel. She slept four straight hours last night. I feel good. I really do. I'm tired yes and I'm sure I'll be completely exhausted by the end of the week, but she's just so precious. Are you coming to see her today? I can't wait for her to meet her Auntie Cara."

Cara thought about the danger she was currently in and debated whether or not she should show up at her sisters. In the end she just needed to see something beautiful so she conceded. "I am coming this afternoon, but won't stay long. I don't want to tire you out, but I can't wait to hold baby Josephine. I might bring someone by though if that's okay with you. They're just a friend," she added as clarification. She could feel her sister's curiosity and excitement through the phone.

"A friend. Mm'kay. Sure he is."

"Who said it's a he?" she asked smugly.

"Puh-lease Cara. You insult me. If it were a girl, you would have said you were bringing a girlfriend by. But don't worry. I promise I won't tell Mom. Or Em. Dear God, or Sterling. Jeez. At least he's out of town right now and won't 'just drop by' when you're here like Em would do. God save us from prying siblings."

Cara could hear the baby stirring in the background even as Lilly giggled. "Well, it sounds like little Josie is waking up so I won't keep you. I'm just so happy for you Lil. I know this is everything you've ever wanted and I'm over the moon thrilled you named her after Nana Jo." She will love that."

After the call was disconnected, Cara moved out to the back terrace. She needed some fresh air. It was hard not going upstairs to check on the officers working there, but knew it was best for her to stay downstairs and out of everyone's way.

It seemed forever before Todd stepped outside, followed by Officer Calloway, Alex, and a female. She was beautiful and Cara stood, uncertain of herself in front of the petite, dark haired woman.

"Cara, this is Rae. She's the best forensics expert the LPD has to offer. I wanted her to check this out because if she can't find something, it isn't there to find.

"Nice to—"

"Ohmygod, I love your hair." The stunning woman

said as she stepped forward and held out her hand in greeting. "Rae Piccadilly. I've heard lots about you from Todd. He couldn't stop talking about you in fact, and now I see why."

Cara regarded Todd in confusion.

"She's exaggerating, Cara. I just mentioned you in regards to your case."

"Sure, that's true, but seriously, Cara, it's more *how* he talks about you."

Cara took the woman's hand. "Nice to meet you. I've heard about you as well. Todd says you are the best, so you must be the best. Thanks for your help in this. Did you find anything?" She asked the question to the group, searching for answers from one face to the other and back again.

"Some fibers for sure, but we won't know if they're supposed to be there, or if they belong to the perp. Sorry, that's perpetrator. I try not to use inside lingo when speaking to those outside the biz."

Cara smiled in spite of herself. She couldn't help but like this woman who could clearly hold her own in what has for centuries, been a man's world.

"Can I get y'all some sweet tea or lemonade? Or coffee if you prefer. I have cold brew or can make regular if you prefer hot."

"Oh sweet tea for me, thanks so much," Rae answered. "Let me help you get it. Beau? Coffee as usge? Todd? Alex? I don't know yours. What's your reg?"

Cara smiled. This woman had energy and saved time by using short forms for many of her words.

"Come on, Cara, let's get these guys some bevys before they get faint in the heat. They got pretty parched upstairs. Guys can't handle the heat like us girls." She linked her arm through Cara's then leaned close and whispered "Wusses... all of them." She winked. "And while we get it, you can tell me how you get your hair so freaking gorgeous. Mine is a hot mess if I don't straighten the hell out of it." She sighed. "I so wish I had curly hair like yours, but alas my mama had bone straight hair and daddy had curly. They cursed me with a perpetual state of frizz that is the bane of my existence. I use a straightener every single day."

She finished with an exaggerated sigh and Cara couldn't help but laugh. It felt good to laugh again.

When they returned, the guys were back examining the perimeter, like there might still be something out there or something would magically appear that would give them a clue.

"Whoever was out here, knew the yard well. I would guess they've been here before."

Cara sucked in her breath and stopped, standing still in the air already heavy with humidity.

"You think it's someone I know." The words sounded flat to her own ears.

"We've talked about this being a potential before," Todd responded first, "but it's not a guarantee. It could be someone who just knows the house and yard. They have been here before. My gut says you have met them though. This feels more personal. Have you had anyone in for service? Cable? Phone? Electrical? Plummer? Anyone?"

She shook her head. Not since I moved in. There's been literally no one here recently except the women I mentor a couple times. Even dates were offsite."

She could feel a blush creeping up her neck and face and turned to set down the tray of drinks.

"No dates have been by to pick you up or see you home?" Beau asked.

Did Todd just stand a little taller? Alex's head swiveled back and forth between Todd, Beau, and Rae-who had no filter and also jumped into the fray.

Even as Cara was shaking her head no, Rae piped in with "Besides Todd? Sorry. I don't mean to embarrass you or anything but if he hasn't taken you out, he's an idiot."

Cara was trying to take a sip of her sweet tea and choked on it, struggling not to spew it out her nose.

"Sorry." Rae smiled clearly not sorry in the least.

The phone rang and Cara went to answer it, followed by each of the men, and Rae who pulled out a tablet from a bag sitting by the back door, began tapping on it.

"Hello?" She watched Rae who was motioning with her hands in a circular motion to keep whoever was calling talking.

"I see you have guests. Enjoy them while you can."

"Who is this? Why are you calling me? What do you want?" Cara yelled into the phone but they had hung up. "Mother trucker," Cara cursed slamming the phone down.

Chapter Sixteen

"I'm pissed." Cara watched the people staring back at her. "What?"

"Well, we did kinda want to keep the dude talking so I could trace the call," Rae added when the guys just stood there, saying nothing. "Honestly, you guys. She's not a delicate flower, ready to wilt. She's pissed at this guy and the situation. Not at you." Rae turned back to Cara. "Seriously. Men don't know how to deal with a woman when she's mad. I swear."

"I'm so done with this guy." Cara paced. "Clearly he's seeing what's going on –probably from the equipment in the attic. OMG is it possible there are more bugs hidden that you didn't find?"

Todd appeared affronted. "I promise you there's nothing else in the house. We can do a search outside as well, but it's possible he was lurking in the neighborhood, or drove by."

"Don't get your panties in a knot, Todd. It's a valid question," Rae interjected, enjoying Todd's discomfort. She turned to Cara and continued, "It's also likely he noticed the video and sound going down and realized he's been made. Or maybe he saw us find it. Either way, he knows his trap has been found and his viewing has been shut down."

"My suitcases are ready, but I have a question for y'all. I am wondering if it wouldn't make more sense to stay here and set a trap. That's probably the fastest way to get this done. What do you think?"

Todd immediately jumped in saying "No. No way. It isn't safe. I won't let you be bait for a trap. It isn't going to happen, Cara."

"It isn't really your choice, now is it?"

Todd placed his hands on his hips, feet spread at hips distance apart and a clear sign of 'you won't win this' arrogance shining through but Rae placed her hand on his arm adding "Stand down, superman. It's not a horrible idea and we can keep her safe."

"She knows nothing about how this could play out. She isn't trained to do this kind of thing."

"You've been teaching me self-defense, Todd. And y'all will be near-by. I can handle this. I know I can. And I'm so sick of living in fear. I don't need anyone to just 'rescue' me and make it all better. I've always taken an active part in my life plan and this should be no different."

"Cara," Todd, added, moving toward her and taking her hands in his, "I couldn't bear it if anything happened to you again. You were attacked already. I can't risk it."

Cara let out the breath she didn't even realize she had been holding until it expelled. "I appreciate your gallantry, but this dude took away my power once. I can't let them do it again. I feel as though I have been violated and this will give me back my own power. You can train me more in self-defense and I promise I will practice at every opportunity. I know I can do this. I will take my life back and do this."

"Cara…"

"Wait…don't say no. Just think about this for a minute. It's me he wants. Me he wants to pay for whatever transgression I committed in his warped mind. This is going to be the fastest way to get this done. I need to prove to myself that I still have control over my own life."

"She's right, Todd," Rae added.

Beau coughed and Alex raised his hand as though in class. "Don't mean to interrupt but can I just add that I'm happy to stay with Cara? Just throwing it out there…"

"That won't be necessary. I will cover Cara. I have the knowledge and this guy has already seen me with her so it won't cause any suspicion. I've got this Alex."

Rae laughed and Todd appeared as though he was ready to spit nails."

"Not to throw a wrench into anyone's plans or you know…cause any bumps in the road of y'all trying to take over my life –which seriously boys…not that I'm not grateful for your help and all, but take a beat here and remember that I have to appear alone if this is going to work. Maybe a public fight or argument with Todd, since he's been around so much and this dude won't be suspicious when I appear to be alone. We have to create an opportunity that is too good to pass up so he will fall into the trap. Then we nab him. I just can't take this anymore. Time to stand up and fight for myself.

The house is clear, right?" She glanced at Todd for confirmation. "You did a sweep and there's nothing here. You will check outside, so I will feel like I have my home back -although I'm still going to sell when all this is over. Let's get this plan worked out so we can end this. I want it done ASAP. We have a party to go to next weekend for my parent's anniversary and I want to be able to enjoy it fully without looking over my shoulder. So how will this work best? Let's do some brainstorming. Gosh I wish Miranda were here. She is really good at brainstorming."

Cara searched the faces of those around her. They were the experts but she wasn't just leaving this to them. She would have input into this. It was her life and she would not just hand over control.

"Miranda writes fiction. This is very much real life," Todd interjected.

Cara stared at him until he fidgeted.

"Just clarifying," he added.

"I think it would be a good idea to stage a fight or argument with Todd," Beau added. I would agree with that. Maybe at work, since this person seems to follow her everywhere. We don't know who it is, but that's a public place and more people will see it. Besides, we have cleared listening devices from here so we know they aren't going to be listening while you're at home anymore."

"Work it is," Alex added. I doubt anyone has seen me around Cara before so I should hide out inside the house to protect her from here. We can have someone follow her to and from work. I can't get this approved through work but I have some personal time saved that I can use."

Beau also added that he would be willing to help and he could allocate work time given it was an ongoing case but Cara disagreed with that. "Everyone in town knows you work for LPD so you probably shouldn't be seen around me too much unless there's been an incident I need to report or you're being open about investigating something. That would be too much of a red flag."

Was that pride Cara saw on Todd's face? That was just silly. She didn't need a man's approval anyway. If her heart felt a little fuller, it had nothing to do with any approval from anyone.

Beau reluctantly agreed. "Copy that."

"Can I just say that it might make sense for me to stay?" Rae offered. "I mean, I'm a woman and men – especially this kind of man- wouldn't be thrown off by having little ol' me here on occasion. I could just be a friend here to console Cara on her break up."

"It's not a break up," Todd argued.

"Of course not," Rae agreed, patting his arm.

"Okay so it's agreed that tomorrow Todd and I will have an argument and go our separate ways."

"I don't like this." Todd crossed his arms over his chest. "It doesn't feel right to me."

"It's only temporary, sugar," Rae added.

****

Why was this bothering him so much? Todd scratched his chest as he pondered that. It was just a pretend break up. Hell, they weren't even a couple. Sure he was comfortable in the relationship-enjoying it even- but he needed to keep in mind that he was moving on. Nothing could be permanent. His career was his priority. Why then was he so edgy every time someone mentioned them breaking up?

"We can't stage a fight until Monday," he added, relieved he still had the weekend with Cara. "If it's going to happen at the office, it can't happen until Monday. There aren't enough people around today and tomorrow is Sunday so…" He let that trail off as he mentally began planning the time he would spend with Cara this weekend. He would make every moment count.

Rae rolled her eyes.

"Okay then, Monday it is. So what do I need to do

now? Just go on as if my life is normal?" Cara asked.

"We spend the weekend like a couple. We will spend all our time together and do couple things. Just like we have for the last week." Had it only been a week? It seemed like they had been together for much longer than that. She had worked her way into his life and had become a priority -the center of his thoughts and feelings. How had that happened? Really? Only a week?

"Deal. But we do need to go out to the house to check on things today so a little work thrown in too. Charlie wants to meet us there to ensure everything is going as planned and get confirmation to move forward. We can do that together."

"Okay, so after the breakup—" Beau began before he was interrupted by Todd.

"It's not a break up."

"Copy that, but after the argument, Alex you should be watching Cara's place to see if anyone tries to add more listening devices, and Todd, you, will have to stay away for a bit while we work this out."

"Like hell I will." He hadn't meant to shout –hadn't even meant to say it out loud, so to cover his surprise, he scowled. "And wipe that grin off your face, Rae."

Her grin turned to a laugh, and Todd's face darkened.

"Sorry, Todd."

She didn't look sorry. His eyes squinted and his brow furrowed. "I will not stay away. We can argue and we can make it appear as though she's alone, but she will not, for one moment, be left alone until this is done. Plus," he added as he mentally patted himself on the back, "I still need to work with Cara on Hunter and Miranda's place so I will still need to spend some time with her."

Cara's eyes narrowed and her lips pursed. "Let me remind you that this is my life. I will have a say in how this plays out." She paused. "Now that we have that out of the way, I have a question. Is there any way we can escalate this to up the timelines? Now that I've resigned myself to taking charge of my own life, I want it done."

"If we push too fast Cara', we may spook him. He seems to think the timelines are his and his alone, so we want to walk that fine balance of pushing him –even pissing him off a little- without provoking him so much that he goes all Unabomber on us."

Cara sucked in her breath, clearly shocked.

"Jesus Christ, Alex, do you ever think before you speak?"

"Sorry, Cara… I just mean that we want to be able to control his reaction as much as possible to keep you safe."

"Thank you, Alex… Todd… Rae… Beau…" she looked each one in the eyes, pausing before continuing to ensure she had their undivided attention. "Y'all are the experts. How do we do that? What do you need me to do? Besides break up with Todd."

"We are not breaking up."

"We aren't really a couple so yes, I agree, but you know what I mean. We will have an argument Monday and then I will leave and come home to follow my normal routine –which fair warning will be boring for those of you watching. If he calls, I will provoke him? Placate him? Patronize him? What is going to get the right reaction? Maybe I should invite him over for a face to face conversation. Chicken-shit coward, hiding behind a phone…he needs to step out in the open."

"We can talk while we drive." Todd grabbed her arm and advised the rest of the group to check the perimeter of the house. "You finish up here and we will do our thing. We don't want to change things up too much and cause suspicion. As a profiler we don't know how much of her life and routines have been documented so far, nor how much of our plans have been overheard. If we make too many changes right now, he could go into hiding and we want to draw him out. I'm sure my being here has pissed him off, so we want to piss him off a little further before our fake argument."

The group agreed and while Cara and Todd got into the car, and prepared for their drive to the beach house, the rest of the team went about scanning the terrace and the garden beyond, and checking the front and sides of the house including trees that may have had surveillance cameras set up. They found two trail cameras facing the driveway and the back gardens and pool area but pretended not to find them, leaving them in place. They could use these to their advantage. There were none, however, facing the terrace area, close to the house. The locations of the cameras left in place would be easy enough to skirt, when doing their own surveillance and they would give the perp a sense of control. That could cause them to make mistakes and they would all be ready when that happened.

As the group continued their inspection, Cara settled into the car. "First up the beach house?" she asked, fingers shaking as she tried to buckle her seatbelt.

Todd covered her fingers with his own and took over the task but she pulled away. "I can do it myself. I need to do it myself," she repeated, successfully inserting the buckle into the slot. "I know you won't get this, but I feel very strongly that I need to be part of the solution here. I need to know I can take care of myself…that I can control my own life."

Todd watched her as she searched for the right words to convey her thoughts. The expressions were changing rapidly on her face as she worked to control her emotions and her fear. He could only imagine everything that was going through her mind, but he would be patient and give her the time to gather her thoughts. He wasn't going anywhere any time soon. He had time.

"When I was involved in the trial for Tommy, I was only sixteen. I didn't have control over anything that happened to me. I mean, I did what was right, but when the harassment started and the threats had me terrified, I had no control over any of it. I still did what I had to do… Tommy deserved that…but I was so scared… Nothing stopped the threats and Mom and Dad kept me pretty much under lock and key. I was never left alone –and I was okay with that -but the choices were never mine." She paused. "I'm not saying this right. It's so jumbled still –the emotions rolling in all over again… I guess what I'm trying to say is I was a victim. I felt like a victim and I felt weak and powerless. I vowed I would never feel that way again –and I haven't. Not until recently. I don't like it. I encourage women every day to believe in themselves and I need to do that now. I need to take back my power. Having said that, I'm not an idiot and I know I can't do this alone. I encourage my group to search out experts for assistance and I will do the same. But don't ever think I will just hand over my life to the care of someone else. Ever. No one will take my power away from me. Or I guess a better analogy would be 'I will never give up my power again.' So don't think for one minute, I won't have input into how this all goes down. I won't do anything stupid, but I won't hide either."

"There are risks and I don't want you to get hurt again. Or worse…" he added hoping it would shock her into being less reckless.

She searched his face, eyes intent. "I get it. I really do. I don't like it. I don't wish it on me or anyone else for that matter, but it is what it is and now we deal. Don't shut me out of decisions and don't try to take the safest route, just to protect me. We will find the balance and we will survive."

She stared out the passenger window and they backed out of the driveway. She seemed intent on watching every moving thing or maybe she was memorizing the beauty of her neighborhood. It was the kind of neighborhood he would love to live in -if he ever settled down. There it was. The thought. No, the hope. That settling down dream- and a dream it needed to stay for a while. He had career goals to achieve. Once those were ticked off his bucket list, he would maybe come back to this area to get a house and start a family.

Todd shifted the gear of his car and tried to shift the thoughts in his mind at the same time. When he was ready to settle down, chances are Cara would be taken and have a family of her own. He figured she wanted that. Didn't every woman? Was that a sexist thought? Was her career more important? Did he care? *Of course you care, you fool. Don't delude yourself while you try to dupe everyone around you. You're hooked. No going back now.* But there had to be a way to go back. Long distance relationships didn't last. He knew that from past experience. They fizzled or exploded with someone always getting hurt. He didn't want that for him nor for

Cara.

First things first though. He had the weekend before they had to argue and go their separate ways. He would make every moment count.

"What time does Charlie need to meet us at the house?"

"She will be there until two this afternoon, so any time before then will be fine. She's got some people there working today because they were delayed by the framers. There was an issue with the foundation before that and having to level it or something. I don't know exactly what the issue was but we need to go see. If there's one thing I know about Charlie and Davenport Construction, it won't be done until it's perfect."

Todd knew Charlie had made a good name for herself as a builder. She was above board and didn't take any shortcuts when building. Everything was by the book. He had checked her out thoroughly. What he found interesting, was Charlie had requested the site visit today; right after they had found the video surveillance equipment. Had he missed something? Could she be involved somehow? He didn't think so, but he'd missed the recording device and now was second guessing himself. He didn't like the feeling. Time to play his cards close to his chest with everyone around Cara. Someone she knew was doing this. He would bet his life on it.

His phone rang then, and he pulled it out of the cradle on his dash to raise it to his ear.

"Mitchell," he answered briskly.

"Mitchell, your next assignment has been approved. You're getting that team you've wanted but they want you in the international division. You'll be stationed in the UK office and are expected to report there a week from Monday. Congratulations. I'm sorry to lose you but this is a good move for your career."

"Can I get back to you on that?"

"What? This is what you've been begging for. Your own team. We need your tech expertise on this one and I went out on a limb to get you the lead. Don't embarrass me by turning this down. That would be career limiting."

Chapter Seventeen

"Cara, so good to see you again," Charlie Davenport said as she held her hand out in greeting. "It's been a while. Appreciate the business you've been sending my way. I hope everyone is happy with their results."

"Come on, Charlie. You know they are. There's no one better in the Lightcastle area and you know it. Maybe no one better in the entire state of South Carolina."

"No maybe about it," Charlie stated, laughing.

"You are always my first choice. I'm constantly thrilled when you're able to take on a project."

Todd stood back, watching the exchange. She seemed at ease and not in the least concerned about anything out of the ordinary.

"Do you always arrange client meetings on Saturdays?" Todd asked bluntly

"If it works for everyone, sure. We have a crew here working so I thought it might work. Was it a bad time?" she asked, confused. "Sorry if I inconvenienced you, Cara. I know you are pretty busy through the week."

Cara glared at Todd, letting him know he was being rude, then smiled a radiant smile at Charlie. "Not at all. Just a kerfuffle at the house this morning and Todd is a little on edge, but it worked perfectly. We were going to come out to see progress today anyway. Let's do a walk through and see where everything is. I have to say, I didn't expect you to be this far when you said you were delayed. You're making great progress as far as I can see."

Charlie reached for Cara and everything tensed in Todd's body. He braced for attack, but Charlie just gently placed her hand on Cara's forearm.

"Is everything okay? Do you need anything? A problem with that gorgeous home you live in? Oh my, it's not the baby, is it? Lilly is good?"

Eyes narrowed, Todd responded, "Nothing like that."

Cara reached over and placed her hand on Todd's arm while she expanded on his response. "Lilly is great." She beamed. "Baby Josie has arrived and oh my goodness, Charlie, she is beautiful. My heart just melted when I saw her picture. We are heading over there to see her when we are done here. I can't wait to hold her."

Charlie looked to Todd and then back to Cara. "Everything good otherwise?" she asked with an expression shooting some underlying message at Cara that Todd couldn't decipher. She turned her shoulder, giving her back to Todd and the next thing he knew, Cara was laughing. He was pretty sure Charlie had pointed to Cara's eye.

"He's fine. I promise you." She snickered again.

Todd was confused. What was going on here? Cara didn't seem to care, and in fact seemed to be enjoying the situation.

"Okay, why don't we do a walk-through. I still can't believe you have all the framing done. When you said you were getting caught up, you weren't kidding."

"I gave my word. The guys are working extra hard to get it all done. Come and see where the issue was with the foundation. It's fixed, so no need to fret but it did take an extra day to get it right."

Todd followed behind, watching the women as they walked and talked. The foundation wasn't a big issue, and just required some self-leveling concrete to correct the problem. He was impressed with her work ethic and her knowledge but everything he had read about her implied the same so nothing new there. He was curious what she had said to Cara though. His spidey senses were still screaming from the morning's find in the attic.

Charlie was taller than Cara, and thin. She moved like an athlete. Very capable and comfortable in her industry and life in general.

A shot rang out and Todd grabbed Cara before it registered that the roofers had started roofing. He needed to get a grip.

"Are you okay, Todd?" Charlie asked, head slightly tilted.

"Yeah, just some stuff going on and it's been a minute since I've been on the jobsite."

"Okay, for real now, what is going on? I have such a sense of tension from you both, but especially you, Todd."

He debated giving some false information to her to see if it drew the perp out, but Cara jumped in, telling her way too much.

"I've just had a stalker following me so Todd is being over-protective. Nothing to worry about. We have it under control now."

"My God, girlfriend, is that how you got that shiner? You have to be careful going forward. If you want, I can assign some of my guys to do some work on your house, so you're not alone there."

Cara sighed, reaching up to touch her eye, wincing

when she touched the bruise a little too hard. "Thanks, Charlie, but I have it under control. I promise," She added when Charlie appeared as though she was going to insist.

Charlie turned to Todd, "I need to apologize for thinking you had done this to Cara." She pointed toward Cara's eye. "I was ready to take you out, if need be."

"You couldn't, but I appreciate the candor." He was still on edge.

Charlie laughed. It irritated him. He wasn't on top of his game at the moment so he couldn't blame her for laughing.

The three of them worked their way through the house, Cara commenting on where light switches would go for convenience and esthetics. When they got to what would be the kitchen, Cara inhaled. "I can just see it all. It's going to be so beautiful. Miranda wants Mediterranean style cabinets and a huge island, with seating. We want outlets in the island as well, Charlie, so make sure the electrician knows that. I want them to be on the side of the island. Miranda doesn't like the waterfall edge, so that won't be an issue. We debated the pop up ones that hide in the countertop, but she wants a smooth surface without anything marring the look. I have to say I agree with her on that."

"There should be a window behind the sink though. That will go here." She grabbed a marker and placed a big 'X' on the wall, then wrote 'sink' below it, with an arrow pointing down. Sorry for that change order. I just sent the measurements for that late yesterday, but with Miranda wanting that smooth island surface, and given the plumbing isn't started, it shouldn't be too much of a pain to change. That's really going to open this up."

Her hands were held upward, like a ref calling a touchdown. He enjoyed watching her in her element. She really was good at what she did. As she narrated the lifestyle each room would embrace, describing the feeling each space would emit, he knew both Miranda and Hunter would have a beautiful life here. They had chosen well.

If he felt a twang of envy for his cousin and the life he now had, he didn't pay much heed. It wasn't his time yet. He had things to do, first and foremost was keeping Cara safe and getting her stalker caught.

****

"Do you want to drive?" Todd asked when they got back to the car.

"Are you kidding me?" she asked, her voice high with excitement. "I would love to drive. I was going to ask but, well, I thought that would be rude." She smiled as she snatched the keys from Todd's outstretched hand.

She drove to her sister's home, thrilled with the feel of the car and how it handled. "My Grandfather would have loved this."

"He sounds like he was an amazing man."

"He truly was. I know everyone thinks their granddaddy was the best, but everyone loved him. He could come across as being a little gruff sometimes but he was a softy at heart. Heaven forbid if someone crossed him though. He might forgive you, but you would never get the chance to cross him again. He loved my grandmother to distraction and gave her anything she wanted." She sighed. "She, on the other hand, would be very cautious about what she mentioned, knowing that he would move mountains to give whatever it was, to her. They were true soul mates."

"You believe in soul mates then?"

"Of course I do."

"I'm not convinced, though I have seen a few love matches that seem to work better than others. For the longest time I didn't even believe in love lasting forever, but I think Hunter and Miranda have found one that will last. But he had to give up his career to make it happen."

Miranda pondered that, then asked "Do you think he sacrificed too much for Miranda?"

"I don't think he feels he did. He was ready to give up his career, but someone always has to sacrifice to make a relationship work."

"Has that been your experience then? Because I don't think my parents did, nor did Grandma and Granddaddy. They compromised, and made decisions that worked for the two of them, but I don't think they felt it was a sacrifice."

"Let's just say I haven't seen a successful relationship in my line of work. It just can't work. We get moved around and long distance never works, as far as I've seen."

"Well I think if a relationship is meant to be, it will all work out. But I also believe in the happy ever after. Not that it will always be easy –it won't- it always takes work and communication. It's worth working on though. Running away is a guaranteed failure."

Did she sound as hurt as she felt inside? Was he prepping her for their break up? Prepping himself? Did he think that she was becoming too dependent on him? She could fix that and would be mindful moving forward. Or was he worried that she was thinking they would have a happily ever after? He'd been upfront with her about not being around forever so she had no delusions there. Did she wish there could be more? Of course she did, but she was a realist, even if she was a romantic, and knew this wasn't a forever kind of love.

Love. There was that word again. Her breathing became shallow and she concentrated on the road to calm herself. Breathe. Just breathe.

"Are you okay?"

"Fine. There's a stretch of road up ahead where I can let this baby fly, if you're good with that. I would love to see what she's got."

"Have at'er. Just don't get stopped by Beau. We don't need a ticket."

She pressed her foot down on the accelerator and felt the blood flow through her veins along with the wind in her hair. The gears shifted and she gained speed. It was exhilarating. Life affirming. All was right with the world as she controlled the car and felt the power flow through her. She was in charge. She had control. She had the power. Her. Not anyone else. Just her.

She needed this drive. Had he known that? He was intuitive and probably sensed she needed some control. Bless him, no matter the reason.

Around the bend, she drove, leaning into the curve.

"Deer."

"Yes…babe," she responded with a grin. "Just kidding, I see it." She safely slowed the car and grinned as she glanced over at Todd. "We're almost there."

As they pulled into the drive of the beautiful two story home, the door opened and a woman who looked much like Cara stepped outside, holding a baby. It was Lilly. She stood taller than Cara-her hair straight, and blonde, but you could definitely tell they were related.

A flock of turkey vultures circled overhead.

Chapter Eighteen

Cara felt a shiver down her spine. Was it an omen? She didn't even believe in omens but there had been signs she hadn't paid attention to in the past and look where she was now. They were in the country. It made sense something could be dead nearby.

"You see them too," she commented with as much nonchalance as possible when she noticed Todd was also watching the sky.

"I do. I'm sure it's nothing to worry about. Things die in the woods."

Cara pasted a smile on her face and got out of the car. Todd followed. Lilly greeted Cara with a one arm hug; her other arm full with baby Josie.

"My God, she is beautiful. Look at her little nose. Her fingers are so long."

"Don't say she's going to be a pianist. Everyone has said that. Not that I would mind, but I don't want anything imprinted on her that she doesn't choose herself. And she has your nose. Look at her. She looks like you did when you were a baby. Mom brought pictures of all of us to compare. Oh, Cara, isn't she just beautiful?"

"I think I need to hold her to tell for sure. Come on Lil, what gives? You get her all the time. Give her to me for a minute."

Cara held the baby, staring into her little angelic

face. Her nose was pert, her eyes deep blue. Her little cheeks were full and rounded out her face. There were wrinkles across her forehead that made Cara smile. "She looks like she has worry etched into her forehead. And what could you be so concerned about already little Josie? Your every wish will be granted by your Mama and Daddy. You have nothing to worry about little one."

Cara pulled her close and inhaled her scent. "Oh the smell of babies."

"You'll be next, I swear it." Lilly added, a sly glance shifting towards Todd. "Hi, I'm Lilly. Nice to meet you."

"Sorry, Lil, this is Todd."

"Nice to meet you, Lilly. I've heard wonderful things about you."

"That's funny," Lilly returned. "I've heard nothing about you until Car mentioned she was bringing you by. When did you two meet?"

"Enough with the cross examination, Lil. We met a week ago. Todd is a client's cousin and working on a job with me."

"You haven't brought client's cousins by before. And what do you do, Todd? Contractor? Are you in design as well? Ooh, a stripper maybe?"

Todd laughed out loud while Lilly batted her eyes trying to appear innocent. "I assume you mean furniture stripper, but no. I'm a Federal Agent."

Lilly's eyes immediately narrowed and her head turned to Cara. "Why do you need an agent? What's going on? Has Jeremy gotten out of jail already? They were supposed to let us know. He was vying to get out for good behavior but Dean, at the prison, said his behavior was horrid. He promised he would let me know. And what happened to your eye?" she demanded, pulling her sister's face and turning it toward her.

Cara pulled her face back and shrugged it off. "It's nothing to worry about. And as far as I can tell, he's still there, but no, Todd is acting as overseer on a build in addition to his day job."

"Oh. Well. Okay then."

Lilly appeared both relieved and disappointed but changed the subject back to her little bundle of joy.

"Come on in. I'll get you some lemonade or sweet tea. What do you prefer?"

She turned and opened the door, expecting everyone to follow her into the house. It was a beautiful home and Cara took pride in helping to design it. It was a perfect combination of Lilly and Morgan, her husband.

"Where is Morgan? I thought he would be here."

"There's been vultures circlin' all mornin' so he's gone out to see what's goin' on. That's not a normal occurrence. He just wants to make sure nothin' is sufferin' out there. You know him. He's such a softy. Can't bear to think about anything hurtin'."

Cara turned to Todd who was standing ramrod straight, staring out the window.

"Here he comes now," Cara pointed out, seeing her brother-in-law walking across the yard, rifle in one hand and a cell phone in the other. He was talking to someone on the phone. His expression was grim.

Todd walked back outside, and stood on the verandah; tension exuding from every pore. "I bet he found something," he stated plainly as Cara followed.

Cara's phone rang, startling her and causing Todd to glance over his shoulder.

"Blocked caller," she said as she held the phone up for him to see.

"Hello," she answered, putting the phone on speaker and bracing for bad news.

"I see you found one of my gifts. There are still more. I told you I would know when you found them."

"He hung up. Dear God, do you think he's done something to my sister's property?" She glanced down at her niece, placing her hand on the side of her head to cover her ear while she held her tight. It was an action meant to protect, but it made Josie squirm.

Lilly exited the house carrying a tray of sweet tea with a bowl of lemon wedges beside the glasses for anyone who wanted them. Her gaze locked on the faces staring back at her.

"What is it? What's happened? Is Josie all right? She set the tray on the table and grabbed the baby from Cara.

"She's fine. I promise you."

Morgan reached the steps and shoved the phone into his back pocket, staring at Todd. "Cara, good to see you again." He gave her a half-hearted hug, while staring at Todd.

"Hi Mo, this is Todd. Todd, Lilly's husband, Morgan."

"He's a federal agent," Lilly added as though that would be important to Morgan.

"Well maybe you want to come with me and have a gander at something. I've already called the police."

"What is it?" Lilly and Cara chimed together. Any other time, they would have shouted 'jinx' at each other, but neither did, given the somber expression on Morgan's face.

No one answered, and Todd followed as Morgan turned and retraced his steps back into the woods. Cara sat down, taking Josie back from her mom and hugging her close, shielding her from the hateful things going on around her.

"I shouldn't have come," she whispered.

Todd, who hadn't gotten far, heard her and turned, "This isn't on you," he responded, finger pointing for emphases. "Don't panic. We will be back in a bit."

"What's going on?" Lilly said, taking the baby from Cara. "Just tell me what's going on."

"Come on, Lil, have a seat. They're going to be a while."

Chapter Nineteen

The men returned just as the police arrived. Beau stepped out of his car and nodded toward Cara and Lilly before following Todd and Morgan back into the woods. Cara tried to explain what had been going on, swearing her sister to keep her secret so as not to worry her parents before their anniversary party.

"But, Cara," Lilly explained for the third time, "they need to know so they can protect themselves. So do Sterling and Em deserve to know. You can't carry this all on your own. It isn't just happening to you. Remember last time? It changed everyone's life, not just yours. We all lost a friend that day and we all worried about you when the threats started. We all felt threatened. You should have told us." Her voice was gentle, even if her words were delivered with a stoic firmness. There was no mistaking Lilly's opinion that this was now a family affair. "You can't shield us from it. That isn't fair to anyone. Not you, and not us. We care and will be there to help you through this. You can't do this alone."

"But I have to. Don't you see? It's all my fault. This is directed at me. I need to make sure none of you get hurt in the crossfire."

"You have always done that, you know."

"What have I always done, Lil?" Cara asked a little annoyed with the lecture her sister was ramping up to.

191

She'd experienced them often enough she could probably recite it.

"Tried to protect the family from hurt and disappointment. We all love you, Car. You have to understand that what affects you, affects us all, whether you try to keep walls up, or not."

"I don't…"

"Here they come." Lilly stood, cutting off Cara's words.

****

Cara was wringing her hands as Todd and the others walked back toward the house. Beau wasn't sure the incident was connected to Cara, but Todd knew it was. Especially given the call she had received and the fact there were trail cameras located nearby. This was not a coincidence.

"There's a lot of blood on a few trees, like a ritual of some kind took place. No way to tell if it's human or animal but whatever it is, it's bad."

"Remember Mrs. Fangrad's dog? It was half wolf and looked like a coyote. Remember how it barked and growled whenever that rat bastard Flaxton walked by or was anywhere within sight of the house? That dog had a sixth sense about people, I swear. I don't know why that just popped into my head."

Cara's head swiveled toward her sister. She appeared pale and a little ill, like she had been sucker-punched. "Mrs. Fangrad said her dog had a heart attack, but I wonder now if that was true. He wasn't that old. Maybe six years old."

She turned to Todd, who was fighting a bone weary exhaustion. "Do you think it's related? You do, don't you? I can tell you think it's related. Couldn't it have been a deer or something that someone shot and cleaned or whatever they do after they kill it? A hunter or something?"

"The reality is, you got a call, mentioning finding a…" he paused, searching for the right word and unable to find it. He refused to call it the 'gift' it was referenced to previously. "Well finding something, right after Morgan finds this. That can't be a coincidence. I've said it before, and I'll say it again, I don't believe in that kind of luck. Draining a deer, wouldn't cause the blood to be spread like that. There aren't usually symbols painted on trees like that when you're just hunting. That place was arranged specifically to highlight them. There are cameras watching it so they would know when it was found. What concerns me most right now, is how did they know you would be here."

"Everyone knows Lil was expecting. That's not a secret. Find out she's delivered, and it's a no brainer to think I'm going to come by to see my new niece."

He ran his fingers through his hair, resting his hand on top of his head for a moment while he thought.

"We will clean it up after Rae's done with her forensic sweep. This is hard on her. She struggles with animal cruelty. Whatever happened, it was done by a truly sick bastard. I hope he resists arrest when we finally catch up to him," Beau stated, his voice flat.

"You and me both," Todd responded quietly.

"Hey, you guys," Cara jumped in. "We should go and let you spend time with Josie. And Lil, you're probably exhausted. You need rest. We will get out of your hair and I will pop in next week one evening to see how you're doing. I will bring some food so you don't have to cook and I want to bring a gift for Josie too. I can't believe I didn't stop off and get one before coming today."

"Don't be silly, Car. You can come by any time and you don't need to bring a thing." She grabbed her sister's hand to get her attention. "We've always got you."

The sisters stared at each other for a moment, until Cara nodded and gave her sister's hand an extra squeeze. "I know you do. And same goes. I will see you later this week."

Todd watched the by-play between the two women. He didn't have any siblings of his own. Hunter was his closest family, and he guessed their silent communication was similar, but now Hunter had had his own family to take care of. Was that a twinge of envy again? He pushed the thought away and reached for Cara's arm, guiding her toward the car. While they walked, he constantly surveyed the bushes around the property for any signs of movement or the glint off anything metal. He couldn't be too cautious. And this would change their plans. Cara wasn't going to like that, but she didn't have a choice in the matter. He couldn't let her end up enduring the same circumstances that occurred in the woods. He wouldn't.

****

They drove back toward town in silence. Cara felt nauseas at having brought evil to her brand new niece's life so early. She shouldn't have to experience that kind of energy so soon. Not ever. No one should have to. The world was a crazy place though and there were crazy, evil people in it. Life wasn't fair.

"I swore I would never allow myself to be dragged into that web of evil again. Yet here I am."

"It isn't your fault. It's the wack-job's fault,

whoever he is –and we will find him. And when we do, we will stop him."

"I can't risk him hurting my family. Do you have any idea how terrified I am right now? What if he attacks one of my sisters -or my parents? Or my good God, Baby Josie? What if—"

"No what-ifs, Cara. We can't live in what-ifs. It will drive us crazy. We deal with what we know. We deal in facts."

"Well, it is a *fact* that he was at my sister's. And it's a *fact* that she could be at home alone with the baby on any given day. Before it was just me, but now he's targeting my family."

Todd took a deep breath. He was working on maintaining control of his own emotions while he also tried to calm Cara.

"And don't give me that look that says I'm being irrational about this, because I'm not and you know I'm not. You saw how close he was to my sister's house."

"I did and I get it. In the interest of full disclosure, it's a real concern, but you are still his focus and he wants you. Even though he took his fight close to your sister's home, it was still all for you. Still to keep you off balance and yes, to freak you out. We have to remain rational about this."

"Rational? There is nothing rational about any of this and don't go thinking I'm just being an irrational female and blowing things out of proportion. *Anyone* would be freaked out by what's going on. It wouldn't matter if they are male or female, so don't go all macho 'I'm a man and I'm the only one who can take care of this' nonsense. And also don't think this is going to change our plans either. I will still lure him out and we will end this."

Todd cringed inside realizing she wasn't going to let him alter their plans. He scanned the horizon and the bushes near the road as they drove while he tried to figure out how to best handle this situation next. His eyes caught a car in the rearview mirror. As it gained on them, he reached beneath his seat for his gun, continuing to rest his hand between his legs, once he grabbed it, but keeping it out of site so he didn't alert Cara.

It didn't matter. She saw him reach for it and pointed out the car behind them anyway. As it passed them, and kept on going, he settled a little-not much, but a little.

"Is this what it's always like in your line of work?" she asked. "Because I gotta tell you, it's not any fun for me. Always on edge. Watching every car. Scanning the bushes—yeah I see you do that too. I need more Zen in my life than this."

Her head hung as she stared at her hands; her hair covered her face. He felt for her. He really did -and he would do everything within his power to keep her safe. The whole thing was too much for someone without experience. He was concerned she wouldn't be able to hold it together.

"You know, I was thinking," she all but whispered, "We did all that practicing for self-defense and he never commented on it. That seems weird to me, don't you think?" She glanced up at him then and he didn't see tears or anxiety, he saw intelligent processing of information. The wheels were turning.

"Correct. What are you thinking?"

"We didn't find any bugs or video cameras on the terrace near the house, and it's clear he didn't find it safe to set up listening devices there. I wonder why that is?

I've talked about renovating the terrace off and on over the past year or so, and maybe he knew that. Maybe he was afraid if I started that project, the bugs would be found and ruin his plans. I haven't talked with just anyone about it, so that should lessen the pool of possibilities, right?"

Her eyes were gleaming with excitement that she'd made a connection. She was taking back her life and she would participate in that process. She had a point, too.

"Interesting. And great work too, by the way. We can use this to narrow down the pool."

"Thanks, but I don't need your kudos. I just want my life back." A flash of anger flared in her eyes and then it was gone.

"I didn't mean that as—"

"Sorry I didn't mean that to sound snippy, I'm just angry at this situation and people trying to take over my life. If I were a man, would the situation be the same? I doubt it. And again, I know that sounds waspish, and I know I can't do this on my own. I don't have the expertise to do that, but I do have valuable input. I won't just run away and hide waiting for 'the men folk' to fix it."

He couldn't blame her for the sarcasm. He'd seen women get ignored and men take credit for their work time and time again –especially in his line of work, but he wasn't one of those men. He could feel his back getting up and worked to take a step back and breathe through it. He cared about her. Dammit. He didn't want to fight. Not when he had to stage it on Monday, and certainly not now.

He could see the pride she had in herself and she should. She was a successful woman who was intelligent and beautiful. She was kind and caring and didn't deserve what she was going through. And she was right. She should be involved in the decision making when it came to her own life, but he wouldn't allow her to be put in harm's way. Even as the thought entered his mind, he could hear her rebuttal of *that's not your decision to make*. Again, she wouldn't be wrong.

You're getting it, baby boy, was the next thought that popped into his head. His Grandma Hailey was working daylight hours now?

"You're absolutely right. You should have input into the decisions that affect your life. I get it. And you are the one who has the information we need. If I tried to take over, I'm sorry. I just want to keep you safe."

They stared at each other for the briefest of moments until Todd glanced in the rearview mirror again and saw another car speeding toward them. It could be the same car but that wasn't possible. They couldn't have looped around so fast. Maybe they had stopped at the gas station they had passed about a mile back. He wasn't too concerned until it drove right up their ass and stayed there.

Cara turned around and the color drained from her face; her hand flying to cover her silent scream.

Todd hit his brakes and the car backed off, then sped up again. This time, it pulled beside them, where it stayed for the briefest of moments and then passed them. Todd sped up to trail them but someone popped up in the back seat and aimed a gun back at them out the window.

As Todd grabbed his gun and stuck his hand out the window to fire back, a bullet hit and cracked his windshield.

"Goddammit."

The car swerved but Todd gained control and fired back.

"You drive and give me the gun," Cara screamed.

"Get your head down," he shouted back.

"I'm a great shot! Trust me. Give me the gun."

Todd stared at her, feeling the indecision that in his field of work could cost a life.

Against regulations, he handed her his firearm and true to her word, she fired and shot out the car's back window.

"Nice shot," he yelled over the roar of the car engine and the gunfire as she shot again, this time hitting the license plate. "Aim for the tire," he yelled.

"I was," she responded annoyed. "You swerved or I would have hit it."

At that moment, the shooter hit his tire and he grabbed the wheel with two hands, arms tightened and mouth grim as he worked to bring the car safely to the side of the road.

"Son of a bitch," he shouted as he banged the steering wheel. "Son of a goddamn bitch." The second was louder as frustration surged through him. He opened his door and stepped out, slamming the door behind him.

Cara got out and walked to where he was kicking gravel on the side of the road. She placed her hand on his arm, giving pressure until he turned to look into her eyes.

"Sorry about your car. And sorry I missed the target. Grandpa would be disappointed given it was he who taught me. I used to be very good, I swear."

"Your grandfather would be so goddamn proud of you right now. I am so goddamn proud of you right now."

He turned, walking away and cursing into the wind.

With his hands on his hips, feet spread hip width apart, he tried to relax the tension in his shoulders. It wasn't working. He had never been so terrified in his life. Not because he'd been shot at. That happened on the regular in this job. He couldn't stand to think of what might have happened had Cara been shot. That scared the shit out of him. He turned then and grabbed her in a hug, holding her tight.

****

"Don't live in the what-ifs. Isn't that what you told me?" Cara could feel the tension in his shoulders. He was almost vibrating with his anger and frustration. "At least now we know who is behind this."

Todd grabbed her shoulders and held her away from him so he could see her face. It happened so fast, he almost knocked her over, so he tightened his grip to steady her.

"What? You saw who it was? You know them?"

"It was Jeremy. I don't know why the system says he's still in jail, but I can tell you straight up, he isn't. It's strange you know…knowing he's out. I would have thought that would have made me feel worse, but somehow it makes me feel better. At least now I know what's going on. He did swear he would make me pay. And just in case it hasn't been clear, he won't rest until he's dead or…" she paused. "… I am."

Todd pulled out his phone and contacted Beau. "We know it's Flaxton. Cara saw him." He paused while he listened. "No, she's sure."

Cara tugged on his sleeve to get his attention, frustrated because she couldn't hear what Beau was saying. "Speaker please."

Finally, Todd heard her and moved the phone to be

face up between them and hit the speaker button. "You're on speaker now, Beau. Cara is here too."

"I'm sending a picture of Flaxton to be sure. Maybe he's changed enough that her memory isn't accurate. It's been a few years since she's seen him."

"It's been twenty years but trust me, Beau, I still see his smarmy face in my sleep. I would know him anywhere."

Todd's phone pinged and he opened the picture.

Cara shook her head, confused. "That's him. I don't understand. That's who I saw driving the car."

"Is it possible that in the excitement of the moment, you thought you saw him but it wasn't? Maybe just someone who looked like him?" Beau asked.

"I guess… I mean… Maybe… Except I recognized him before all the shooting started…but I guess anything is possible."

Did she recognize him, or was her traumatized mind playing tricks on her? She didn't like not being certain. When she made the decision to abandon law, and move to design, she was certain it was the right thing for her. When she chose her office space, she was certain. When she started her mentoring program, she was certain. When it came time to make all her life decisions, she was certain. This being unsure, made her feel off balance.

"I just don't understand. How could there be two of them?"

"He had a brother, who is deceased, but you said he had a cousin. Did they look alike?" Todd asked.

"I don't remember the cousin. I just know he had one. They were a few years younger. I can't remember them at all. Can you ask for a picture of the inmate? Is it possible they made a mistake?"

"Let me make a call to my contact at the prison and just confirm. I wouldn't think it would be possible for him to get out without them knowing it, but like you said Cara, anything is possible. Stay tuned."

"Copy that," Todd added and hung up.

Cara's phone rang almost immediately. She fumbled with it as she pulled it out of her pocket and answered. "Hello?"

"Having fun yet? Your boyfriend almost shit the bed with his driving. Too bad his car didn't blow up. Maybe next time."

"Listen, Flaxton, I don't know how you got out of prison, but you're on your way back. There is no place you can hide where you won't be found."

"Flaxton? I don't know what you're talking about."

The laugh that followed was horrific. So sick and twisted and downright evil. Cara shivered.

"Cold? Or is did someone just walk over your grave?"

"Bite me, you bastard." Cara hung up and turned off her phone completely, searching her surroundings to see where they were.

Todd walked toward the woods by the side of the road. "Bastard has to be close by."

Something shone in the sunlight, just inside the tree line and Cara ran toward Todd, yelling for him to get down. "Gun," she screamed as she tackled him.

Todd took her tackle in stride, twisting and grabbing her to ensure she went down with him, shielding her from the fall, then rolling on top of her to protect her. They waited in the tall grass for the sound of gunfire, but none came.

Their breathing was hard and fast, as Cara tried to

catch her breath. She couldn't get enough air into her lungs and panic swelled inside her.

Todd, rolled off her and helped her sit up. "Are you hurt? Are you injured?" he shouted into her face while his hands scanned her body with a swipe and search method, searching for what she only assumed was blood.

"Breathe, darlin'. Just breathe. You're okay. I probably knocked the wind out of you. Just breathe." He grabbed her by the shoulders staring directly into her eyes, maintaining visual contact with her. "Okay now, that's it. Just breathe. Good girl. You've got this. Deep breaths."

She realized she was indeed breathing again. She had control. Concentrating on each individual breath she continued until they became deeper, and the panic eventually subsided.

Reaching up with her hand, she wiped the hair from her eyes, removing some grass that had become tangled in it.

"Stay here," Todd ordered. "I want to check out the flash of metal I saw."

"You saw it too. I was beginning to think my mind was playing tricks on me again."

Staring straight into her eyes, he responded, "Don't start second guessing yourself now. I believe you when you say you saw him. Don't let him steal your confidence. We will get through this together."

With a nod of his head, Todd crouched and moved toward the woods once again. Cara got up to follow him and he turned to remind her to stay down.

"I thought we were past all of that," she mumbled but lowered herself to make a smaller target. "What happened to all the 'we'll get through this together' stuff you just spewed?"

"I don't spew," he whispered back, turning his head to make sure she was listening.

She wasn't, of course. She wouldn't just sit back and wait for someone else to manage her life. She was a new woman. Fight or flight would be fight from here on in.

When they arrived at the spot where they thought they had seen the gun Todd scanned the trees, keeping Cara behind him. She pushed her way beside him, sticking close to the trees to better be able to use them as cover, if need be.

Todd's head tilted as though listening to the forest. She did the same, realizing that if someone had been there, they may be on the move. There were no sounds except the chirping of birds and the babble of a stream nearby.

They found a footprint in dried mud beneath a branch that had tinfoil wrapped around it to glint in the sun as the breeze blew. It hadn't rained in days so the print had to have been there for half a week, at least. Probably longer.

"It looks like this footprint has been here for a while, but I don't get the tinfoil. Why would that be here?" Cara asked chewing the inside of her cheek while she processed what she was seeing.

"I've got no idea. It's not like they would have known we would be here and could have staged it."

"Right? I mean, seriously, no one would know Lilly would have delivered and we would be visiting today. But what if they thought she would go earlier or set it up in advance, just in case?"

"That would take a lot of planning and a whole new level of obsession. I'm calling Rae and Beau to come investigate here as well, when they're done at your sister's. This guy is escalating."

****

"Do they suspect anything, yet? I thought they were smarter than this."

"Nothing," was the response. "She's such an idiot and he's no better. They won't figure it out. Not until it's too late. And then, it won't matter."

The two laughed together over the phone.

"You should see them now, checking the trees out and ogling the boot print, like they're going to find something. They're probably trying to figure out the tinfoil, but they haven't found the blood yet. Idiots. We are dealing with idiots. It's kind of funny to watch them though. Wish you could see it. I will send the video to you. You will find it very entertaining."

Chapter Twenty

"We're missing something here," Todd grumbled as he carefully searched the bushes once Rae and Beau had arrived.

"Rae will find it," Beau added confidently.

"Rae is doing her very best, but she's getting a little annoyed with you getting in her way," Rae responded, standing and bumping into Beau.

"Give the woman some room. You said she's the best. Let her do her job," Cara chimed in. "Wait, what's that?" She asked pointing upward to the tree. "Everyone is looking down, but isn't that a trail camera? It's hidden in the leaves, but…"

Todd jumped to grab a branch on the tree and swung himself up, then climbed over to where the leaves were bunched. He was about to grab it but stopped. "There's a wire attached."

"What the hell?" Beau asked. "Don't touch it man. I'll call the bomb squad." He walked away pulling his phone from his pocket.

"Todd don't move," Cara whispered. There's something above your head. It looks like a tarp. It could have the bomb in it. If you jiggle the wire, it may blow. Just be still please."

"I've got a step ladder in my truck," Rae added. "Let me grab it. Todd, just stay still. Do. Not. Move."

"Trust me, I'm not moving."

Cara could hardly breathe. Panic was beginning to rise again.

"Cara, I want you to take a step backward and move away. Head toward the creek, where there's a drop off and crouch down. If this goes off, I don't want you anywhere near it."

"I won't leave you here to face my battle—"

"Cara, now is not the time to argue. Just go," he gritted through his teeth.

"No. Where is your 'we are in this together' now? I stay and we face this as a team."

"Dammit, Cara."

Rae returned with her ladder and carefully placed it by the side of the tree. She climbed up carrying a roll of duct tape, then with great care, wrapped the wire where it lay along the branch securing it in place.

"Okay, you should be okay to come down now. Then we can wait for the bomb squad to get here."

Cara ran to Todd once he had climbed down from the tree. She clung to him, both absorbing his strength and sending her own to him as well. He held her close, his face buried in her hair.

"Let's get out of the way, darlin'. I don't want to trample any potential evidence and we need to leave enough room for Rae to do her job. And Rae," he said turning his head away from Cara, "watch the area for any more triggers. We don't know what the hell this dude is up to. It might even be best to wait for the bomb squad to get here and do a thorough search of the area."

"Like they could do a better job than I could. Give me a break." She was annoyed, but she complied. "Beau, make sure they bring the dogs, just in case. I want a search done of the area to be sure we aren't leaving anything behind for anyone else to find. They can search more efficiently than any of us, and do it much faster."

"Rae's ability to search an area can only be outdone by the sniffers." Beau piped in after hanging up the phone. ETA is twenty minutes."

"Gawd save us from this snail's pace." Rae sighed.

****

When the bomb squad arrived, they followed the dogs, searching for potential targets. They didn't alert to anything except for Louis, one of the new pups in training who wouldn't leave the hanging tarp area alone. He kept sitting beneath it and barking. Todd got a stick with which the pup then wanted to play but Todd ignored him. He grabbed some of the duct tape from Rae and taped his phone to it on an angle, then switched the camera on and started a video. He talked into the camera stating his name and the location, date and time, then raised the stick enough to record what was in the tarp. When he pulled it back down, and viewed what he had recorded, he cursed.

"What is it?" Cara asked trying to see his phone.

"Appears to be a tarp full of blood to me. Rae? Thoughts?"

He held the phone toward Rae and Cara, and they both moved so they could see better.

"Ew. That's gross."

"No kidding, girlfriend. Gross is an understatement. If I had to guess, I would bet on blood. It could be paint –and dear God, I hope it's paint- but I gotta be real with y'all. I would bet on blood. I just pray it's not human. We can tell it hasn't been here long. No flies yet," she added.

Cara shivered again and Todd reached for her,

pulling her close to him to share his body's warmth.

Cara's phone rang, startling everyone in the somber silence of the woods.

"I thought I turned that off," Cara stated, confused.

"You did," Todd responded, taking her phone, and answering with the speaker button.

"I see you have found my lair. Well we both know it's not really my lair, but let's just say for today that it is. You found it because I wanted you to. Because I let you. In fact I had to lead you to it. Your boyfriend isn't nearly as smart as he thinks he is. He needs to get out of my way before I kill him too. Time's a wasting."

Cara grabbed her phone from Todd yelling as she did so. "Listen you bast—"

"Cara, he's hung up." He gently pried her fingers from her phone and placed it in an evidence bag.

"What are you doing? That's my phone."

"It's evidence now Cara. I should have thought of it sooner. It's either been cloned, or there's malware in it. Your caller has probably been listening in through it and that's how he's known so much about what you're doing. We will run diagnostics on it and see for sure, but for now, we need to put it away. We can get you another phone. One that won't put your life in jeopardy."

Rae and Todd stared at each other, communicating something silently that Cara didn't understand. "What? What is that look for?"

"We will need to do a sweep of your computer at home and work. Do you have a smart system in your home? You know, where you can change the temperature, unlock the door using your phone?"

"We have one at the office but it's not hooked up. I never added it at home."

"Well small mercies, I guess," said Rae, with a sigh.

"Have they been listening and monitoring me through my phone? Then why didn't they know about the self-defense training?"

"We didn't take our phones outside. We left them on the coffee table so they wouldn't get broken while we sparred.

They probably didn't care we found the surveillance equipment in the attic because they still had a backup, right? Oh my God. I can't believe this is happening. Why? What did I ever do to deserve this? And oh my God, I hooked my phone to my smart TV so do they have control of that too? I can't believe this. It just isn't real."

Todd bent his knees so he was eye level with Cara. "We will check that out too. Everything with smart capabilities will be searched/scanned/cleaned. And you did absolutely nothing. This isn't your fault. This is the doing of a sick bastard. Don't let him steal your sunshine darlin'. Don't let him steal the joy from your day. Don't give him that power."

When they arrived back at Cara's, Todd did a sweep of the house again, and then led Cara out to the terrace. "You okay sitting out here? I feel like it's a safer bet, given there are definitely no bugs out here. Well not of the listening kind," he added as he swatted at a fly that landed on his arm. "We need to have a chat about all of this. And I think your sister is right about looping in your family. They all need to be on alert, yes, but they would also want to know what's going on. Keeping this a secret is only going to hurt them at best and risk them at worst."

"I know you're right. I just feel like a problem. I don't like being a problem. I'm going to turn my family's world upside down again and ruin my parent's anniversary party. That's not fair to them."

"What's not fair," Todd responded with a gentle voice, "is thinking that you have to endure this alone. You aren't on your own and cutting them out of the picture, only hog-ties them. They're adults. They've seen this kind of thing in court before, I'm sure, and maybe they will remember something you don't. You were only sixteen at the time. You could have blocked something out that they may have insight into."

"Fine we can tell them tomorrow, but I do it."

"I'm coming with you," Todd insisted.

"Of course you can, but I tell them. Not you. That's a deal breaker."

****

Cara had called her parents to arrange brunch on Sunday. She was nervous about how best to tell them. Would they think she'd been careless? Would they become over-protective again? She wasn't sure how they would react. In the end, they took it far better than she had anticipated.

They had met at her parents' favorite new brunch place, 'Breakfast at Tiff 'an Eason's', a bistro by the water. It would allow her to swing by the house again to see how much progress was made the previous day. Gosh, was that only yesterday? So much had happened since then. It seemed like a lifetime ago.

When they had all been seated together, Todd had shaken her parent's hands, while they both sized him up. He held his own, saying it was good to meet them and mentioning her mom's most recent win in court. He had details too. It was clear he had done his research prior to meeting them. She wasn't sure how she felt about that, but her mom was smitten with him. That was no easy feat given her abilities to see through someone's bull, and get directly to what was behind every word. Not that Todd was kissing up. He wasn't. He approached them both with the respect of a colleague.

Her dad on the other hand, seemed colder. It was as though something was simmering underneath his façade of amiability. She wasn't sure what it was, but Todd seemed to sense it to and aimed to head it off at the pass, as her granddaddy would say.

"Sir, I sense you have concerns and I want to assure you that I won't let Cara out of my site until we have this guy in custody."

"Dead or alive?" her father asked, succinct in his speech.

"Honestly, sir, I don't really care at this point. Of course I will do my best to bring him in alive so justice can be served, but that's up to him, not me."

Her father gave one nod in response. "Good. And what about you?"

"What about me, sir?"

"What are your intensions toward my daughter?"

"My intentions sir?

"You heard me."

"Daddy, please. Don't do this now. Seriously. This is why I don't tell you when I'm dating someone."

"So you are dating him then."

"Daddy." Cara turned to Todd. "Don't pay any attention to him."

"It's a fair question, Cara. I like to think that if I'm lucky enough to have a daughter one day, I would behave in the same way." Todd turned back to her father, his gaze forthright. "Let me speak plainly sir. I have feelings for your daughter. I care for her more than I expected, but I won't be around for much longer. I've received an opportunity for my next assignment, and am weighing my options. I just finished the paperwork on Friday for my last case so I have to make my decision. I don't know where I will end up next, but I do want to be able to continue a relationship with Cara, if she's open to that. I just can't offer any guarantees."

Cara sucked in her breath. "Don't you think this is a conversation the two of us should have before you discuss this with my dad? When are you supposed to leave?" She looked at Todd and he appeared a little... was that fear? No, it couldn't be. "We will talk about this later," she continued then rolled her eyes turning to her father. "And I'm serious, Daddy. Leave it alone. I'm not a baby anymore. You can't protect me forever. My life, my choice. You taught me that."

"I did teach you that but not so you could throw it back in my face. I have a right to ask about the man who is dating my daughter and you can't stop me."

"Daddy...look at me. Do I, or have I ever given the impression that I can't handle my life? Present situation excluded, I've done well at managing myself. I have a successful business. I've built a good name for myself. I think you have to agree I've done well."

"You've done very well at business and that's a good thing –a great thing even. But you've also done well at protecting your heart and that worries me. I always worried you wanted to marry Tommy and had shut down after he died."

"He was murdered, Daddy. You can say it how it is. He deserves the truth to be spoken. I didn't back down then, and I won't back down now. Not from this and not from life. I've never closed myself off. I just hadn't found the right man."

Her dad smirked, like he'd won something but she couldn't figure out what it was. Then he enlightened her.

"Until now."

Todd dropped his spoon, and her dad beamed more.

"Daddy, just stop. Mama please make him stop." She rolled her eyes after imploring her mom for help.

"Y'all know I have no control over him. He does what he likes, when he likes. But he loves you. And like me, he gives his stamp of approval to Todd."

"Lawd, Mama, you too?"

Todd choked on his coffee.

****

"They're all having brunch. She's probably telling her parents about everything. They still don't have a clue. I said they wouldn't, and they won't."

"They underestimated you –and me. That will be the downfall of them all. I wish we could hear what they're saying. I want to know what they're planning."

"I can try to get another bug in the house."

"No too risky. They will be on guard. It's too bad they figured out we had control of her phone. You shouldn't have turned it back on again. That was a slip up on your part."

"Yes, but I wanted to follow along in the conversation. It was an impulse to make that call but it was fun. Did you see the look on her face? I nearly peed myself, I was laughing so hard."

"If it burns us, you will pay, and pay dearly. Don't you underestimate me too."

Chapter Twenty-One

"Well that went better than anticipated," Cara said as they left the restaurant. "Sorry about my dad's third degree, though. When I said that was why I didn't bring dates around, I wasn't kidding."

"I can understand that, but it was to be expected, under the circumstances."

"You didn't need to lie to him though."

"Lie? I didn't lie,"

"What? You mean you meant what you said about continuing to see each other even after you're transferred? I mean... I would like that but it wasn't expected. You said long distance never works. Where are you going next?"

"Of course I meant it. I don't say things I don't mean. And I'm still weighing my options." He appeared irritated and it made no sense but it warmed her heart.

Grabbing his arm she swung her other arm wide, while she danced in the wind and sunlight.

"What a glorious day. Let's go by the beach house now and maybe we can take a walk along the shore. I need some sunlight in my life right now and I do feel better after talking to my parents. You were right about that."

"I'm happy they're letting us add extra security to their anniversary party, just in case we don't catch him before then." He held up his hand, palm out when she started to protest. "Just in case. We have no control over how he's going to react between now and then."

"Right. Tomorrow when we have our fight—"

"Oh we are not having a fight anymore. Let's get that straight right now. We have no need of that. He's already made his move when I've been there. He will move and he will move fast. Mark my words. He's unravelling."

****

They were walking through the house when Todd's phone rang. "Yeah, Rae, you're on speaker and Cara is here. What have you got?"

"Maybe take me off speaker?"

"Rae, it's Cara. If it's about my case, I need to know. I thought we were friends. You know. I am woman, hear me roar and all that."

"Fine. Been working with Beau. The man who is in prison in Flaxton's cell isn't Flaxton. He looks like him. He's in the infirmary at the moment. Prison personnel don't know when the switch was made, exactly, but they thought it was weird two cell mates had the same rare blood disorder. They did DNA testing to confirm when we asked them to review it. They do look a lot alike, but I can confirm Flaxton was released a week ago, in error when they thought they were releasing his cellmate Richards. Richards had to have agreed to the switch. Not sure why at this point but Flaxton must have something on him. Anyway, Richards –or Flaxton as it were-completed his initial meetings with his probation officer but has been AWOL since Friday. We're talking radio silence -off the grid completely. Cara, I'm sorry the system has let you down. We will catch him though. At least we know for sure. Not that Cara wasn't sure already… I'm babbling. Sorry, Cara. I really mean that. They're launching a manhunt for him and about to hold a news conference. He's about to go underground, I'm sure."

"Can we stop the news conference? Delay it a day or two maybe? Give us some time to get him? He definitely will go underground if we don't."

"I tried Mitchell. Sorry man. I even used both your name and your cousin's to try to get approval but no one would bite. He's a murderer. A felon. And he's dangerous. To keep it quiet would be fool-hearty and put the public at risk."

"She's right," Cara added, taking a deep breath. "At least about him hiding, but it won't stop him. He will just take a beat to regroup and make his last-ditch effort a big one. It just means the games will stop. He'll be playing for keeps next time. One last effort –winner takes all. And he can't be doing this all alone. He has to have help. I've been feeling like I was being watched for weeks – months even. If he just escaped a week ago, that part couldn't have been him."

"We need to bide our time then until they find him. We can wait him out. We have the upper hand now."

"For what outcome? If he runs and we don't find him, then I'm watching over my shoulder for the rest of my life? No. That doesn't work for me. We can hold our own press conference and sweat him out. Play to his ego. Offer a dare or something. You know…challenge his manhood. He always was a sucker for a dare."

"Thanks, Rae. We appreciate the heads up." Todd kept his eyes on Cara as he spoke into the phone.

"Wait, that's not all I have. The blood in the woods, was chicken blood."

"There's a chicken processing plant just outside of town when heading South on the interstate. It was abandoned for years but started up again a couple of years ago. I know the couple who opened it up again. I helped them with their home."

"Were they someone you would have told about re-doing your terrace?" Todd asked, zoning in on a possible accomplice.

"No, I didn't know them that well. While I did have them over to the house one evening, when I was hosting clients, I didn't talk to them about any renos I was planning. In fact I didn't even think about making any changes until after that cocktail party when I realized there could be better flow when entertaining."

"Could they have heard from someone else?"

"Anything is possible but they aren't in town much that I've seen. Their home is in the country even further out of town. They probably go into Charleston for shopping."

"Rae, ask Beau to head out there to investigate. See if he sees anything. I'll get Alex to join him."

"Copy that."

Cara felt an energy flow through her. She glanced around her, searching for anyone watching. She was on alert. High alert. She felt in control. The end was near and she would be victorious.

The sun shone on the water, creating the appearance of diamonds sparkling as far as she could see. The waves rolled in and out soothing her. Calming her. She was in charge of her life and she would win.

Todd was on the phone with Alex, but she could still see him scan the beach and the crowd that was walking toward them. "Come on, Cara," he said after he'd hung up. "Alex is heading out to help Beau and I want you off the beach. There's a crowd coming and I don't want anyone getting hurt should anything happen. We don't know what Flaxton will do now that he's desperate."

With his arm around her waist, he held her close to his side, continually scanning the beach, then the parking lot. He walked Cara to her door, and held it open for her while she got inside, then closed the door, still scanning.

The car's engine roared to life and gravel spewed out behind the tires as they left their spot. Back on the road, he rotated his vision flicking over the side mirrors, the rearview mirror, and the horizon. Always on alert.

Their trip back to Cara's was uneventful and collectively they both let out their pent up tension, Cara with a deep sigh and Todd with a quick perusal of the house.

All windows and doors were locked, but he had anticipated that. Alex had said there had been no sign of anyone while they'd been out. That was a good sign. Cara was safe; at least for the moment.

"I put a pizza in the oven. It will be ready in twelve minutes. I know it's not gourmet or anything but it will do in a pinch."

"It will be perfect. Now come on outside, so we can practice some self-defense. I want you as prepared as you can possibly be if anything happens and I'm not around."

"You mean like after we break up."

"We are not breaking up, Cara."

"You know what I mean. When we have our fight tomorrow."

"Again, that's off the table. I am not leaving you alone until this ass is found. I get that you're independent and can handle yourself, but that's non-negotiable. And before you say something about it being because you're a woman, you're wrong. If any of my partners were in the same boat, I would do the same thing. We have each other's backs, right?"

"Right. Okay, we have ten minutes now. Let's go,"

The pizza was a just this side of overcooked but it tasted delicious just the same. Todd swore he preferred a crispy crust. They'd gotten a little carried away with practice because Cara kept pushing to do better; to learn more.

"I'm getting better, no?" Cara asked licking some cheese that had strung a little too far and landed on her chin.

"You're doing great. More confidence in your moves means more success, provided you don't get cocky."

"Moi? Cocky? I abhor cocky. Cocky is beneath me. But next time, you're going down."

Todd laughed in spite of himself. He felt like he was seeing the Cara he had originally met, just before all of this started.

"Just promise me you won't go anywhere by yourself. And I mean anywhere. Not so much as to the mailbox. Promise me."

"Believe me, I promise. And I'm happy we aren't breaking up tomorrow."

"We were never breaking up, Cara."

****

The days passed quietly. It was unnerving, how quiet. There were no calls. The feeling of being watched was gone. Todd was beginning to feel like the perp had run and they would never hear from him again.

He drove Cara to work every morning since she

insisted she work from the office, and then picked her up and brought her home. He had enlisted the assistance of Alex and Beau to tag team her surveillance when he wasn't available. The story hit the news, with the whole backstory and Cara was badgered for interviews all over again. He was sure it was like reliving the loss of her friend for a second time. It couldn't have been easy, but she felt, and he agreed, that it would piss off Flaxton and force him out. So far, it hadn't, but it was only a matter of time. While others believed that maybe he really had fled, Todd insisted that wasn't likely. He was too obsessed. It would have been the smart thing to do and Flaxton seemed smart in his surveillance of Cara but Todd would bet money on the fact that Flaxton wouldn't give up that easily. Psychopathic brilliance was hard not to notice. The attention to detail was undeniable throughout the whole ordeal, but so was his obsession. No way would he run until he'd finished what he started.

Every evening he worked with Cara to prep her, with lessons. Where to hit, how to use her body weight to her advantage, how to escape holds. Over and over and 'one more time'. Again. Through exhaustion and sometimes tears, Cara kept up. He was proud of her. She was beyond tired but he wouldn't rest until she was ready. *Will she ever be ready enough for your liking?* His mind asked, mocking his own determination to push.

At night, he held her close, arms wrapped around her in protection and knowing their time was limited. If she were close to him, he would sleep well and better be able to protect her. He was driving himself crazy through the process; pushing himself to his own limits along with Cara. It wouldn't be enough until she was safe and she wouldn't be safe until Flaxton was caught.

****

When Friday arrived and the party was eminent, he was ready to ask Cara's parents to call it off. Cara, of course, vetoed that. She refused to allow her parents celebration be tainted or dimmed by the actions of a psychopath.

She stepped out of her car, grabbing the briefcase that was in the back seat and had been for over a week now. It was heavy so she opened it to see what was in it. The most horrific smell hit her in the face. She gagged, dropping it, bending over to throw up in her camellias.

"That won't do them any good," Cara said as she wiped her mouth.

Todd was by her side in an instant. "What happened? Are you okay?"

"There's something awful smelling in my briefcase. I'm betting it's another 'gift' from Flaxton."

Todd carefully opened the briefcase and nearly tossed his own cookies. His gag reflex was strong, but he managed to hold it together by setting the case down and walking away to catch his breath, breathing deeply to inhale clean air and clear out the smell one could never mistake for anything but death.

"Bet you dinner?" he joked, but the joke was on him when he gagged again.

His phone rang and he pasted a smile on his face, causing clear confusion for Cara. "Cousin, how's the honeymoon? Loving Italy?" The smile dissolved in an instant and Cara was concerned. He held up his hand to let her know all was fine.

"Yes, I have it under control. Alex has been helping and Cara is safe." He paused, holding the phone out from his ear and Cara cringed listening to Hunter scream at

Todd. "Listen, Sloan," Todd continued, a firmness in his voice that Cara hadn't heard before. "You will not come home early. I didn't call you for this very reason. You can't ruin Miranda's dream vacation, not to mention your honeymoon. She would never forgive me."

He rolled his eyes at Cara and made a puppet movement with his hand insinuating that Hunter wouldn't shut up. Cara snickered as intended.

"Fine, put Miranda on the phone. Oh hi, Miranda," he said immediately. Cara reached for the phone but Todd just lowered it and hit speaker. "You're on speaker now and Cara is here."

"Hi, Miranda, I hope you're having an amazing time, taking lots of pictures."

"Cara, are you all right? I swear if Todd lets anything happen to you, I will never forgive him. You're my best friend. You be safe. Listen to Todd. He knows what he's doing. And don't think I believe you can't take care of yourself but I've read what they're saying online about this lunatic and you need to be careful. Trust me this is not the time for that 'I can handle it myself' stuff. Hunter is going to rebook our flights and we are coming home early. We should be there tomorrow afternoon if we can get the flights changed."

"Don't change your flights, Miranda. I love you for wanting to rush home to help protect me, but I swear by the time you get home, this will all be over and you will have ruined your vacation for no reason. Todd has a strong lead," she added, shrugging in Todd's direction.

"He better have more than a lead on this," Hunter yelled from the background. His voice sounded like he was in the next room.

"Seriously, cousin, go and explore museums and

fountains. Relax at the villa and make bread or pasta or whatever it is you do in Italy."

"We've been to so many museums already. We don't need to see anymore. We'll come home and help. You were there for me when Miranda was in trouble. I'm here for you now. That's how it works."

"Ah, you're bored and missing the action a little?" Todd asked but didn't wait for a response. "Listen to me. I've got this. I'm not letting anything happen to Cara."

"Take me off speaker," he ordered, then continued assuming he had been obeyed. "I hear it in your voice, Mitchell. Don't deny it. You've fallen for this woman. I can hear it. Your tone is a dead giveaway, so I know you will move mountains to keep her safe. Don't screw this up. And also, I want to add that I'm happy to have lost this bet. Miranda said Cara was the perfect match for you. She said as soon as she got the two of you together, you would forget about all your superficial beauties who are more concerned about the name on their shoes than real conversations –my words, not hers. I'm happy to concede."

"I don't know what you're talking about."

"You do and you know it. And don't go blowing it by spouting all that crap about your career. There are options. There are always options. Don't let your pigheaded brain mess this up. Love you, man. Gotta go. Keep Alex in the loop. I'm calling him next to ball him out about not letting us know what was going on."

The call was severed and silence ensued.

"Well, that was enlightening," Cara said feeling smug.

"Sorry, didn't get that off speaker in time."

"Are you blushing?"

"Sunburn. Listen I was just about to call the police to have your briefcase gone over. They should send Rae but I want the call logged through the proper channels."

"Fine but we will discuss this later. While you do that, I'm going to go brush my teeth. Blech."

Rae showed up with her forensic kit along with Beau and Reilly. Todd figured the ass would show up now that the news was on top of the story. He'd called Todd several times asking if there was any news –any new leads. He needed to do his own work. The chief would hear about what a great job Beau had been doing. He deserved that promotion to detective.

"If I were to guess, I would say it's a snake, but hard to be one hundred percent sure until I examine it. And no way to tell what kind right now, given everything is kind of soupy, but it was pretty big." She didn't have a trigger happy gag reflex, thank God. She'd seen too much.

"I can't tell if there will be anything of use in here, but I will go over it when I get it back to the lab. Will call as soon as I've got anything, good or bad. For now, though, I'm outa here since Cara said the case has been in her car for over a week. We know he hasn't been by recently or you would have seen him." She offered a slight nod toward the trees lining the driveway, while turning her back to them. I'm sure he's been watching though. If you want me to pull them down, I can try to see if there's any way to figure out where they're transmitting to. No promises though."

"Do it. It will piss him off to not be able to see her. We should have done it sooner."

"Shoulda, coulda, woulda never helps. We'll do it now. Let the pissing off commence."

Chapter Twenty-Two

Saturday morning started bright and happy. Cara woke beside Todd, happy despite the stress they had both been under. She'd been working hard at her self-defense lessons and was feeling fit. Feeling strong. But today was all about her parents' party. It seemed like forever since they had started planning it, and today it was here. Finally. She wouldn't let anything dim this day for her parents. They deserved this celebration. The whole family did. It was a real accomplishment for them. Fifty years was a long time to stick with a marriage in today's day and age. She hoped to one day have a relationship that strong.

Things were great with Todd and all, but it had an end date and she knew that. Even if he was stationed close, it was still very new for both of them. People changed. Changed their mind. Changed their goals. Grew. While she knew their relationship had progressed faster than it might have had they not been under such stress, she also realized that once that thing that united them was gone and dealt with *please God make it happen soon,* the attraction might no longer be there for him. She had no doubt about her own feelings. She had accepted that she loved him. Even knowing that he was moving on to another appointment. She was surprised he had heard about his next appointment but he hadn't said anything to her. Then again, she wasn't really his girlfriend, so there was no commitment. He needed to make his decision about his job based on his own dreams and wants. She wouldn't be stupid enough to think he would give anything up for her and she wouldn't want him to even if he was willing. What would she do if she were in his position? She didn't have an answer to that.

That was a problem for future Cara to worry about. Today she was going to live in the moment. Embrace all that was, and enjoy the festivities. Maybe Jeremy had moved on by now. It would have been the smart thing to do. It wouldn't matter for today though. Her dad had hired a security firm to monitor things. Sure it would appear weird, but the world was a crazy place and they were important people. Everyone would feel more at ease with them there given the news that was everywhere. The papers, the TV. Radio… You couldn't watch any news outlet without seeing his picture and hearing about his escape. She said a silent prayer he would be caught soon.

She pulled her hair up, capturing it in a messy bun so it would be out of the way when she met with the florist at the venue. She glanced at the clock.

"I gotta run. I'm going to be late," she called to Todd as she ran down the hall and into the kitchen where he was drinking coffee.

"I'll drive you. Hold on one second. Then I will swing by my place and pick up my suit."

"You have suits here already," she interrupted. "Sorry…continue." She giggled.

"I have a particular suit I want to wear and it will give me a chance to check on my place. When I'm done there, I will come help with whatever needs doing, though I'm sure the event planner has everything under control. I'm sure you want to oversee everything to be sure it's perfect. Then we will come back and change for the party. I don't want you there alone though. Who else will be there? I can always stay and help and then we can swing by my place."

"The caterer, the florist, the event planner."

"Any of them certified in martial arts?"

"I don't believe that was a prerequisite on the initial questionnaire, nor in the interview, so I don't know. But I'm sure the security company, which will also be there getting things checked out, will be able to handle anything that comes up."

"Still, wait for me. I want to drive you."

She was happy for the time together, especially given they had an end date. It didn't matter what he had told her dad last weekend. She knew better than to believe in forever when he had said it was temporary and was moving on.

As they drove to the venue, Todd held Cara's hand. His was a large hand, compared to her small one, with strong fingers, but a gentle touch. Their fingers were entwined and he let go, only to change gears.

The houses in her neighborhood were large century homes, with oversized manicured lawns. Some had children playing in them and others were quiet, bikes left haphazardly strewn in the drive. Some homes were locked up tight and others had doors wide open, welcoming the beautiful weather. Dads washed cars with kids, spraying them at random and making them run. She didn't roll her window down because she didn't want to risk her hair turning into a hot mess, so she couldn't hear their squeals but could tell by the smiles on their faces that they were having fun. It reminded her of her own childhood. It had been idyllic until she was sixteen and the hatred of the world ruined everything.

"What's going on? You were smiling and now you look sad. Are you worried about Flaxton? There's been no reported sightings of him anywhere. I'm not letting my guard down, but it's possible he's in the wind."

"You said yourself, as a profiler, his personality was too focused on me for that to happen." She stared out the side window, trying to capture the feeling of joy she'd had only moments ago.

"And you pay far too much attention. I have been known to be wrong before." He paused. "But you're right. I don't think he has, to be honest, so I want you to promise me that you will be careful. Not just tonight, but until we catch him." He squeezed her hand for emphasis. "And we will catch him, Cara. I promise you that."

"That isn't really a promise you can make and we both know it, but I can promise I will be careful."

Cara noticed that Todd kept checking the rear view mirror and her brow furrowed. "Is there someone following us?"

"No, just being vigilant."

The venue was stunning. It was a grand estate, with a large property, giving it privacy for any event. The ballroom was glorious and the flowers had already arrived and been set up. Cara proceeded to shift things slightly, then groaned as the event planner walked over to make sure everything was okay.

"Fabulous, thank you so much for all you've done," she told her. "I'm just that person you probably hate doing parties for. I just need to tweak things slightly to make them perfect."

The event planner moved on to direct the caterers

who had arrived and were unloading in the kitchen. Cara followed to ensure all was going well there too, but stepped back out when she almost got smacked by a swinging door. Served her right for sticking her nose in where it didn't belong.

With everything going as planned, she checked her phone for the time. Todd should be back in about fifteen minutes or so. Just enough time for a check of the gardens. She exited through the French doors to the terrace and down through the gardens. Everything appeared in order so she went out front to wait for Todd.

He looked glorious in his '57 Corvette. She was secretly happy he'd changed cars when he changed suits. She suspected he had wanted to do that given his other car still had a cracked windshield and bullet holes in it. She cringed inside, thinking about that day, then shook it off, promising herself she wouldn't think about it again, at least until tomorrow.

****

Todd was dressed and ready to head over to the party, but Cara wasn't ready yet. He wanted to enjoy the party, but he'd gotten a call from his boss's assistant and was told to expect a call. It couldn't wait until Monday? What could be that important that he had to take a call on a Saturday night. It made no sense. His mind raced, wondering if he was getting fired for declining the promotion. He would be disappointed, but he had decided it wasn't the right move. Something else would turn up. He'd worked hard to get ahead. He deserved his own team and old Todd would have jumped at the opportunity to be on the elite international team. Then his mind sprinted in the other direction and he was afraid he would be transferred somewhere else like Los

Angeles, or Seattle. He didn't want that either. Maybe he would see if there was an opening with DEA. They had an office here in Lightcastle. He didn't really want that either. He was FBI through and through. But he would deal with it, no matter how it turned out.

Cara walked into the kitchen then, and his jaw dropped. Something weird happened to his stomach and it dropped too. *Those are the butterflies, Baby Boy,* his grandma whispered in his ear. He refused to check to see if she was standing beside him. She couldn't be. It was just his imagination. He whistled, reaching for Cara, but she turned sideways and away from him, making a full spin for his viewing.

"Wow. You look absolutely incredible, darlin'." He heard his southern voice drawl a little more, but he didn't care. He took her hand and spun her around again, then pulled her to him, placing his lips against her throat. "You smell amazing too," he whispered.

Her dress was deep green and highlighted her blue eyes. It was an incredible contrast. The dress was form fitting across her body with a V at the neckline and a deeper V down her back that went all the way to below her waist. It flared slightly at the hips and fell to ankle length, moving freely as Cara twirled. A slight sparkle at her ankle caught his attention. It was visible periodically as her dress moved, indicating she was wearing jewelry there. Her heels were high stilettos, black patent, with a red sole. The bracelet on her wrist was delicate and white gold. Her ring on her right hand was an emerald cut emerald, plain but elegant. At her ears, she wore dangling diamond solitaires earrings. Her hair was up in what she would call a messy bun with tendrils, hanging down, giving her a very sensual appearance. Every detail matched perfectly well and suited what he had come to know of her. She was gorgeous.

"You're pretty delicious yourself," she responded nuzzling his neck and inhaling. "You smell amazing too. But we better get going or we will be late. Thanks for coming to this."

"Mia cara," he whispered, "I would do anything for you."

He felt her shiver and offered a gentle squeeze before stepping back and walking her to the door. Before exiting, he scanned the street, then stepped aside and ushered her to his car. It was an exquisite evening for a date with a stunning woman, but he wouldn't let his guard down no matter how much he wanted to enjoy himself. His gut was on alert. He had met with the security team earlier and everyone had a picture of Flaxton. No way would he be getting inside. Cara had arranged for invitations for Alex and Beau so they would be there as well, keeping watch.

Ever vigilant, he continued to scan the street. To the right and left, and then the rear view mirror. Alex was going to watch the street behind them and then follow at a distance, just in case. His gut was saying, as stupid as it sounded, Flaxton was going to try to make his move tonight. From a psychotic standpoint, it would be the perfect time and produce the most damage should he be successful. It would hit all of Cara's family and friends, who Todd was sure, were all at fault for Flaxton's troubles in his twisted little mind. Todd doubted he had taken responsibility for anything in his life…ever. People like that never grew to become good people, and he would never reform, no matter their opportunities for change.

Cara placed her hand on his thigh while he drove. "You seem a thousand miles away right now. I won't ask what you're thinking about because I'm pretty sure it's Jeremy. Hey...plus side though...you don't have to call him my caller anymore." She smiled. "Okay, that was lame. I admit it."

Todd took her hand and raised it to his lips, glancing toward her out of the corner of his eye. "Ever the positive one," he encouraged. "Don't you worry. Tonight will be glorious for your family and your parents in particular. We've got this."

There were cars everywhere when they pulled up in front of the villa again, this time all dressed and ready for the party. It was almost dusk and the place was magnificent with lights and flowers all over the yard. The windows were beacons of welcome, lit as they were. When the Kane's threw a party, they sure went all out.

Cara reached for her door handle, but Todd tugged on her arm. "Just wait there."

"I can appreciate the diligence of protection, but there is security everywhere. Unless someone swims under water, across the lake, they are not getting in. I'm fine."

"Anyone would be an idiot to do that given there are gators in that lake, but not to worry, I have the lake covered too. I just wanted to get your door for you."

Todd hopped out of his side and scooted around to open Cara's door, then held his hand out to her while she exited the car. When she stood, he reached into the glove box and pulled out a box. "I want you to wear this tonight." Her eyes lit up at the sight of what appeared to be a jewelry box.

"It has a tracker in it-just in case," he continued.

"Please. Do it for me. For my peace of mind. And your parents too," he added quickly when she appeared as though she might protest.

"What is it?" she asked as she opened the box. Her inhalation was quick. "Oh, it's stunning."

It was a crystal brooch about three inches wide and two inches high. There were crystals in swirling patterns that sparkled with the slightest movement. When she held it up to her shoulder, it didn't suit. She tried the V at her chest, then her waist and glanced up. "I think it's too big. Don't get me wrong, it's gorgeous, but where would I wear it?"

"May I?" he asked holding his hand out.

When she handed it to him, he gently turned her around and clipped the brooch to the bottom of the 'V' at her back. It was made for the dress. What was a classic look became nothing short of glamourous. A quick picture with his phone to show her, and she agreed.

"It does look amazing. Thank you. But are you that worried?"

"Just a precaution. No one will know it's got a tracker and it suits the dress flawlessly. I can't lose you, Cara."

"I agree to wear it, as an exception only. I don't want someone tracking me on a daily basis. That isn't normal."

"Of course. That's understood. But humor me for tonight. Please."

"Cara... Sweetheart..." Cara turned searching for her father, recognizing his voice immediately.

"Daddy, everything is wonderful. Where's Mama?"

"She's with Emily, ordering the caterer around in the kitchen. They'll be out shortly. You and your sisters have done an amazing job helping with this. Your mother and I are grateful. Have you seen your brother? He's around here somewhere too."

"Sterling is here? Gosh I haven't seen him yet. I heard he made it home –and just between you and me, I would have smacked him if he hadn't."

"You couldn't hurt a flea," a voice said behind them.

Cara turned around squealing and launching herself into an embrace with a man. "Sterling, you've been away too long. You're getting thin. It's obvious you're needin' some of Mama's cooking to fatten you up a little."

"I just told him the same thing," Emily added.

"Why is everyone so concerned about my weight. I'm fit. Not skinny. Just mind your own business."

"Oh, there's Paige and Ivy. I just want to go and say hello. Sterling, this is Todd. Don't be mean to him please," she added and then strolled across the floor. Todd kept his eye on her the entire time.

"So that's how it is, is it?"

"Excuse me?" Todd asked.

"You're in love with her."

"Sterling," his dad said in his clear and warning tone.

"It's okay, Mr. Kane."

"Call me Rhett. And don't laugh. My own mama loved that old movie, lucky me."

"Rhett, I can admit that I do love her. I don't know what's going to happen in the future-no one does- but I love her and will protect her with my life. You have my word."

Cara's dad nodded and Stirling whistled.

"Nice maneuvering, Todd. Well played."

Todd wasn't really listening, he was watching Cara

and tensed when she was stopped by Charlie. Was she Flaxton's accomplice? He didn't think so but no one was above suspicion.

"You going to stare at her all night, man? Can I get you a drink?" Sterling asked.

****

Charlie grabbed Cara's attention on her way to see Paige and Ivy so she stopped for a moment. "Gosh Charlie, you're stunning. And not a work boot in sight. This isn't a look I'm used to seeing on you, but it suits you. Your dress is stunning. And who is this, you've brought with you?" She turned to Charlie's date. "Sir, I don't believe we have had the pleasure. I'm Cara. The one who keeps adding to Charlie's workload."

Charlie's date introduced himself but Cara didn't really pay attention to what he was saying. She was trying to see what Charlie saw in him. She hadn't dated much and certainly didn't bring dates to events, so this was a big deal for her. Cara didn't care for him much. Something was off. Or maybe he was just shy. In any case, she dismissed him, hoping Charlie wasn't serious about him, and extricated herself when she was able to do so politely.

"Ivy and Paige. So happy you could make it. Mama and Daddy will be so thrilled to see you. It's been a while. Be sure to pop over and say hello when you have a minute." She gave each woman a hug and kissed their cheeks. "Isn't it just the best here? Gosh if I ever throw a big party, this is where I want it to be."

"They do weddin's, you know, Sunshine." Paige glanced in Todd's direction, pointing with her lips. "You know…in case you decide—"

"Paige, have you heard of the term boundaries?"

236

Cara laughed in shock, "You do know what the word means, right?" Cara interrupted, following the direction Paige was indicating.

She saw Todd reach inside his jacket and pull out his phone. He glanced in her direction as he answered and smiled at her. It was an intimate moment between the two of them no matter that they were in a crowded room. She melted inside. If there were any barriers left, and she was honest enough to admit there weren't any, they would have crumbled in that moment.

"Just teasing you, Sunshine. All in good fun." She glanced over Cara's shoulder and then excused herself. "I see a hot property by the bar. Back in a jiff." She winked and was gone.

"Are you enjoying yourself, Paige? I hope you're feeling better. You were missed at the office and were pale when you returned. Is everything okay?"

"Yes. I was just feeling overwhelmed with everything including you being attacked. I just needed some time alone. Besides, y'all were too busy to miss me anyway." She winked, trying to tease but it fell short.

"What's going on Ivy? Talk to me. Something is bothering you."

Ivy scanned the people around her then shook her head. "Not here. I don't want anyone to overhear."

Cara took Ivy's arm and led her out to the terrace and down the stairs to the garden where they would have more privacy. "It will be quieter out here. Now talk to me, girl. Tell me what's going on."

Ivy raised one eyebrow and stared. Her whole demeanor changed and a chill when up Cara's spine. Ivy smirked then and Cara glanced down, seeing for the first time, the gun Ivy had pulled from her pocket.

"I think it's pretty clear, don't you? Payback's a bitch but it's time to pay the piper."

"I don't understand. I did nothing but try to help you and encourage you. Why are you doing this?"

"You really don't remember me, do you?"

The words flashed through Cara's memory and it finally started clicking together. "It was you? This whole time it was you? You put the doll in my office and the disintegrated snake in my briefcase? You killed the chickens and put the blood everywhere? I thought it was someone else."

"You thought it was Jeremy Flaxton. He's my cousin and because of you, I had to move. I had to leave Lightcastle and all my friends. I had to move to Idaho where no one knew me and I had zero friends. They made fun of me in school until I figured out how to get the boys' attention. Can you imagine what that was like? Don't get me wrong, Jeremy is waiting for us and helped once I got him out of jail but yeah, it was all me. I was so nervous when I first started working at your office building that you would recognize me. But you didn't. I looked up to you all those years ago but you didn't even remember me. It was like I didn't exist. Didn't matter."

"You're doing this because I didn't remember you? Are you crazy?"

"Move," Ivy ordered. "Now, or I shoot your parents and your sisters. Maybe even that new baby of Lilly's."

Cara moved away from the venue and the people there. She had no choice. She would get Ivy away from everyone and then would grab the gun. Her mind was racing, trying to figure out exactly where she would have the highest probability of success without risking anyone.

"This is a mistake, Ivy. Todd will not rest until he finds you and he won't go easy on you."

"Don't be naive. He will never expect little ol' me to be in on this. Everyone underestimates me. All your bullshit talk of believing in myself and relying on brains instead of beauty pissed me off, by the way. Even you underestimated me. Bitch, you will pay for that too."

Cara noticed that Ivy's voice was sinister and the cadence of her speech –well it was just like the caller, even when it had been distorted. She should have recognized it before. It was true she clearly had underestimated her, but that wouldn't happen again. But Cara was also sure that Ivy had underestimated her and that would be her downfall.

"Around that corner over there. Move faster. You're pissing me off."

Cara felt the jab of the pistol in her rib and winced.

"Hurt, did it? Oh hell, bitch, I owe you much more than that. You blackened my eye in the parking lot and scraped my face. That's why I was off work. I had to heal. I knew you probably wouldn't suspect me even with a scraped face and I could have said I was attacked too, but I just didn't care enough. Besides it gave me time to plan things to perfection. Todd will never find you. Nor will anyone else. You will just vanish into thin air. Poof," she said waiving her hands in the air. "Just like I had to do when you screwed up my life and Jeremy's."

"But—" Cara felt a blow to her head as she rounded the corner and fell to her knees. She couldn't black out. She couldn't. She had to stay alert to be able to fight back.

"Well hello, Cara. Nice of you to drop by. I've missed you. Have you missed me?"

She glanced up, into the face of the man who killed one of her very best friends. She saw his fist racing toward her face and then all went black.

Chapter Twenty-Three

Todd's phone buzzed and he reached for it. This would be the call he had been waiting for. As he lifted his phone to his ear, he realized Cara was staring at him. He could see the attraction shining in her eyes and it warmed his heart. He loved this woman. There was no way around that. He knew in that moment that he would do everything within his power to make her happy. Even with that though, was he willing to give up his career for her so he could stay and build a strong enough foundation for their budding relationship? That was the question of the day. Or…could they work together to come to some kind of compromise when her business was here and not easily moved. She was worth the effort to try.

"Hello?" he answered, placing his finger in his other ear so he could hear better. It didn't help so he worked his way out to the hall and then to the entrance way so he could hear.

"Mitchell," his supervisor said. "I'm not happy you turned down the job in the UK. I warned you it would affect your career. I have some news and there's not a lot of time on this. I know you've been gunning for a team of your own in Washington, but something has presented itself and it's moving fast. There's the possibility of a new satellite office opening up in Lightcastle, given the activity that's been going on down there. I know this wasn't on your radar but I want someone I can trust there to get things going. It's a Special Agent in Charge position for now. I want you to think about moving into management and potentially… eventually run the region. How would you feel about that? Are you interested in being a SAC? Staying in Lightcastle? I know you grew up in the area and that pain in the ass cousin of yours is there, though I hear he's retired –we'll see if that sticks, 'cause I personally don't think it will…"

Todd was reeling from the news. He was still being offered a promotion and the opportunity to stay. His heart swelled, both with pride and excitement. This was everything he'd hoped for. No, more than he'd hoped for. He'd worked his ass off for his career and he was now being rewarded for it. And as an added bonus, he could have his heart's desire too. It was too much to absorb all at once, and he had to share the news with Cara. Then he would call his cousin Hunter to share with him as well. It was like all the horrible things that had happened, were culminating in this one moment, and yes, you can have it all.

"Mitchell? You there? I can hear you breathing. Finally speechless?" His supervisor was chuckling as Todd made his way back into the ballroom to share the news with Cara.

"Sorry, sir, just absorbing the news. It's a lot to take in all at once and not really what I had expected."

"As I've said in the past, you are doing good work. You're going places and your name has been on the radar since shutting down the LPD leak and a major drug ring all at the same time. I know you didn't want to take on that job but I was right when I told you it would be either career making or career limiting, depending on how you handled it."

"Well I did have help," Todd responded, searching the room for Cara. His gut churned. Something was wrong. He saw Paige at the bar chatting up a guy who clearly had already had too much to drink. He couldn't find Ivy. She'd been with Ivy the last time he'd seen her. She wouldn't have left the safety of the group. They had talked about that. He tried not to let panic set in. She would be fine. She was fine. Nothing was wrong. But no matter how many times he repeated the words, he knew something was wrong.

"Sir... Rhett," he corrected covering the mouthpiece of his phone, "have you seen Cara?"

"She just went out to the back garden with someone."

"How long ago?" Todd questioned immediately.

"A few minutes. Maybe five?" Rhett tensed, becoming more alert and scanning the crowd with Todd. "What's wrong? What's got you all worked up? Is she okay? Did something happen?"

"I don't know. It's just a gut feeling. I'll let you know when I find her," he said moving away and towards the garden.

"I'm coming with you, Cara's father insisted, working his way through the throng of people.

"Mitchell!"

Todd stared at the phone in his hand, confused for a moment as to why it was yelling at him.

"Dammit," he cursed under his breath. "Sorry, Sir. Something has come up. I will call you back."

"Mitchell if this is some sort of leveraging tactic... Let me remind you that saying no twice would kill your career. I—"

Todd didn't hear anymore since he'd ended the call–and potentially his future career as well. Something else would come up. Cara was more important.

The two men ran to the back garden but Cara wasn't there. It was that moment that Todd knew what true panic was. His head swiveled back and forth. "She's not here. She wouldn't leave. We discussed this," he repeated. "Something is wrong."

He turned to Rhett as Ivy returned from around the corner. She appeared to be in shock, and then she stumbled just as her facial expression turned to one of fear. The tears turned on and she ran to him, throwing her arms around his neck. Todd realized then what it was he had never liked about her. She wasn't real. She faked everything to get what she wanted.

"Pulling her arms from around his neck, he held her back. "Where's Cara?" he yelled. "She was last seen with you, leaving the ballroom. Where is she?" he repeated when she didn't answer, holding her shoulders and shaking her.

"Todd, the poor girl is upset. Give her a minute. I'm sure she just went to the bathroom or something."

"They took her. Someone took her." Ivy finally spoke between sobs.

"Who took her? Who did it Ivy?" Todd responded, shaking her shoulders again.

"They just grabbed her and knocked her out and took her."

Ivy crumbled to the ground in a heap. Todd ran around the corner, but no one was there.

"When he returned, Rhett was sitting on a bench, comforting Ivy, who was so overwrought she could hardly breathe. "Ivy, I need you to tell me everything you saw. How many were there? Did they have a car? How did it happen? I know it's scary, but Cara's life depends on it."

Ivy cried harder, turning her head into Rhett's tuxedo to hide her face. She was useless and Todd didn't know what to do to make her coherent enough to provide helpful responses.

"There's gotta be security cameras," he said, walking back into the ballroom. By this point, a crowd had gathered just outside the door and Todd struggled not to shove people out of his way. He had to pass Cara's sisters and mother on his way to find the security team and the venue staff.

"Jesus Christ, where is the damn security team? Beau?" he bellowed "Alex?" he added when he finally saw Beau coming in through the front door.

"Cara's gone. He took her. How the hell did this happen?" he yelled as much at himself as at anyone else. He'd let her down. He had promised her and he had let her down. He knew he was being unreasonable but he couldn't get control of his panic.

His phone rang and he pulled it from his pocket and swiping to answer. "What?" he yelled into the phone, swiping his hand through his hair, then leaving it on the back of his neck.

"Mitchell, what the hell kind of a greeting is that?"

"Sorry, sir. Not a good time."

The phone was shoved back in his pocket and he placed his hands on his hips while Beau, Alex and the head of the security team gathered.

"Beau, call in Lightcastle Police Department. I want this place locked down. Alex, there has to be video surveillance. Review it."

Realizing he needed more help, he called his boss back.

"What the hell is going on Mitchell? I offer you a promotion and you hang up. This isn't the kind of man I want running—"

"Sorry again sir but there's been an incident. A woman was just abducted by an escaped felon. He committed murder twenty years ago and Cara testified at his trial. He's been stalking her for weeks and now he's taken her."

"I'll deploy a team but I need to know who she is and how you're connected. Who is she to you, Mitchell? What I'm hearing in your voice says you're involved somehow. Do you need to stand down? Are you too close?"

"I will not stand down, sir. All due respect, this is my case. She is my heart."

Todd paced while his boss ranted about being too close. He didn't care if his boss ordered him to stand down, he wouldn't. Even if it cost him his promotion. Even if it cost his job.

"It's not going to cost your job, unless you screw it up," his boss retorted.

Todd, hadn't realized, he said that out loud. Now he was sounding like Cara. The emotional sucker punch was unexpected but with it came the realization that they were linked.

His boss asked questions and Todd answered as best he could, with what little information he had.

"You can't be lead on this," his boss continued. "We can't have anything screwed up here. McPherson is taking the lead because he's already been on the hunt for Flaxton. He's currently in Pittsburgh because we received a tip he'd been spotted there, but if you say he's in Lightcastle, the team will be mobilized and be there in a couple hours. Send McPherson your coordinates and he will meet you as soon as they land."

"Yes, sir,"

"And Mitchell, next to you, he would be my choice if it were my daughter or wife who were taken. We will find her."

"The clock is ticking, sir. We don't have much time."

Todd had no intention of waiting for the other team. He would work with his own team, small though it was. Alex was a great asset, as was Beau. And he had the added benefit of having placed a tracker on Cara, which would give them a head start in finding her and bringing her home."

He held his phone up to ensure the tracker was indeed working. A dot appeared on his screen, showing it was in the garden. He ran toward the garden doors but Beau stopped him while he ran with a laptop toward him.

"Mitchell, hold up. You gotta see this." He faced the laptop towards Todd and pressed play.

Todd stood there watching the scene before him. He saw his beautiful Cara walking with Ivy. They were close together and Cara walked of her own accord but she was stiff, and searching around her. What was Ivy telling her that seemed to have her on edge and if she was nervous, why did she walk away, instead of back inside? Ivy's arm jerked a little and Cara winced. Was she hurt? Their pace picked up after that and they rounded the corner and out of site.

Todd raised his eyes to Beau. "Do we have another angle?"

"Unfortunately no, but keep watching." Beau reached around to hit the fast forward button until Ivy walked back around the corner.

"How many minutes was that?" Todd asked. How much time had passed?"

"Approximately four minutes. Then we have this from the front of the building and parking area."

Todd watched as he saw Cara being carried to a car and thrown in the trunk. He stared at his phone again and the dot was on the move. He could catch her.

Running to the front of the building he grabbed the keys from the valet and dove into his car. It roared to life. He drove like a bat out of hell, leaving gravel spewing behind at those who stood staring, confused by what was happening.

With one hand, he placed his phone in its holder on his dash so he could easily track Cara while he continued to speed down the road until he caught up to the car ahead of him. He passed it and cut it off, forcing it to stop but it didn't. It drove off the shoulder and into the shallow culvert, then back up onto the road. Todd kept driving, fishtailing as he pulled his car around and straight again.

His phone rang and he swiped to answer then brought the screen back to his tracking app.

"Talk to me," he barked.

"Alex and I are following behind, but that's not the car we saw in the surveillance video. That's a different car. You're following the wrong car."

"It isn't. I had Cara wear a tracker. I'm telling you, that car has Cara in it."

A woman stepped onto the road in front of Todd's car and he cursed, while slamming the horn and swerving to miss her; barely missing the car in the lane beside him. He never took his eyes off the car in front of him except to watch the little red dot that represented Cara, represented his whole world. They swerved between cars, changing lanes when openings presented themselves. Todd wanted to ram the back end of the car, forcing it off the road, but he was afraid, with Cara in the trunk, he would hurt her. He couldn't cause an accident and risk her life.

"I'm going to get in front of them and box them in," he told Beau and Alex through the phone line he'd left open.

"There's a short cut I know where I can get out in front," Beau responded. "You stay behind and I'll jump ahead."

"Go. Just don't cause the car to roll. Remember Cara's probably in the trunk."

Before Beau could get in front, the car pulled into a parking garage. Wheels squealed at every turn as they worked their way to the top. Just as Todd, pulled up onto the top level, the car still in his sight. Thinking he had them, he watched, in shock as the car continued at high speed driving straight for the edge.

"No," Todd screamed, horrified. When the car bashed through the concrete wall and drove straight over the edge, it was like watching a horrific movie in slow motion. He slammed on his brakes, skidding to a halt, stopping on the precipice of going over himself.

The crash shook the building but he jumped out and peered over the edge in time to see the car below burst into flames. The explosion blew him back onto his back.

No. She couldn't be dead. He couldn't have just found her, only to lose her. His breathing was labored, as

Samantha Quinn

he tried to suck in air. His lungs wouldn't work. He was drowning in his own fear and failure. His heart was broken. This wasn't real. It couldn't be real.

Maybe she survived, his mind screamed. He knew it wasn't possible -not from this height- and not with that explosion, but he couldn't give up until he knew for sure.

"What's happening?" Beau shouted from the phone, still hanging in its holder in the car.

Todd couldn't answer. He didn't have a response that made any sense-would ever make any sense. Sirens screamed in the distance. The sound was hollow in his ears and barely registered as finally Beau and Alex pulled up behind Todd's car. He continued to stare over the edge. At least he could breathe now. It was still shallow, but the much-needed oxygen was at least making it to his lungs.

He had no idea how long he had been standing there when hands pulled him from the edge. He couldn't tell you who it was. It didn't matter. Nothing mattered anymore. He tried to free himself as he watched the flames destroy the life he'd allowed himself to dream of; to hope for. Even if the dream had only just started to flourish, it was a dream that had settled in fast and deep. And in the blink of an eye, it was gone.

Chapter Twenty-Four

"Pull yourself together, man. We will find them and make them pay." Alex had grabbed his lapel and was shaking him. He couldn't focus. "Man, there was no one in the car. At least no one that can be seen through the flames. I admit we can't get very close yet, but I saw it go over the edge and I didn't see anyone in the car at all."

"But, Cara—"

"We don't know anything," Alex enunciated and emphasized the word 'anything', by giving Todd another shake. "Until we know for sure, ya know? Now come on man. Cara needs you to find Flaxton at the very least, and make sure he pays for his crimes. She would want that and you know it. I read the transcripts from the trial. She's my hero too. And if you can't pull yourself together long enough to get her justice, I will do it my damn self."

Alex pushed Todd away then and walked back to his own car. In doing so, he passed Todd's car; the door still ajar and glanced over at Todd's phone still in its holder.

"The dot is moving. The dot is moving. Mitchell. Goddamn the dot is still moving."

Todd, fully alert, pulled himself up from where he'd been leaning against a car and sprinted to his vehicle.

"Son of a bitch. She's still alive. Thank God," he prayed it was true and he wasn't just dreaming now. *Please let her still be alive,* he added silently.

"Alex, with me," he shouted. "Beau, talk to LPD, then I'm going to need you. Call me when you're on your way and we will let you know where we are headed."

Leaving rubber on the concrete, he peeled away, tires smoking in their tracks. She was still alive. He just kept repeating the phrase in his mind. As long as he kept saying it, she would really be okay. He'd nearly died when he thought Cara was gone forever. The state of disbelief –of shock –was horrific but it was okay now. He still had a chance to save her. They still had a chance at the life he'd been too afraid to reach for.

"There." Alex pointed up ahead. "Around that corner. There's an abandoned building at the end of the road. Maybe she knows about it and is hiding or maybe she's trying to find someone she can trust."

"She can trust me," Todd barked back. "Goddammit, she can trust me and she knows it."

"But she can't contact you without her phone. Did she have her phone with her tonight?"

Todd thought about the dress she'd been wearing. There were no pockets. He tried to recall in his mind, a picture of her at the venue. Did she have a purse or anything in her hands? He was sure she did. They could call her so she knew they were on their way. He grabbed his phone off its stand, and dialed her number, all the while keeping his eyes on the road. He couldn't afford an accident now. Cara needed him. No answer.

"Cara, answer the damn phone," he snarled in frustration. He could only imagine how terrified she must be.

****

Cara was pissed. She was nauseated too. And dizzy. She moaned when she tried to move, then held very still when she heard movement not far away. Slowly, she squinted her eyes, trying to see through her lashes in case whoever had tied her hands behind her back was watching. She would rather they think she was still asleep. All she could see was the wood floor she was lying on, and wood walls. Her eyes moved upward toward the ceiling only to find more wood. She searched and finally found a window on the perpendicular wall. Could she get up and dive through it and make a run for it? It would certainly catch Jeremy off guard. She was remembering now. Jeremy had knocked her out. And Ivy was there too.

Her stomach rolled when she remembered Ivy. Ivy was the one who had been tormenting her. She had taken her under her wing and tried to help her, to mentor her, but she'd been using their friendship to gain access to her house and office. She couldn't throw up now. They would know she was awake if she threw up. She needed to get control. She was such an idiot. She felt betrayed for sure but also stupid. She'd never thought of herself as a dumb woman but this proved she was wrong. Frustration coursed through her, making her angry with herself and her situation, but especially at Ivy and Jeremy.

They'd spent so much time together and she'd never recognized Ivy. She hadn't even had an inkling of having met her before. Not even an ounce of familiarity. How could that be? It had been a very troubling time for Cara. Maybe she'd blocked it.

It didn't matter now. Right now, she needed to escape and find Todd and Alex and get herself to the police. She had no idea how long she'd been out so she had no idea how far they had gone or where they were now.

Footsteps crossed what she assumed was a porch outside. The sound of shoes on wood made her think so, and then the door opened and she heard the sickening sound of Jeremy's voice.

"I know you're awake. I heard you moaning. Might as well open those baby blues, Cara. The sooner you wake up, the sooner I can tell you all the ways I'm going to torture you before I kill you. I can hardly wait to get started. We're going to have so much fun. Well, I will. You probably won't enjoy it nearly as much as I do."

Cara kept her head down, hoping if she played possum, he would think he'd been mistaken. Her mind prayed she could keep it together long enough to escape.

A hand grabbed her arm and pulled her upward. The world started spinning and she nearly threw up, but she gulped and breathed her way through it. She wouldn't give him the satisfaction of knowing he'd gotten to her.

He pulled her head up by grabbing her hair. She spat in his face. Shock registered just before he slapped her.

"I don't want to knock you out just yet, dear Cara. I need you awake so you can enjoy all the delicious things I'm going to do to you. Should we start with cutting off a finger, or should we scalp you. I skinned various animals, all of them already dead, but have always wondered what it would be like to do it to a woman. You, my dear, are lucky number one. But I promised Ivy I wouldn't start anything until she got here. She will need to hurry up though because I'm itching to get this party started. In the meantime, how be we have a gander at what we're dealing with. He grabbed her chin, bruising her face, she was sure, and held her head so she had no choice but to look him in the face. She would have spat again, had he not held her jaw closed. Instead she glared defiantly, refusing to back down.

While he tried to size her up, she was taking note of what her hands were tied with. It felt like zip ties because they were cutting into her wrists. If she could get enough traction, enough momentum, she could break them like Todd had shown her. It would be easier if she could use something, like a chair. She wasn't sure she was strong enough to do it from behind her back, especially since her arm had gone to sleep where she had been lying on it.

"What's going on inside that stupid head of yours," Jeremy asked.

Cara just glared. She refused to be cowed by him. Refused to let him think she had given up. It occurred to her though, that if he thought she had given up, maybe he would let his guard down, so she tried to change her face, slowly so as not to create suspicion, to one of fear and intimidation, losing the defiance.

"Ah, I see you are finally registering the severity of your situation. Maybe you're not quite as stupid as I thought."

The anger rolled through her again but she worked to keep it from her face. She needed the benefit of surprise if she was going to get herself out of this.

"Todd is going to kill you for this," she said instead. He will hunt you down, no matter where you go and he will find you. There is not one corner of the world where you will be able to hide, where he won't find you.

"Don't be ridiculous. By now, he's noticed you're gone, of course. That's to be expected. But Ivy has already implemented the other part of our plan and he'll be dead within the hour."

Tears welled up in her eyes. She tried not to let them show, but she couldn't stop them. She had to get away and warn Todd. She had to save him.

"I see the wheels turning in that little head of yours, but there's no way to stop it now. She's got the perfect plan to poison him." He laughed long and deep. It was a laugh filled with hysterics and madness.

"You're insane."

"Nowhere near as insane as you're going to be before this is all over. Now come on over here and sit down. I want to get some pliers out of the shed and we are going to remove those nails, one by one. They aren't very becoming anyway. You're a nobody. I always thought you were the one for me, but you always thought you were too good for me. And look at us now. You're still the one for me. The one I'm going to kill. You can join your precious Tommy...in hell." He laughed again, the lunacy evident in his eyes. There would be no reasoning with him. It was her or him. She would win, or die trying.

No sooner had he walked out the door than she was up and on her feet, using the back of her chair to try to break her bonds. The first try knocked the chair over so she moved to another chair by the table that was closer to the door. If she knocked this one over too, it would be much harder to get free. Could she do it from a sitting position beside the chair? She didn't think so. Instead of using the chair she decided to use the corner of the table. It didn't work. Next was the fridge door handle but all she succeeded in doing was opening the door and letting a horrible smell out. Old fridges should stay closed. The smell almost overwhelmed her as she gagged. She moved closer to the open door again to get a breath of fresh air and decided to go for the chair. Come hell or high water, she would succeed.

With one last reef on the chair, she broke her ties and had her hands free. She rubbed them, chaffed as they were. Blood oozed on her wrist from where the ties had cut her skin when she'd struggled. She didn't care. She was free.

She debated peeking to see if Jeremy was on his way back but decided against it. She would just make a run for it and go out the window on the other side. Even if she made noise when she broke the glass, she didn't care. She needed to get away and save Todd. He didn't know Ivy was evil. Everyone had underestimated her. She had to warn him.

She ran, but a hand grabbed her by the hair and yanked her back. She fell, bumping her head which caused stars to spin around her. She couldn't give up. If she did, she was dead.

Rolling fully to her back and planting her hands on the floor beside her hips she raised her legs and struck out at her captor raising her hips with an extra thrust. She made contact with his chin, knocking him backward. He stopped himself from falling by grabbing the edge of the table, screaming with rage.

Cara jumped up and faced her opponent, bracing her feet apart, hands in fists, and tucked in close to her body. She could do this. Todd had prepared her and she'd done the work.

Scanning and shifting on the balls of her bare feet she waited. *Use his anger against him, Cara.* Back and forth she shifted, moving backward slightly with each shift. *If you have no easy escape, make him come to you.* She could hear Todd talking her through it.

"Jeremy, you seemed to have stumbled. You're not going to let a little ol' girl beat you, are you? Why, bless your heart."

The insult hit home as she knew it would and he charged her, grabbing the chair and swinging it at her. It kept him off balance so he missed, but he swung around fast--faster than she had expected and swung again, making contact this time. The stars floated before her eyes again but she blinked and shifted. She was ready when he charged again, grabbing his arm as she stepped aside and added her own force to the momentum of his movement, causing him to crash into the table, breaking it.

She turned to run out the door, but he tripped her and she fell. Pain shot through her arm instantly but she tramped it down and rolled over onto her back, kicking with her legs, aiming for his most tender parts. When contact was made, he grunted and cried out, bending over in agony. She jumped to her feet and ran but she wasn't fast enough. He grabbed her ankle and pulled her to the ground again.

"You bitch. You will pay for that." The words were whispered through gritted teeth and more menacing for their quiet. She could feel the silent rage emanating from him and grabbed a broken table leg swinging upward with all her might.

****

Todd and Alex followed the signal into an alley with a dead end. Why would Cara go somewhere so secluded? She should be searching out groups of people. She knew this.

The hair stood on the back of his neck. "Something's not right, Alex."

"There. Up ahead -beside the garbage bin." Alex pointed.

Todd pulled his gun from the back waistband of his pants as he got out of the car. "Call it in Alex."

"But it's Cara," he insisted.

"No it isn't. Call it in, dammit."

He heard Alex call dispatch to advise of their location. His gun was in his hand and hidden slightly behind his back while he approached.

"It's okay, Ivy, it's just us. We're here to save you," he called out to her. I promise there's no one here to hurt you. I know you're scared, but I'm here to protect you."

Ivy crawled out from behind the garbage bin. Her dress was torn and her legs and feet were scraped up pretty bad. She was barefoot.

"It's okay, honey, come on out. I've got you."

He saw the panic along with the madness in her eyes and worked to maintain his own calm. She looked like a deer caught in a rifle sight, so he knew her grip on reality was breaking, if not gone all together.

"That's it, honey. Come on. You're safe now. I've got you."

He was prepared when she charged him. He grabbed her arm, syringe grasped tightly as her arm swung toward him. The guttural cry when he stopped her was shocking in comparison to the woman he had seen on a near daily basis since meeting Cara. He hadn't pieced it together until he saw her hiding in amongst the garbage.

He had her hands tied behind her back before Alex got to them. The expression on Alex's face said he'd too been snowed by her act, and likely her beauty. He was sure a lot of men had been taken in by her over the years. What he didn't understand was why. What had Cara ever done to her?

"Grab her purse, Alex, and make sure there's nothing more in there that can hurt us, or anyone else."

"Whoa, isn't this the brooch Cara was wearing on her dress?"

Todd refused to think about where Cara had worn the brooch and why Alex had been looking there.

It didn't take long for Ivy to start spilling it all. She tried to tell them Cara had given it to her but she caved and admitted she'd wanted it because it was so pretty.

"And since Cara doesn't need it, I deserve it. I've worked hard to orchestrate this whole thing. It hasn't been easy.

"Ivy, you have the right to remain silent. Anything you say can, and will be used against you in a court of law. You have a right to an attorney. If you cannot afford an attorney, one will be appointed for you."

Ivy just couldn't seem to stop talking but none of it was helpful in finding Cara.

"Where's Cara?" Todd finally interrupted her tirade, losing patience. That seemed to stop her.

"Come here, sugar," she said in a deep southern accent he'd never heard from her before. "Closer, sugar. I'll tell you where she is."

Todd leaned closer, ever vigilant in watching her for her next move. He knew it wasn't going to be that easy.

"I want a lawyer," she whispered and then laughed hysterically.

"Dammit, Ivy, where is she?" He shook her shoulders.

"Police brutality."

"Hardly but you couldn't prove it anyway, Ivy. I see no witnesses. Just tell me where she is."

"It's too late anyway. Or will be by the time you find her. It's a place we used to hang when we were kids. That's all I'll say. You're a big city dick. Try to find her…if you can. But like I said, it will be too late."

"That means she wasn't in the car and that's all I really needed to know. As for the rest of your plan I will," he emphasized the word, "destroy it and I will find her."

"Good luck, sugar."

The sound of sirens increased and two police cars pulled into the alley, blocking Todd's car.

"Move 'em to the side boys. Move it. Now," Todd shouted

His arms indicated the direction he needed to go, as he hopped back into his car and began backing up. Alex ran and jumped in while the car was still moving.

"I'm coming with you," he huffed, slamming his door closed. "You'll need back up."

Todd eyed Alex but said nothing and dialed his phone calling Lilly.

"What's going on, Todd? Where is Cara?" she asked as soon as she picked up.

"Where did Ivy and Cara hang out as kids? Or where did Cara hang out as a kid?"

"Cara hung at home, but I don't know who Ivy is. Our house was the gathering place. Why? What does this have to do with Cara's disappearance? Is she okay? Where is she?"

"Dammit," Todd muttered. "Ivy is Jeremy's cousin."

"I thought she seemed familiar," Cara's mom could be heard in the background.

"What about Jeremy? Do you know where he hung

out? Does anyone in your family know?"

"Wait, Mom and Dad are here. I have you on speaker. Em, call Sterling over."

He heard her asking her parents where Jeremy had hung out and heard her parents and Lilly say they had no idea. Then he heard Sterling speaking and his voice got louder as he took the phone from Emily.

"There's an old shack out in the woods. It's out Plantation Road. There used to be a path from the dock if it's still even there. I know the way though. Meet me at the bend in the river. It's east of the intersection of Planation and River Rd. If you don't know where it is, track Lilly's phone. I'll take it with me."

"Got it. Alex knows where that is." He peered at Alex for confirmation and Alex nodded. "But you should stay where you are. Your parents need you. This is going to be dangerous and I need to concentrate on Cara and not worry about you too. Stay with your parents and protect them and your sisters, just in case. I've got this. I will bring Cara home. You have my word."

He hoped it wasn't too late to keep his word, but come hell or high water, he would succeed, or die trying.

"Goddammit, it's too far out. We're not going to make it," he yelled after ending the call.

Chapter Twenty-Five

Cara felt sick when the table leg met with Jeremy's head but she didn't let up. She couldn't. She jumped to her feet, supporting her left arm, with her right hand at her elbow. She didn't have time to worry about whether it was broken. She ran toward the window. With Jeremy between her and the door, she couldn't risk being grabbed again.

Before she could get more than a few steps though, something hard smashed her in the back, knocking her over.

"Dammit, Jeremy. Don't make me kill you," she shouted as he flipped her to her back, standing over her, sure of his power.

His laugh was not unexpected. She used his distraction to pull her legs into her chest and kick out with all her might. He stumbled. She might have enjoyed the expression of surprise on his face as he lost his balance, had their situation been different. She watched as he fell to his knees before catching himself. She tried to make her body move faster but couldn't seem to get up to a speed that satisfied her. Everything was moving in slow motion.

Did adrenaline heighten your hearing too? Is that why she heard the click of a pistol? She turned, facing down her opponent, holding a gun.

"Go ahead, Cara, make your move. While I would

thoroughly enjoy the torture, perhaps knowing your lover is at this moment, dying from poison is enough. Did you know that's a very painful way to die? Were you aware of that? Your body shuts down, organ by organ, starting with your lungs. Your throat tightens so you can't get enough air. Your lungs fill with fluid, making it even more difficult. It isn't a long process –twenty minutes maybe –but it's a painful one."

She flinched, debating whether she could knock the gun out of his hand. He wouldn't expect her to make a move. *Use surprise to your advantage.* She could hear Todd whispering in her ear.

****

Todd and Alex left the car at the bend in the road and hiked into the woods toward the dock. He prayed he was heading in the right direction.

You've got this, baby boy, his Grandma Hailey whispered. It was just his imagination, he knew, but it calmed him none-the-less. *Toward the sun, baby boy, but hurry, she needs you.*

"This way," he said to Alex, who followed without question.

They hiked for mere moments, but it felt like hours. Nothing they could do was fast enough but when they saw the shack in the clearing, Todd knew this was it. The front door was wide open but it was silent inside. Still he knew she was there. *Please let her be alive,* he prayed silently.

As they got closer, he heard the rumbling of talking but couldn't make out what was being said. If he could hear talking, it meant she was alive, didn't it? His heart soared with hope.

Holding a finger to his lips, he motioned Alex to the

front of the shack and then pointed to himself and motioned toward the back.

"We'll need a distraction or something but first I want to make a sweep around back to see if there is more than one entrance or a window or something."

"On it."

Todd crept one way and Alex, the other, surveying the forest as well as the building. It wasn't in great shape. A good storm could blow it over. There were no doors in the back but Todd found a window he could use. It wouldn't take anything to get through it. Crouching down, he crept closer, then raised himself slowly until he could see over the ledge.

What he saw horrified him. Cara's back was to him and Flaxton was holding her at gun point. He had blood dripping down his face from what appeared to be a significant gash on his head so Cara hadn't made it easy on him.

A creak on the front porch of the shack had Jeremy grabbing Cara and wrapping his arm around her neck, the gun pointed at her head.

"Hello?" came a voice from the front of the cabin. "Knock, knock. Anyone home?"

"Get the hell out of here man or I'll shoot you. Get off my property."

"I won't take a moment of your time, sir. I am selling vacuum cleaners and wondered if I could give you a brief demonstration."

"Do I look like I need a vacuum? Get the hell off my land."

"I was thrilled to come across your lovely home and thought it must be a sign. I've been thinking about giving up on this job, but I thought…you know…it was a sign.

I have it right here. She's a beauty if I do say so myself. Gets all the dirt up and you can use it to clean walls and windows with a special attachment."

God bless Alex and his ability for improv.

While Todd searched for something to grab onto to hoist himself through the window, Alex kept Flaxton occupied. He noted a branch that would be strong enough to hold him –he hoped- so he swung up, just as Flaxton moved the gun toward the door and Alex's voice.

****

Cara wasn't sure how Alex had found her but bless him, he had. She prayed Todd was nearby as well but she couldn't just wait for someone to save her. She was terrified that she would screw something up and would have to pay with her life, but she also knew if she did nothing, he could pull the trigger any second.

"Get the hell off my land, asshole," Jeremy yelled and aimed his pistol at the door, firing to emphasize his threat.

This is it, Cara thought as she threw her head back while simultaneously grabbing the gun with both hands and heaving all her body weight to one side, throwing Jeremy off balance. She spun around, breaking free as she saw Todd coming through the window. Jeremy grabbed her again, this time facing him, so she wrapped her legs around one of his, locking her ankles behind him and throwing her right arm around his neck, pulling with her other hand to strengthen her hold. She then threw her body back and to the side as hard as she could, causing Jeremy to fall with her. She landed hard on her side, and Jeremy landed with a thud, on top of her.

The sound of the gunshot rang through the woods, deafening her briefly, followed by a ringing in her ears.

"Oh my God," she screamed.

"Cara, are you hurt? Answer me. Are you hurt?"

Jeremy was pulled from her, but she kept holding on tight so she moved with him, her arm still around his neck in a death grip, trying to strangle him.

Todd gently pulled her arms free. "It's okay, Cara, he's dead. You can let go now. He can't hurt you anymore."

Cara opened her eyes to see Todd squatting down beside her, pulling at her arms.

"I tried to stop him, Todd. I tried. I fought back, just like you showed me. I fought him and I didn't give up." Her voice was breathless. Was that even her speaking? She was having trouble piecing together everything that had happened.

"Darlin', you were fantastic. You did it perfect. Now let go," he repeated, pulling her arms toward him and lifting her up from the floor.

"You were fierce and I'm so very proud of you."

She threw her arms around Todd then, and clung, like her life depended on it. "Did I kill him?" she asked, her voice muffled by his neck.

"No, sweetheart, I did."

"But he's truly gone? It's over?"

"He's gone. It's over."

She pulled her head back, panic on her face. "But Ivy—it was Ivy too. She's going to poison you. We have to stop her. No one suspected but it was her. She's evil."

"We have Ivy in custody already, darlin'. No need to worry about her either. It's all over and Ivy will go to jail. You're safe now."

Cara cried then. It was like a damn burst and the tears flowed freely. Todd just held her tight, letting her cry it out. All the emotion, the fear –terror.

"Let it out, darlin'. Just let it out."

He rocked her, pulling her closer to him and she reveled in the love and safety of his arms.

Alex was on the phone outside giving them some space, and updating the FBI team that had just landed in Lightcastle, and then he called Beau, to update him and LPD.

"McPherson's team just landed." Alex entered the cabin. "They're on the way. McPherson said he'll secure the scene and we can leave as soon as he gets here. If you want, I can wait around and you can go. I can catch a ride with someone after we're done here. Take Cara to the hospital so she can get checked out. I'm sure she'll want to clean up after that, so take her home. I've got this."

****

Todd glanced down at Cara's face. She'd stopped crying but her face still wore the tell-tale signs with puffy eyes and tear-streaks where the tears had washed away the dirt. There were bruises showing already and he'd seen her holding her arm when he'd spotted her through the window so a trip to the hospital was a good idea.

"Thanks, man, I appreciate it. If McPherson wants statements from Cara and me, he knows how to find me. I will take her to the ER to get checked out."

In the car, he called Cara's family to tell them Cara was fine but he was taking her to the hospital to get a doctor to check her out. He knew they would meet him there without them saying it. That's what family did, and Cara had a great one. Up until this moment, his family had been Hunter and until she passed, his Grandma Hailey. If Cara would accept him, he could have a real family. A large family.

Cara was resting with her eyes closed. Once the adrenaline rush wore off, it was natural to want to. She wasn't there yet, but she was close.

He carried her into the hospital, even though she protested.

"I can walk myself. For crying out loud, what are people going to think?" she'd asked, but he ignored her and carried her anyway. Setting her down gently and getting her through triage, they waited together for the Doctor to come and get her.

An ambulance pulled up to the door, followed by a police car, and a woman was wheeled in on a stretcher. He didn't think much of it, until Beau followed in, angry and alert. When he saw Todd, he approached, keeping an eye on Cara who was staring at the stretcher.

"What's up? Who's that?" Todd asked nodding in the direction of the stretcher.

"It's Ivy," Cara answered. "What happened, Beau?"

"Reilly had her in the squad car and was about to drive away when I jumped in to go with him. I wanted to keep an eye on her and didn't trust him…or her for that matter. So we were in the squad car together, taking her back to the station after some antics and an attempted escape after you left –long story –and Alex called saying you'd found Cara and she was fine. I turned around to tell her she'd failed but she'd heard already and appeared to grab something from her bra and put it in her mouth. It was a pill or something. She just threw it back before we could even react and then she was convulsing and we had to call the ambulance. She stopped convulsing after the ambulance arrived but was unconscious so we brought her here."

"What did she take? Is she going to live?"

"She was going to poison Todd. Jeremy told me that. I was terrified she would succeed," Cara added.

Todd squeezed her hand. "She didn't succeed though, and now she's done."

A nurse with a cart passed by, and then all hell broke loose. All of a sudden, Ivy jumped up and grabbed the cart and a scalpel that had been lying on top of it. Before Todd and Beau could react, she had the blade to the nurse's throat.

"Cara, you walk your fat ass over here or I slice her throat."

Todd had his gun aimed at Ivy, as did Beau and Reilly.

"There's nowhere for you to go, Ivy. Put the knife down and let her go. You're only making it worse for yourself," Cara responded.

"Cara, do not go over there," Todd ground out as Cara stood.

"Ivy, put the knife down. That nurse was only trying to help someone. She isn't any part of the sick and twisted story you've been telling yourself for years. Let her go."

"Burn in hell," she shouted as she twitched her hand ever so slightly.

She didn't get another chance. She was shot once through the shoulder, and once through the head. Reilly moved in, pulling the nurse, who was screaming, away from the dead woman.

At that moment Cara's family rushed through the door. They stopped and stared at Ivy, then at Cara, whose dress was torn and dirty. Todd saw her as her family was now seeing her. Bruises on her face, her hair askew with matted blood at her temple and blatant tear streaks on her face. Her jaw was swollen and her eye was swelling shut –and she couldn't have been more beautiful to him in his life.

He braced for her family to rage at him for the shape she was in, but it never came. Instead, they ran to Cara and embraced her, all talking at the same time. He stepped back to give them space and then found himself engulfed in hugs from her teary-eyed family.

"We owe you a debt of gratitude for saving our girl." Her dad struggled to get the words out through his own tears. He wiped his hands across his face then gave an extra swipe under his nose.

"She is my heart. I would have given my life for her, but she saved herself. She was ferocious and the victory belongs to her."

"Don't believe him, Dad. If he hadn't shown up when he did, I'm not sure how much longer I would have lasted."

Cara moved to Todd then, giving him a hug of her own, tucking herself under his arm, and standing by his side. "He saved my life."

Alex showed up, taking in the scene, confusion clear on his face.

"Oh and if you ever need a vacuum, Alex is your man." She laughed through her tears.

Chapter Twenty-Six

Cara waited patiently for Todd to finish speaking on the phone in the hall. She was dog-tired but finally able to take a deep breath. She sighed deeply, then winced with pain from her cracked rib and whatever was torn in her shoulder. "Okay, not too deep," she whispered to herself.

"Not too deep for what?" Todd asked, walking through the door and closing it behind him.

"Not too deep for a deep breath. Cracked ribs don't like that."

Todd winced.

"I'm fine," she responded, trying to keep him from getting worked up again. He'd been hovering ever since he'd found her. She was good and she repeatedly reminded him of that fact.

"Cara, we need to talk." Todd turned serious.

"Oh-oh. That sounds ominous. 'Bout what?" Cara asked cautiously

"I have my new assignment but I want to talk to you about it."

"Oh." Cara's heart fell. She knew this was coming. Todd had been completely up front and honest about moving on. She had wished -dreamed even- that he would miraculously choose to stay…but she understood.

"So my supervisor offered me a promotion last week in the UK."

"Congratulations. I know this is what you wanted. I'm happy for you," she interrupted before he could continue. She didn't want to hear him say the words he had to move on. She couldn't stop him forever, but it was going to hurt so much more than she'd ever anticipated.

"I turned it down."

"Are you crazy?" she asked.

"It wasn't the promotion I wanted."

"Oh… I'm so sorry, Todd. You deserve the promotion you wanted. I'm sorry," she repeated, not knowing what else to say.

"He called again last night to offer me another position and this one was better than expected. They offered me an SAC position –Special Agent in Charge," he added before she could ask what that meant. "It's here in Lightcastle, so I'll be staying on. I know I told you we had an end date and if you still want an out, I understand, but I already know what I want. I love you, Cara. You are my heart."

Cara's hand covered her lips and tears filled her eyes. She had so much love for this man and her heart was filled with joy because he could stay.

"Of course, I don't want an out, silly man. I love you too. Oh my Lawd, you're not leaving. I am so over the moon happy about that."

He knelt down on the floor in front of her just as her family burst through the door.

"The doctor said we could come in…" her mother said.

"Oh my Gawd, he's proposing," Lilly squealed.

"No…he's not," Cara waived her arms, embarrassed that her family was putting Todd in this position. "Todd, get up. They think you're proposing."

"Cara," he took her hand in his. "I am proposing, but clearly not well." He chuckled. "Will you do me the honor of being *Mia Cara*, Cara? Will you marry me and spend your life with me?"

Cara was stunned.

"I know we've only known each other for a few weeks but I've known you were the one for me from the very first moment I saw you sitting on the bench holding your face to the sun. Even with the shrill of the fire alarm raging I saw nothing but your beautiful soul and heard nothing but my heart calling yours."

"Yes. Yes…," Cara repeated nodding. "Yes, I will marry you."

Her family lost all control then. Her mother cried engulfing Cara in a hug-a little too tightly, causing Cara to wince, then pulled Todd into the mother-daughter hug as well. Cara's father slapped Todd on the back nearly knocking Todd over, while he wiped at his eyes denying the obvious tears and claiming it was allergies.

"I knew you would be a good one the moment I saw you," Rhett said, finally grabbing a hanky from his pocket and blowing his nose."

"Oh, Daddy, you did not. You gave him such a hard time, grilling him like you were doing a cross examination."

"I was just testing his stamina. God knows he's gonna need it with you. Now don't give your daddy a hard time and let's talk dates. I want to walk my daughter down the aisle, and we have plans to make."

Her dad grabbed Todd's hand again shaking vigorously, then engulfed him in a big bear hug. Cara adored the enthusiasm of her family and reveled in their acceptance of Todd, welcoming him into the fold.

In those moments of congratulations; of excitement for things to come; those moments filled with love from past and present and the hope of future; the web she'd found herself entangled in since Tommy had been killed, was broken. She was free, finally, and her heart was full.

A word about the author…

Samantha Quinn has always loved stories, whether they were from her voracious reading habit, or family history passed down through generations. It was a natural progression to begin writing the stories that swirled in her mind, going on to publish in both fiction and non-fiction. An avid traveler, Sam enjoys visiting other locations, usually in warm tropical climates, where she feeds her imagination and the water soothes her soul.

Sam grew up in a small Canadian town in South Western Ontario and hasn't strayed too far from her family and grown children. She and her husband enjoy tackling the odd home reno and walking their dog, Georgia On My Mind.

http://samantha-quinn.com

www.ingramcontent.com/pod-product-compliance
Lightning Source LLC
Chambersburg PA
CBHW050450070726
47506CB00018B/541